DISRUPTION

Books by Jessica Shirvington

DISRUPTION

JESSICA SHIRVINGTON

HarperCollins*Publishers*

HarperCollins*Publishers*

First published in Australia in 2014
This edition published in 2016
by HarperCollins*Publishers* Australia Pty Limited
ABN 36 009 913 517
harpercollins.com.au

Copyright © Jessica Shirvington 2014

The right of Jessica Shirvington to be identified as the author
of this work has been asserted by her in accordance with
the *Copyright Amendment (Moral Rights) Act 2000*.

HarperCollins*Publishers*
Level 13, 201 Elizabeth Street, Sydney NSW 2000, Australia
Unit D1, 63 Apollo Drive, Rosedale, Auckland 0632, New Zealand
A 53, Sector 57, Noida, UP, India
1 London Bridge Street, London SE1 9GF, United Kingdom
2 Bloor Street East, 20th floor, Toronto, Ontario M4W 1A8, Canada
195 Broadway, New York NY 10007, USA

National Library of Australia Cataloguing-in-Publication entry:

Shirvington, Jessica, author.
    Disruption / Jessica Shirvington.
    ISBN: 978 0 7322 9810 4 (paperback)
    Shirvington, Jessica. Disruption series ; 1.
    For young adults.
A823.4

Cover design by Stephanie Spartels, Studio Spartels
Cover images: Girl by BONNINSTUDIO / Stocksy.com / 779872;
Clouds by Leandro Crespi / Stocksy.com / 124391
Typeset in Palatino LT Regular by Kirby Jones

For Selwa

*Thank you for helping
turn dreams into reality.*

I made myself a promise.

I would do whatever it took. I'd see this through to the end.

Make it right.

I'd been tracking *him* for most of the day. I had other things to do, but it had been over a month since I'd monitored his weekend activity. And sloppiness wasn't an option. Not now.

We were in DC, waiting in Dupont Circle Metro. He'd opted for a rare driver-free day, making it easier than usual to tail him, and I wondered why. Perhaps because he'd spent the morning touring Georgetown University and wanted to appear normal – not that everyone didn't recognise him and point. I suspected it had more to do with not wanting to explain to Daddy why he'd explored a university other than Princeton. His family hailed from a long line of Princeton graduates and I knew it was assumed he would attend, like his brothers, after graduation. He probably already had a wing named after him.

Hidden beneath my faded blue baseball cap, I fidgeted with the edge of my sweater as I studied his movements carefully, with calculated interest. Carrying out my plans wasn't going to keep me up at night. Not after all the things I'd already done.

He never noticed me anyway. Not once. Not even when the large lady with the foghorn voice asked me if she was on the right platform for Chinatown. It wasn't because I was particularly stealthy. It was just that, standing there in his waist-hugging suit pants and waywardly untucked white shirt, he simply had no need to see me.

A commotion erupted at the other end of the platform. All eyes turned to watch as five M-Corp security guards stormed down the escalators, closing in on a short, balding man wearing wire glasses. I had barely registered the man before he was blocked from my view.

My attention returned to *him*. He had only just turned eighteen, but his obvious wealth combined with the way he projected confidence made him look older. I heard one of the M-Corp guards demand the man with the glasses activate his Phera-tech. The command was followed by a number of feeble attempts at refusal. Of course, the balding man knew it was futile. You could already hear the whispers of the nearby commuters.

'Is he?'

'He must be.'

'A neg.'

'I hope they take him away.'

It wasn't that I was immune to the situation. I'd just seen it a whole lot worse. A whole lot more personal.

He on the other hand …

My interest heightened as I watched his reaction. Oddly, he observed the situation with a kind of reluctant curiosity, even taking steps towards the scene others were quickly distancing themselves from. His eyes widened as the guards restrained the man, fixing plastic ties to his wrists. One guard plugged in a portable link-up system to the man's M-Band so that they could hack into his personal data while another recited the Negative Removal Act.

My view to the man cleared briefly. He was visibly shaking. He attempted to drop to his knees, though the guards held him up. He begged them to let him go, crying out in broken sobs for a chance to make right whatever it was he'd done – or was going to do – wrong.

No one made a move to help him, even though I heard one or two heart-rate monitors sound an alert. People's hearts weren't racing for him; it was fear for themselves that caused the spikes.

The man's pleas fell on deaf ears.

I knew my expression gave away nothing but detachment. *He*, conversely, watched everything with a look of revulsion, and I felt a sick sense of justification that he should see this now. Nothing could better prepare him.

The spotlights that lined the platform began to pulse red, indicating a train on approach. I glanced one more time at *him* and noticed he was moving towards the guards. I straightened, suddenly intrigued. Was he going to step in? Surely not.

I never found out.

The sounds of struggle intensified and I turned my attention back to the balding man in time to see him break free of the guards and leap straight off the platform.

The man – the neg – collided instantly with the oncoming train.

Nine years ago ...

United States of America
Individual Identification Act

Part I

In the interest of public and individual safety the government of the United States has approved the compulsory use of microchips for GPS, identification and potential medicinal purposes.

As of October 1, all residents and permanent or temporary visitors of the United States of America are required to be fitted with a current M-Corp issued microchip.

Failure to do so is viewed as a criminal offence and is punishable by law.

For further information on the Individual Identification Act please go to:

http://www.m-corp-systems.com/mchip

One

Crouched in the shadows, I scoped the underground parking garage again – one of Arlington's inner-city lots. I kept my focus on my surroundings, even as I took the time to pull my hoodie over my head. I wouldn't need it for long. Soon, I'd be sweating. Running for my life does that.

I glanced down at my sleek M-Band, missing the days when a simple wristwatch sat in its place. When life wasn't dictated by whatever data it spewed out. But those days are gone. It had only taken nine years for the world to change completely. And forever. You'd have thought we were better than that. You'd have thought we'd fight harder and stronger. But it turns out being able to rate ourselves against one another, being able to scientifically map the way our pheromones interacted with every individual we crossed paths with, was more important than any of the other values we'd once held so dear. Like honour. Time. Family.

Like falling in love.

I had no desire to be told by a factory setting who was and wasn't compatible with me. If anything I despised the technology, but that didn't make me Pre-Evo. The Preference Evolution supporters might have felt like they had safety and power in numbers, but being a team player got you nowhere in this world.

I stood up and took a series of deep breaths to calm myself, watching as my M-Band instructed me my pulse was dropping to an acceptable level. I hated that I still got anxious, but even raw determination doesn't dampen nerves. I'd never bothered with the mute zips that concealed heart rate and pulse beep-offs – it was cheating. I prided myself on my ability to control the M-Band readings that seemed to control everyone else. I wasn't going to let a glass bracelet control me. It was a sign of how far I'd come these past two years that I could master the discipline.

Especially at moments like this.

I stubbed my booted toe into the concrete pylon I was hiding behind and reminded myself it would all be worth it when I had him back. A sound to my left caused me to flinch and spin defensively. I let out a breath. It was just the digital advertisement on a far wall shifting. My shoulders began to ease only to tense again when the new 3D ad came into view.

Rehabilitation leads to reintegration.

Bullshit. The rehabilitation farms for negs looked idyllic; images of sprawling hills, meditation rooms and team sports. The last image showed some loser with a cheesy smile on his face as he waved goodbye to the other negs before apparently heading back out into the world. All propaganda.

My eyes fixed on the words at the bottom of each image – *An M-Corp Initiative* – and my hand itched to rip the digital panels off the wall and replace them with the real pictures I kept stored away. Instead, I clamped my fingers closed and looked back towards the parked cars.

Pulling out my old-fashioned handheld, I called the only number I used the phone for.

'You set?' Gus answered in a flat voice. I could hear the sounds of his engine in the background as he shifted gears.

'Not quite. Two to go and one of them is an unknown,' I explained, my tone hushed as I glanced back at the mystery cherry-red convertible. It could only be a woman's car. 'I need you to run the plates.'

I heard him blow out a breath. 'Have I mentioned I hate your guts lately?'

'Every day.' I grinned.

Silence met me at the other end. I waited. Gus needed these few moments. They made him feel like he actually had a choice. I could give him that, even if it wasn't true.

'It might take a bit of time,' he said, sounding defeated.

I rattled off the convertible's plate details and Gus hung up without another word. It didn't bother me. The terms of my relationship with Gus were clear. He worked for me until I said otherwise. No warm fuzzies. A friend was the last thing I needed.

When I started down this path two years ago, I knew there was no point unless I was willing to give it everything. I might've only been sixteen at the beginning of all this, but watching my family fall apart little by little, hearing the gossip escalate until we were forced to change over to Mom's maiden name and eventually leave our home – it was devastating. What choice did I really have?

And I had given *everything*.

My M-Band sent out a low beep. I glanced around before looking down and sighing at the message that scrolled across the screen.

Mom.

She'd picked up another shift and would be home even later than planned. I leaned my head back against the pylon and swallowed past the tightness in my throat. The message was no surprise. Mom worked crazy hours at the hospital for barely anything, and what she did get all went towards paying off debts we never should've had.

I'll leave you some dinner in the oven.

I sent off the message to her, wishing, yet again, that the world hadn't changed. The ad to my right taunted me again and my jaw flexed. Things would only get tighter now that the government was introducing the Poverty Tax.

All because of a microchip that was smaller than a grain of rice.

It had been up for debate for years, the public protesting the invasion of privacy vehemently at first. But once the Identification Laws were passed nine years ago and every man, woman and child was implanted with an M-Chip at the tip of their spine, people swiftly forgot to argue. Instead they became obsessed with, *addicted* to M-Bands and their must-have accessories. And soon enough, M-Bands became law too.

Of course, all of this paled in comparison to the biggest discovery.

Phera-tech.

A stumbled-upon tech that changed the way everyone interacted. Even me. Now, every relationship was a definitive statistic.

Taking another deep breath, I shook the jitters from my hands and waited. It was all about timing. I had enough experience to know it was foolish to waste time looking over my shoulder when the real danger was usually straight ahead.

The elevator doors at the far wall chimed. Without thinking, my tranq gun was in hand. My finger on the trigger just in case.

A middle-aged man stepped out of the elevator. The tread of his polished brogues echoed through the parking garage as he tapped his M-Band to open his Mercedes.

'Wanker,' I whispered.

I waited for him to slip into his car, worth more than the shack we rented on the outskirts of west Arlington, and watched as he reached over to open the glove compartment and pulled something out.

I was already smirking.

I stuffed my tranq gun in the front pocket of my hoodie, shuffled into a better position, and opened the camera zip on my M-Band. I may have only been eighteen, but the last two years of my life had given me a solid education. I'd learned to see these things for what they really were. This guy was seriously funded and worked late. Add the wanker component and likelihood he had some lowbrow connections ...

Sure enough, he pulled out another M-Band and began switching it with the one on his right wrist.

'Tsk, tsk,' I admonished, taking a few photos as he made the changeover. By law, people were only permitted to own one M-Band. If you bought a new or upgraded M-Band, you *had* to hand in your old one on delivery.

Mr Polished Brogues had a black-market M-Band, which meant he was up to no good.

My guess: he was cheating on his wife. By wearing the black-market band he was creating a kind of alias, covering his tracks so his unsuspecting wife would never know if he spent the night trawling bars. No matter what people claimed M-Chips and Phera-tech could do, no matter how many long-term matches they created, or how many negative relationships they supposedly protected people from, you can't stop a bastard being a bastard.

Storing away the photos in my hidden cyber drawer, I closed down my camera zip. You never know when such evidence can come in handy. Information is power, and I'd made compiling and exploiting it an art form.

'One down,' I muttered as Polished Brogues started his engine and screeched out of the parking garage. I turned my attention back to the six cars remaining on this level. Thanks to the last few weeks of surveillance, and some expensive intel, I knew five of them weren't a concern. The owners of those cars always worked late and it wasn't uncommon for them to stay overnight – hell, half of them had pull-out beds and bathrooms in their offices.

The convertible however … I gnawed on the inside of my cheek, knowing Gus wouldn't have had time to complete the plate search yet.

Decision time.

It wasn't simply getting into the elevator unnoticed that mattered. I had to be able to get back out too. I let go of a deep breath. I didn't like unknowns. What I *liked* was a sure thing. A scientifically proven fact. I got that trait from my father. He was also the one who'd taught me that information was power.

Then again … 'Chance favours the bold,' I mumbled. I got *that* from myself.

It was nearly 10 p.m. I'd waited long enough. I pulled out my phone again and made the call.

'The search isn't done yet,' Gus answered.

'Don't worry about it. I'm ready.'

I could hear Gus tapping away on his laptop, but that wasn't all I registered. There was music and the distinct sound of chatter in the background.

'Where are you?' I asked, suddenly suspicious.

'Drinking my way into oblivion. I'm hoping when I get there, you aren't.'

'You'd better not be drunk,' I warned.

'You know, Maggie, there are places for people like you,' he said, and I noted with a sense of relief that he wasn't slurring his words the way he did when he'd had a few drinks. It was more likely he'd opted for a crowded place in case his transmissions were traced. 'They bring you food and little round pills and you get to lie in bed all day and talk about your feelings. I think you'd like it.'

I bristled. 'There are already enough people locked away who shouldn't be,' I said, my words clipped.

'Whatever,' he grumbled.

After one of his trademark pauses, Gus made a grunting sound. 'You're good to go in thirty seconds and you'll have a thirty-minute window. Hope you get lost down there.'

He hung up and I kept count, unfazed by his moodiness. Gus hated me. So he should. But catching him red-handed ten months ago had felt like Christmas. And regardless of what he thought of me, I owned him.

'Thirty,' I counted. I adjusted my grey hood and took off across the dark parking garage, knowing, without question, that the security cameras would show nothing but an empty lot for the next thirty minutes. He might hate my guts, but Gus had mad skills.

TWO

I lunged at the elevator button, relieved when the doors opened immediately. Every second was precious. Inside, I hit a few buttons, smiling briefly when nothing happened. Gus had the elevator under his control, so I climbed up onto the mahogany railing and pushed open the hatch in the roof.

I levered myself through the ceiling of the elevator cabin and stood on the roof. The door was exactly where our intel promised – between floors, blended seamlessly into the wall, making it all but impossible to see. Unless you knew it was there.

I slipped the M-Corp card that Gus had programmed into the door's unmarked scanner. Of course, if I were actually authorised to be there the elevator would've delivered me to the door directly. After exactly twenty seconds, the lock clicked and the door slid open. Calmly, I slipped into the dark transit tunnel, letting the door slide shut behind me. The air was stale and moved against my skin, reminding me of two things: it was recycled, and it was limited.

The intel we'd paid for assured me that there would be no guards in this area, but I still took the time to palm my tranq gun and listen out for any nearby sounds. Nothing.

Before long the passageway led to a larger underground system, and I couldn't help but be in awe of the elaborate network. It was all but out in the open. I quickly scanned in each direction as far as the low lighting allowed. There were no security guards manning the discreet entry / exit points nearby. *That* alone was a big part of why the doorways remained so well hidden.

It had taken over a year, a great deal of underhanded dealings, and my lucky new 'partnership' with Gus to finally discover the key to getting access to these transit tunnels.

Parking garages.

Who would have suspected that within parking garages, all the way from Washington DC to Fairfax and beyond, were doorways into an underground transit system?

The system connected hundreds of small hubs, each of which could house up to a thousand people. Originally built for FEMA as part of their emergency strategy in the case of Armageddon or nuclear warfare, the design revolved around a complex layout of self-contained 'hubs' which were rumoured to link to a 'core' hub built beneath Mount Weather in Bluemont, Virginia. If you believed the whispers, the core alone could house up to twenty thousand people.

I hadn't seen that far.

Too many guns in that direction.

The hubs were where M-Corp locked up the negs. Those rehabilitation farm ads were a complete lie. And tonight was my best chance to find what I was looking for.

I closed my eyes briefly, slowed my breathing, and lined up alongside the metal tracks – not dissimilar to railway lines – to wait for a passing pod.

Transit pods were bubble-shaped vehicles made of bulletproof glass, wicked fast and near impossible to hitch a ride on. On my first attempt, almost nine months ago, I'd nearly snapped my neck. I *did* break my arm. Fun times.

Squinting, I recognised the glow that was beginning to warm the far east of the tunnel. My pulse started to race and my M-Band let off a warning beep. I ignored it, my eyes fixed on the fast-approaching pod.

'Don't die today, Maggie,' I ordered myself, as I moved closer to the tracks.

Even when it was close enough that I could see it was unoccupied, there was no time for relief. I was already running. My arms and legs pumped harder and harder, knowing that my leap would need to count. When the front of the pod lined up with my shoulder, I sprung into the air, stretching my arms in front of me.

My hands and feet scrabbled for something, *anything*. My left hand made contact with the pod's barely there grip point at the back, but my right hand missed, flying across the silken surface.

My entire weight hung from the tips of four fingers. I couldn't stop the small cry that fell from my lips as I dug deep to hoist my right arm up and into place before I lost my ride. Panting, I manoeuvred myself into a better position and prepared for the fast-approaching drop.

Getting off is unquestionably easier. It just hurts like hell.

A large 74, painted on the tunnel wall in white, loomed ahead. My junction. I jumped. My ankle twisted as I hit the ground and rolled. Denim ripped and pain shot into my butt and knees. I sat up, attempting to dust myself off and refocus. I managed to tug my ponytail tight and double-check my M-Band hadn't been damaged before I dropped my trembling hands into my lap and let go of a shaky breath.

Would anyone ever find me if I died down here?

Would Gus even tell my mother what happened to me?

Would I *want* him to?

God, I didn't have time for wallowing. I jumped to my feet and rotated my ankle a few times before setting off again. The clock was ticking. I had to move.

I dashed through the intricate tunnels, heading west, following the map I'd memorised. It didn't take long to reach the opening I was looking for.

I stared, still amazed – still angry – each time I discovered another neg hub.

The area below was hard granite, but a huge crater had been carved out of it like many of the other hubs I'd seen, reminding me of a black salad bowl. In the centre of the bowl was a series of interconnecting buildings. And only two direct entry / exit points: the large open tunnel down at their level, which allowed for truck access, and the open stairway accessed from my elevated position. Both had steel doors closing them off.

The community wasn't the largest I'd found, but close. At first glance, I would guess the hub was big enough for around eight or nine hundred people. Too many to search every face, but I didn't need to. Down here, everyone knew everyone – a survival strategy rather than a need for companionship.

I hovered around the upper edge of the settlement. The trick to not getting caught was getting in and out fast. Even if the steel doors weren't enough, there were heavily armed guards posted at the access points, making entry via the staircase impossible. No problem. My way was faster anyway.

Ignoring my ankle, I jogged towards the darkest corner, yanking my rope free from my pack and quickly spying a large boulder to tie it to. I hooked it to my belt and launched myself off the edge. I barely utilised the support of the abseil until just before the rooftop of one of the smaller side buildings. I landed sharply, grimacing as I hobbled towards one of the air vents that had become my preferred way in and out of these hubs. Pulling another length of rope out of my pack, I prepared for my final descent.

I landed inside a cold concrete corridor. I hid in the shadows for a moment before inching my way towards a T-junction ahead. On the way I passed an open door – the room inside was no larger than a college dorm and nothing at all like the quaint 'farming estates' the government advertised. I shivered. The hubs had an on-edge feeling that I'd never gotten used to. The people in here knew. Just like I did. They would never be truly free again.

Negs had what scientists called a 'pivotal flaw' – a chemical imbalance that left them unable to rate positively with others. While it wasn't uncommon for people's Phera-tech to show occasional negative ratings with other individuals, negs only *ever* rated that way. When the flaw was first discovered, scientists found that a concentration of negs were already in prisons across the country, often for violent crimes. During the period of their research, many who hadn't at first appeared dangerous showed a developing tendency towards wrongdoing. It wasn't long before the scientific community branded negs 'the pollution to society'. And when they proved that a neg's continued interaction with non-negs would ultimately result in volatile and often aggressive outcomes, people agreed that they were the worst of mankind.

The government had turned a blind eye to what they couldn't fix, handing over the reigns to the increasingly powerful firm that had first invented M-Chips and M-Bands. Now, beneath the ground, too many lives were in the hands of M-Corp.

My father's life was one of them.

I froze a few metres from the top of the corridor. A man had just turned the corner and was walking towards me. I knew he was a neg by his grey uniform and bare feet. He caught sight of me, his pale green eyes assessing yet unafraid. Cold.

He tilted his head a fraction, his overgrown dark hair falling back, exposing a streak of dirt on the side of his neck. He didn't look much older than me, but I knew not to underestimate him. I stood still, feet apart, hands loose but ready by my sides.

'New?' he rasped, stopping a couple of metres away from me.

I shook my head, risking a quick look over my shoulder to ensure we were alone.

'What city are you from?' I asked, my voice even.

The line between his eyebrows creased. 'Chicago, why?' He was studying my clothes, no doubt wondering where my uniform was. If I wasn't dressed like a neg, I should've been wearing M-Corp credentials at the very least.

'White Sox won last week,' I said, grateful that I always took the time to stay up to date on sports results.

His eyes lit up, just for a second. He looked around. 'You're not M-Corp?'

I kept my voice low. 'No.'

He rubbed the back of his neck, trying to decide if he would ask. They always did.

'How?'

'The Yankees are asking the same question,' I said, causing his eyes to narrow and his hand to twitch. I should have known better than to antagonise him. Negs were prisoners. Being trapped underground with no light, no escape, no hope, did things to a person whether they were good or not.

'You know what I mean,' he said, his voice dropping to a growl.

I did. Even if I was a new inmate, I should've been held for at least a few months before being delivered to a hub. And, since the first thing that happens to negs is to be shut off from the real world, I should most definitely *not* know last week's baseball results.

I shrugged, and pulled a picture out of my pocket – the only one of Dad that I'd managed to save. All the digital images had been erased for his 'future well-being'.

'How long have you been underground?' I asked.

He took a step closer to me, his suspicion morphing into curiosity. 'Coming up to a year and a half,' he answered. 'You?'

I pushed up my sleeve and checked the time on my M-Band. 'About eighteen minutes.'

Before his jaw dropped all the way, I held the picture up for him. 'Listen, I don't have long. I'll tell you the final score and give you a zip with today's news if you tell me whether you've ever seen this person.' When he stared back at me and crossed his arms, I added, 'The zip's black-market.' In other words untraceable.

The guy glanced around nervously and licked his lips. He wanted that news zip bad. I felt a pang of guilt that it had to be this way. Even worse that I couldn't just grab his hand and take him with me. I could save him right now. But if I did … my way in and out would be blown. I couldn't take that chance.

I was out of time, but I waited.

When his eyes lowered to the photo again, I knew I had him.

'Who is he?' he asked, probably trying to work out if this was some kind of trick. For the zip, he'd probably tell me whatever I wanted to hear.

I shrugged. 'Someone I need to find. Dead or alive.' I added the last bit to give him permission to tell me bad news and still get his prize. 'He was taken in a little over two years ago.'

He raised an eyebrow and I knew what he was thinking. I wasn't a fool. I'd seen enough to know there was a chance I was already too late. But that wasn't going to stop me. I was going to find Dad, or find out what had happened to him, no matter who I had to bribe, blackmail or destroy along the way.

The neg cleared his throat. 'I know the face of every animal in this shithole. Never seen him.'

I fixed him with a challenging gaze. 'Then why did the girl I just spoke to say he was here?'

Confusion touched his features, his nose crinkling. 'Seriously, I don't know what she told you, but this guy is *not* in this hub.' His cold eyes locked on mine. They sent a shiver down my spine, reminding me that while the system was terribly flawed, some negs really were very frightening. But he wasn't lying.

I put away the photo and pulled the coin-sized zip from my pack. I flipped it in the air and he quickly snatched it. 'Scores are in the sports section,' I said, turning.

'Wait! You're leaving here, aren't you?' His breathing picked up and he moved towards me, causing me to step back cautiously. 'I ... I'm Ben,' he said.

I looked at his chest, avoiding his eyes, and winced. I hated it when they told me their names. It made the nightmares so much worse.

He reached out and grabbed my left wrist in a fierce grip, making it clear he had no intention of letting me go anywhere. I could see the thoughts flitter across his face – fear, anger, mostly desperation – as he tried to work out what approach to take. I'd seen them all.

His grip tightened, but I didn't try to pull away. 'Take me with you. Please. Take me with you!' he pleaded, settling on begging.

I turned my right arm slightly and glanced at my M-Band. I had less than twelve minutes to get out.

My fingers curled into a tight fist and I closed my eyes briefly. When I opened them, I knew they were emotionless. Much colder than his had been. The way they had to be.

'Sorry,' I said. 'Can't.'

Three

'So you just knocked him out and left him there?' Gus said after I gave him a brief rundown of the night on my walk home.

I put my hand over the receiver as I blew out a tired breath. 'Yes.'

The door to my attic room above the garage was stuck and I had to kick it to get inside. It wasn't big and barely had any ventilation – forget about insulation – but it beat sharing a room with my mom or brother in our tiny excuse for a house. And there was the added bonus that no one could monitor my comings and goings.

'You're a callous piece of work,' Gus murmured.

'Yes,' I agreed, my voice flat. I'd learned to shut down and justify my actions a long time ago. I was just glad the neg hadn't been fast enough to put up a fight and cost me precious seconds. As it was, I only made it back into the elevator at the thirty-minute mark, which also turned out to be exactly three minutes before the blonde driver of the cherry convertible barged through the stairwell door with building maintenance, complaining that the elevator wasn't working.

'Someday one of them is going to catch you, or tell the right person about you.' He meant one of the negs.

I kicked off my boots and sat down on my mattress, only to jump up again and yank down my jeans. 'Damn it!'

'What?'

'I've got gravel in my ass.'

There was a pause on the other end as I inspected the damage, then, 'Oh. Well … that made my day a little better.' Gus sounded genuinely pleased.

'Just get me the map for the next quadrant.'

I could hear him jamming something into his mouth. 'I can try, but I lost my contact. I'm asking around, but if I ask the wrong person, we're both toast. It could take a while.'

When Gus said he'd lost his contact, it meant the contact was probably dead. I couldn't wait to be done with all this.

I wriggled out of my jeans and kicked them into the open garbage bag in the corner. Another pair totalled. 'How long, Gus? And don't mess with me.'

'Even once I find a new contact, you know we'll have to set up a dummy trade to build the trust. It could take a couple of months before we find the right source.'

Silence.

'Maggie, you there?'

I'd been watching *him* for so long. I was ready. But still, there was a part of me that had always hoped I wouldn't need to do it.

'Are you in place for the M-Band distribution next week?' I asked, a stillness coming over me. A resolve.

I could hear Gus's sharp intake of breath. He understood what this meant. 'Maggie … Jesus.' He took another moment. When he finally spoke again, his voice was tight. 'Even for you, this idea is insane.'

'Gus.'

He sighed. 'I'm scheduled for tomorrow. But when we get caught for this, which we will … a neg camp will seem like a holiday in the Bahamas.'

I turned on the shower and cast a quick glance at myself in the mirror. The person staring back at me was a stranger. Someone who'd taken the girl I was two years ago and stripped her down only to rebuild a different person. Now I was strong, I was capable and smart. They were the good qualities. But I was also calculated, manipulative and selfish. They were the things I promised myself I wouldn't be. After I found him. After we put this right.

'Quentin Mercer is a spoilt little rich kid. I've been watching him for the past three months, Gus.' Actually,

I'd been watching him for the past two years. 'He won't be a problem once I hook him. This is my best chance.' I swallowed back the truth. This was my *only* chance.

Gus snorted. 'It's times like this I miss the old days when a girl could just shove her tits in a guy's face to get what she wanted.'

That *would* be much easier. But in a world dictated by pheromone ratings, the magical power of tits and ass had slid down the scale.

'I'll call you tomorrow,' I said, finishing the conversation.

'Hope that gravel burns like hell when you're pulling it out.'

With a half-smile, I hung up and hopped in my minuscule shower with a pair of tweezers.

Gus got his wish.

It wasn't the familiar surroundings of our old home, or the smell of one of Mom's cakes burning in the oven that made me realise I was dreaming of the days before Dad turned neg – it was seeing myself from a distance. It was the only way I had these dreams now, as if I'd become so different that I could only view myself from afar.

Mom always baked on Thursdays. It was her one night shift of the week, and she liked to leave something out for us to have as a treat. We used to toss a coin to see who would do the taste test after she'd gone to work.

Samuel had skipped out with his friends again, leaving Dad and me alone. It was surreal to see him, and I recognised the ache in my chest. He looked like he always did; his hair was long and he was wearing a shirt tucked neatly into his pants. I couldn't look away from his eyes. They had the kind of warmth that comes with time, family and hard work. I found myself studying him with a familiar awe.

Dad sliced off a bite-sized piece of Mom's cake, casting a dubious glance towards my sixteen-year-old self. 'Do you think it's chocolate?' he asked, a glimmer in his eye.

My younger self laughed heartily. 'That or she's burned it evenly all over.'

Dad chuckled. I could see the joy reflected in my younger eyes that I'd delivered a good comeback. He popped the piece of cake into his mouth. Chewed. Glanced briefly towards me with a grim smile. Then grabbed his keys and wallet off the counter. 'Wanna eat out?'

I was out of my chair in a flash.

In the blink of an eye we were sitting in a small booth in the diner two towns over. Dad and I talked about my school, friends and how annoying Samuel had become – though Dad didn't exactly participate in that part – and then we both turned as one of the customers started to give a young waitress a hard time.

'Max, surely you can get some help in here that doesn't put us all on edge,' he said to the manager. 'She never rates well. Barely friendly.'

I observed my dream version, watching how my forehead crinkled and I turned back to Dad, whispering, 'She seemed really nice to me.'

Dad smiled softly. 'It's all because of the M-Chip, Margaret. We're a lost cause now,' he said, ignoring my brief scowl at the mention of my name.

'What do you mean?' I asked.

He rubbed his eyes, watching the waitress closely even as he responded. 'People have left their fates in the hands of corporations. The individual desire to be in the know, connected, included, to possess the latest technologies … It's a disease.'

The alarm on my M-Band sounded and the dream slipped away from me. I swung my legs over the edge of my bed and dropped my face into my trembling hands. I missed him so much. That was the first night Dad had taken me to Mitchell's Diner.

Securing a place in America's most selective private school, Kingly Academy, had not been easy, especially given that I couldn't afford to buy my way in. But I had viewed it as a test of my dedication. I knew if I wasn't willing to put in the time and effort to ace the entry exam, then I wasn't going to be strong enough to do any of the things that would follow.

I jumped off the bus – wishing I'd managed more than a couple hours of sleep – and headed towards the front doors, lingering on the entrance steps.

It was game day.

It had taken eighteen months of studying and six months of my savings – savings Mom believed were going into a college fund – for credible cheat sheets. But it was worth it when I received the full scholarship. I might've made the cut anyway; my GPA was now well over the 3.0 required. But I'll never know. Didn't matter anyway. I hadn't busted my ass for the academic satisfaction. I was there for one reason.

Quentin Mercer.

He probably never had to sit an entrance exam in his life. His name alone opened every door he'd ever need. His older brothers, Sebastian and Zachery, had both been head boy and valedictorian of Kingly. Judging from what I'd seen of them, their cheat sheets had been the best money could buy.

Quentin, on the other hand, coasted. He did well at everything, but didn't particularly excel. Yet even his cruising level was in the top fifteen per cent of some of the most promising minds and sporting potential in the country. I figured he just couldn't be bothered to read his cheat sheets all the way through, which made him even lazier than his amoral brothers.

Out of the corner of my eye I saw his black SUV, equipped with the latest bulletproofing, pull up at the corner. I never understood why he didn't have his driver drop him right at the front doors. Possibly it was an attempt to fit in with his peers. Clearly he hadn't noticed that most of them were delivered to the front doors in chauffeur-driven cars themselves.

I watched him walk up the entrance steps. He was the picture of ease; with himself, his surroundings, with what he projected to others. Quentin Mercer knew who he was and felt no need to fit anyone's expectations. His shirt hung half untucked. His tie was perfectly knotted, but hanging on an angle. His shoes were polished to a high-gloss shine, with one lace untied. He was a walking contradiction and that seemed to be exactly what made him comfortable.

I studied his face. Soft features with hard eyes that he wasn't afraid to unleash on others. He was handsome, sure, but the addition of a scar down the edge of his hairline tilted everything from just right to not quite. He could've easily grown his hair long enough to cover the mark. He'd certainly look prettier for it. But instead he kept his hair buzz-short, as if refusing to hide it. It was the one thing I liked about him. The one thing I hoped meant he would have enough backbone to get through this day.

I stood in his path on the steps. One of us was going to have to move, and I knew full well that Quentin expected the world to move for him. I mean, why wouldn't he? He was an heir to M-Corp after all.

Just the thought strengthened my determination and my jaw clenched.

Head down, earphones in, he didn't even raise his eyes to look at me. He just stopped when he saw my feet blocking his path.

I almost laughed. Did he really think he didn't even have to look at me to get me to scamper out of his way? I leaned back against the wall and crossed one ankle over the other, settling in.

I could just about feel the shock bounce off him. Slowly, he lifted a hand to take out an earpiece while simultaneously lifting hard blue eyes to mine. More steel than ocean.

Oh, I felt it – the sting of his stare – but I didn't flinch. He raised an eyebrow.

I stared right back at him, bored.

His brow furrowed. He gestured to my booted feet. 'Those aren't regulation,' he said. They were the first words Quentin had ever deemed me worthy of.

I glanced at my black army boots – laces untied, my grey skinny jeans jammed into them – then back at him, still bored, still not moving.

His eyes narrowed, but I thought for a second the corner of his mouth might have twitched.

He leaned towards me. I think it was supposed to unnerve me, but the more this dance went on, the more comfortable I became. 'I'm sorry, I don't know your name, but if this is some attempt to …' His lips definitely twitched. 'I have a girlfriend.'

My own amusement came to an abrupt halt. Did he really think I was *hitting* on him? Today of all days? *Seriously?* And did he really think I cared that he didn't know my name? I'd made it my business to never be noticed by him before today.

Holding back a snort, I kept his gaze, lowering my voice to mirror his. 'And I have a spot that I'm happy standing in. There are three other entry doors that no one's using.'

'I'm sorry?' He actually didn't know what to do.

'Apology accepted.'

He blinked, anger now starting to show. 'I wasn't … *apologising*. Do you mind? I need to pass.'

'Well then, I suggest you walk down the stairs and take the next door. That, or you could try to move me yourself.'

I was sure in that moment that no student *or* teacher at Kingly had ever spoken to Mr Mercer that way. And the fact that it was over such a small thing made it even better.

I kept my breathing even and maintained the same expression, even when I heard the satisfying sound of his M-Band beeping twice, registering his increased blood pressure levels. Yep, I was pissing him off.

Finally, Quentin Mercer turned tail and moved to the other side of the railing before re-climbing the steps to access a door I wasn't blocking. His steely eyes stayed on me the entire time.

'That went well,' I whispered to myself as I watched him walk down the school hall. His girlfriend, Ivy Knight, wrapped her tall, annoyingly busty body around him as soon as she saw him.

I hitched my bag onto my shoulder and made my way to the day's first class, my hand unconsciously caressing the small vial in my jacket pocket.

By the end of today, Quentin would never need to ask my name again.

Four

It was a day of building blocks. Very carefully placed blocks that I'd spent the past two years collecting. If one thing slipped off kilter, everything would come crashing down. And that simply wasn't an option. I'd never get another shot at this.

After a mind-numbing hour of American history, I spotted Thomas Mayer heading for the library. He wasn't an overly popular guy, but he was one of the most outspoken at Kingly. He was the head of the debating team and had already received an early offer of full scholarship at Harvard Law. He was also, like most people now, a health freak.

I followed him to the library, noting that on top of his books he balanced a bottle of SwitzWater. I couldn't contain the eye roll. As if rainwater collected from peaks of the Swiss Alps was going to provide the miracle 'pheromone cleansing' it advertised.

The school librarian, Ms Cooper, was tapping away

on the computer at her desk. I bit back a smirk when I saw her flinch at the sight of me. My trip to the library had just become dual purpose.

Eighteen months ago I'd begun shadowing a number of Kingly's teachers. It was a lucky day when I'd spied Ms Cooper attempting to negotiate her way out of some heavy gambling debts with one of Arlington's less forgiving loan sharks. Unlike many of the older generations, Ms Cooper had taken to the new world of M-Chips and their many uses like a duck to water. In particular, gambling. Seeing my opportunity, I'd stepped in and made her an offer she literally couldn't refuse – unless she was okay with seeing her dog's throat slit that night.

Tough choice. She really loved her dog.

'Hello, Ms Cooper,' I said, smiling.

'Ms Stevens,' she said curtly, straightening her frumpy dress at the waist, avoiding my eyes. I might have paid off her debts, but she – like many others – definitely didn't appreciate the repayment schedule.

'Everything arranged?' I asked, resting my elbow on the high bench and keeping an eye on Thomas.

She pursed her pencil-lined lips unhappily. 'You're an intelligent girl. If you spent as much time studying as you do … God knows what, you wouldn't need to cheat,' she hissed.

I shrugged. 'Probably true, Ms Cooper. But those other things I have to do keep me awfully busy. When will the papers be ready?'

I liked Ms Cooper. She had fight in her eyes and I respected that. But she and I both knew we were already in way too deep together.

'Tomorrow,' she said, looking back at her computer. She was finished with me. I nodded, making a mental note to return for the copy of my midterm questions tomorrow. She might not like helping me keep my place at Kingly Academy, but like Gus, she always delivered.

Thomas had set up his books and laptop at one of the deserted communal desks, placing his water bottle on the edge. He obviously had a free period and was settling in. It was almost too easy. After about five minutes, he disappeared into the boys' bathroom. As soon as he was gone, I whipped by his table and cracked the lid on Switzerland's finest.

Pheromones don't begin to register in human bodies until after puberty. When scientists first discovered how to access and decipher pheromone data, it was quickly decided that children would not be given access to Phera-tech until the age of eighteen. This would allow teenagers to complete puberty before relying on the new technology to make positive and negative matches.

Once you turned eighteen, you were fitted with a new M-Band containing the Phera-tech zip. In activation mode, the new M-Band would take a pheromone reading off people within a two-metre radius, rating them according to their chemical signature. Ratings were given as percentages and included everything from friendship to lust potentials and long-term relationships – as well as the rare one hundred per cent true match.

It remained a person's right to choose whether or not to leave the Phera-tech on – some turned it off when they found their long-term match, or in the golden cases their true match – but it was compulsory for every adult to be fitted with the Phera-tech zip and to register a minimum of four ratings per calendar month.

Why?

So that negs could be detected.

Along with four other students, I'd celebrated my eighteenth birthday this month. Which meant we were all required by law to have M-Bands with Phera-tech. And today was the day M-Corp was sending in one of its technicians to upgrade our M-Bands.

Walking through the halls during lunch, I sensed people's excitement. An upgrade day always created a thrill, and today wasn't just an ordinary upgrade day. Ratings ruled futures and preparation had become key. Gone were the days of the rave parties. Underage sex was scarce and no one smoked or did drugs. These days, the biggest trend was gambling. Predicting other people's ratings was big business and Kingly was no exception.

Today was a *major* payday for the school's punters – in just over an hour, everyone would know whether Quentin and Ivy were the ideal match they appeared to be.

I'd placed a hefty bet myself.

I had every intention of turning my Phera-tech off the moment I could. But aside from long-term – usually married – couples, deactivating was seen as a Pre-Evo statement. My choice would put me in a highly judged minority of the population. Not a problem as far as I was concerned.

Preference Evolution supporters were still fighting against M-Chipping and pheromone technology. They were the only ones left who stood by the idea of the God-particle – claiming that each person should have the chance to bend against science and explore love for themselves.

I agreed. But I wasn't one of them. Their methods were too slow, too righteous and result lacking.

I sat in the back corner of the lunchroom, watching the 'in' table. Quentin and Ivy were the focal point, flanked by some of Kingly's highest and mightiest. It was surprising there wasn't a green aura surrounding the table given the amount of money wafting off them.

Ivy and Quentin had been together for the last year and were *the* couple everyone drooled over. They appeared to have it all: great looks, intelligence, high-flying families, connections, money-money-money. And the list went on ...

Ivy was stunning, of course. No one snags the high-school hottie without being equally as attractive – at least, not without Phera-tech on her side. Ivy somehow managed to portray a demure image, and I had to give it to her, she knew how to put herself together without looking overdone. In fact, with her slender frame, naturally golden hair and restrained makeup, which showcased her smattering of freckles, she really did paint the picture of a natural beauty. There were not many guys at the school who did not covet her. And more than a few made passes at her, despite the fact she was clearly Mercer territory.

Quentin seemed unbothered by the male attention Ivy received. He appeared to be more than content to sit beside her, earplugs in, while everyone chatted around him. He was that arrogant. The odds were high in favour of a Quentin / Ivy seventy per cent plus match – which would put them in the 'happily ever after' category.

If today went my way, not only would I hook Quentin, I'd bankroll Gus's attempts to secure our new contact.

The final bell rang and students began meandering towards their classes. All except for Ivy, Quentin, Nathan Bennett and me.

Despite my best efforts, I was nervous. But then I looked over at Nathan Bennett, who was sporting his usual angry-at-the-world expression, and I couldn't help feeling a little smug. He was the perfect person to round out our little group.

Feeling eyes on me, I turned back to the centre table and caught Quentin staring at me with – what? Morbid curiosity? I wondered briefly if I'd made the right decision that morning, challenging him that way. But then he turned his gaze away – not embarrassed, he'd simply finished looking. I rolled my eyes. Yes, it had been the right decision. He had to know I was strong, that I could stand up to intimidation and power. It was the only way he was going to trust me.

The cafeteria door swung open and in strolled Headmaster Edwards, followed by a familiar face.

'Right.' Mr Edwards nodded, taking in our presence. 'We're all here, good. You'll note Mr Mayer is not present. He appears to have become quite unwell and was taken home. Therefore …' The principal cleared his throat uncomfortably and I forced a neutral expression. No one else needed to know I was giving myself a mental high-five. 'We will be continuing without him.'

Without a fifth person to attend the upgrade, Principal Edwards was walking a fine line. Many people would consider a postponement. But today was no ordinary upgrade day and, like Ms Cooper, Mr Edwards enjoyed a side wager. I'd had no doubt he would've bet big on the Quentin / Ivy match. I had counted on it.

'This is Mr Reynolds. He will be fitting you with your upgraded M-Bands today.' Mr Edwards cast his gaze over all of us, settling disapprovingly on Nathan. It may have had something to do with his black skinny jeans teamed with a formal suit jacket. He almost pulled it off too, in that kinda rocker, kinda emo way. Almost.

'For the sake of clarification,' Mr Edwards continued. 'Let me reiterate what I am sure you already know. Included in your new upgrade will be pheromone technology. It will be your choice whether this accessory remains active or not. However, everyone is required to register a minimum of four pheromone readings per calendar month. As I am sure you are aware, if you register more than three negative ratings in any one-month period, you will be liable to further inquiry. Now, before I leave you in the capable hands of Mr Reynolds, does anyone have any questions?'

Faced with our silence, he went on, 'Very well. Lastly, please remember, teachers keep their Phera-tech inactive during school hours. We ask that you respect their privacy if you should see them outside of school hours and not attempt to take a reading.' His eyes narrowed in warning, as we nodded awkwardly. Pheromone ratings had caused some inappropriate relations between students and teachers in the past. Satisfied with our response, he spun around and disappeared through the swinging doors.

Everyone stared at Mr Reynolds.

Or as I knew him, Gus.

At the age of twenty-two, Gus was young to be in the position he was. He clicked the top of his pen, uncomfortable with the attention, and concentrated on the folder in his hand. 'I've um … I've set up in room 212 just down the hall.' He glanced at me and I stared back impassively. Damn it, he was not normally nervous. I narrowed my eyes in the hope of aggravating him. Anything would be an improvement.

'All your preliminary data has already been uploaded. It will only take about five minutes to link up your new bands. You can come in at five-minute intervals.'

Was he *sweating*?

'Upon entering the room, you will be required to use cleansing inhalers to clear your system before testing.

Please ensure you inhale these fully.' Gus cleared his throat, but was finally warming up. 'I'll see you in reverse alphabetic order. Maggie Stevens first, then Quentin Mercer, Ivy Knight and Nathan Bennett. Any questions?'

Ivy leaned forwards in her seat and smiled. 'Will you have your Phera-tech on active?'

The obvious come-on was a surprise. I didn't see it myself, but girls seemed to find Gus's genius rebel look a turn-on. Even more surprising was Quentin's complete lack of care. He actually looked slightly amused. Either way, it gave Gus what he needed to get his mojo back.

His shoulders loosened and he gave Ivy a lingering look, which had her turning pink. 'I see no reason why I should. Do you?'

Oh, poor Ivy. She was so out of her league.

Ivy's pink blush turned red and she shook her head, suddenly finding her shoes fascinating.

'Let's get this done then. Miss Stevens?' Gus prompted.

I nodded, my mouth suddenly dry, and followed Gus out of the cafeteria.

Five

O nce we were halfway down the hall, he glanced at me with an are-you-sure-about-this look. I raised my eyebrows in a don't-make-me-hurt-you response. He shrugged and kept moving into room 212, positioning himself behind the desk where his computer and M-Band equipment were already set up.

'I see our testing group is missing a person,' Gus said slyly.

I shrugged. 'Poor Thomas. Must be something in the water.'

Gus grinned even as he shook his head. Having five people in the room would've made things considerably more difficult, not to mention Thomas was altogether too opinionated and forthright. He could've ruined everything.

'You look like a nerd by the way,' I threw at him, giving his navy blue suit the once-over. Gus had a particular style – a unique expensive yet somehow thrifty look that I'd never admit worked for him – but this suit was not part of it. At least he'd kept his haphazard hair.

He tugged at his sleeves, scowling. 'Blondie out there liked it enough.' He flashed a brief smile. 'M-Corp policy when representing the company. Baggy suits with pillow-sized shoulder pads should be outlawed.'

I refocused my attention as I closed the classroom door and stood in front of the plastic tray holding the four small inhalers. Everything around me faded away as I studied the small vials, taking slow steady breaths.

Pheromones are released through our glands, and we register them via a receptor located between our nose and mouth. If there was a blockage to a receptor then a pheromone reading could theoretically be faulty. The inhalers, taken through the nose, were intended to cleanse and ensure there was no interference.

Reaching into my pocket, I extracted the tiny vial I had carried with me for the past two years. It was all I had left of my father. Dad hadn't even known I'd taken it. I swallowed, thinking back to that day. I was only just sixteen and didn't understand. Dad and all his crazy experiments were nothing more than fun times to me. It had been our secret. Our special time together. I wished I'd paid more attention, or at least told him how much I admired him.

I often wondered what Dad would tell me to do if he knew I still had the vial. Given what it was capable of, he'd probably expect something sensible, like delivering it to the Pre-Evo's. But I couldn't part with it. Especially when I knew it could make all the difference.

I picked up the inhaler labelled Quentin Mercer, opened the top and dumped the contents into a nearby flowerpot. With a deep breath and a glance towards Gus, who had turned a pale shade of grey, I poured in the vial's contents and resealed the lid.

Gus groaned. 'We're going to burn bad for this.'

I licked my dry lips and tried for a smile. 'You worry too much.'

He shook his head, turning back to his keyboard. 'Sometimes I think I would've been better off taking the jail time than getting into bed with you.'

Now my smile turned spiteful. 'The day you and I get into bed together will be the day I'm buried in the ground.'

'Gives us both something to look forward to then,' he hissed. 'Turn off your band.'

I did as he instructed and heard the ensuing beeps as my new band uplinked with my M-Chip.

'Here.' Gus tossed my new M-Band at me. 'It's up and running. Put it on.'

When he saw my hesitation, he smirked. 'Nervous you might be the one to test neg?'

It hadn't been what I was thinking, although it wasn't as if the idea hadn't crossed my mind. With all the choices

I'd made lately, the things I'd done to people, wouldn't I be the perfect candidate for a neg rating?

Instead of answering his question, I eyed him suspiciously. 'You're inactive?'

He scoffed, looking like he was on the verge of laughter. 'Baby, trust me when I say, I don't need a pheromone reading to know you and I are never going to be compatible in any way. Inhaler.' The last was an order.

I grinned. 'True.' I picked up the inhaler labelled as mine and breathed it in, following protocol. It was important I didn't do anything out of the ordinary – other than what I'd already done, that is.

We heard footsteps and then the door opened. Quentin Mercer strolled in, super suave. Guess knocking isn't required in his world.

'You ready for me?' he asked Gus, his voice as smooth as his walk.

Gus nodded. 'Just activating your band.'

Quentin moved in, giving me a wide berth, which gave me confidence. I sat on the edge of one of the classroom desks and studied my new band. It looked exactly like my old band, but the touchscreen had more accessories. I cheered myself internally when I noticed that my heart rate was cruising exactly where it should be.

There was a beep from Gus's direction; Quentin's new M-Band was online and attempting the uplink to his M-Chip.

Gus's brow furrowed and he looked up at Quentin. 'Have you still got your other M-Band turned on?'

Quentin nodded.

'Turn it off, please.'

While Quentin followed Gus's instructions, I opened up my new Phera-tech zip for the first time, noting the side diagram resembling a thermometer. It provided the visual gauge of any rating, while the dial in the middle offered additional information such as gene types and health data. Phera-tech didn't automatically entitle you to have access to other people's medical history and gene typing, but if authorised by the individual, it was all there for the taking.

I shook my head at the thought and heard another beep; Quentin's M-Chip linking correctly with his new M-Band that was resting by Gus's computer.

This was it. The moment of truth. Two years of planning. Two years of doing things that would forever haunt my dreams. If this failed ...

Out of nowhere, my band flashed and released a three-beep blast. Startled, I looked down at the screen. The air left my lungs in a rush and another series of beeps sounded. Heart rate, blood pressure – I was going off like a freaking fire alarm.

Feeling faint, I grappled to turn off my Phera-tech while out of the corner of my eyes I saw Gus reach for Quentin's band, which had also beeped.

I took a breath and dug deep for equilibrium before looking up. Both Quentin and Gus were staring at me suspiciously. I swallowed, reassuring myself that now that I had deactivated my Phera-tech any data would be erased from both of our bands.

I'd almost ruined everything.

'What?' I said, my voice too pitchy for comfort. I took another breath and pulled it together. 'I'm nervous and my heart rate spiked.' I tilted my head towards Quentin, recovering my mask. 'Surely you know what that's like,' I mocked, referring to his heart rate beep-off earlier.

Quentin kept watching me, again with a curiosity that seemed to unsettle him. Gus was flat-out staring at me. Hands on hips, I narrowed my gaze on him until he looked away.

Gus turned his attention back to Quentin and pointed to the inhaler. 'Inhale.'

Quentin picked up the inhaler and I could feel the blood pumping in my chest and rushing to my head. I had to work hard to control my breathing so my M-Band didn't go off again. With a fast snort, Quentin inhaled the small dose. This *had* to work.

'All set,' Gus mumbled, looking back and forth between Quentin and me.

Quentin took off his old M-Band, handing it over to Gus and replacing it quickly with his new upgrade. He used the touchscreen to check a few settings, seeming anxious to make sure everything was correct. Then, as if surprised, he looked up at me. 'Your Phera-tech's off …?' It was a statement and question in one, though I wasn't sure exactly what he was really asking.

I shrugged, unfazed. 'I'll turn it on for the testing.'

His brow furrowed, and then he surprised me by tapping his screen. 'Me too, then.'

Before I had a chance to wonder about his response, Ivy pushed open the door. 'Ready?' she asked, smiling at Quentin excitedly.

Gus motioned Ivy in and followed the same process, setting her up and linking her M-Chip to her new M-Band, and then again when Nathan entered.

Our records were uploaded and codes for our new M-Bands were scanned into the system to hook up our GPS and health history. Then, as the privacy act stipulated, Gus cleared all of the old M-Bands. Each one of us had to fingerprint-sign on his computer screen that the band was now inactive. When I signed mine, I used the opportunity to give Gus a wink, reminding him why he was here, *why* he had no choice. It was his fondness for rebooting discarded M-Bands and selling them on the black market that had given me the perfect leverage against him.

I felt more than *saw* his seething hatred.

'Your new M-Bands will be on factory settings,' he told us. 'Check your heart rate and other health monitors are operating as per usual, ensuring that if you have any prescribed medicines these are picked up through the link.' Everyone complied, nodding when they'd checked.

Gus took a deep breath. 'Okay. Let's turn on the Phera-tech and run a test. Please stand within a two-metre radius of one another. It's easiest if you form a small circle. When you are ready, if you haven't done so, turn on your new tech.'

Nathan moved forwards first, surprising me by his eagerness. His angsty attitude always made me assume he was a Pre-Evo, or at least against the technology. But for the first time he actually appeared to be … excited. Willing.

Huh. I'd had Nathan Bennett all wrong. He wasn't against it. He was one of the quiet hopefuls. There were a lot like him, teenagers who'd never been much more than average and hoped their new rating potential would open doors. Until now Nathan had done a good job of keeping his desires hidden.

Ivy scooped up Quentin's hand and they moved into their positions. 'This is it, baby,' she said excitedly, planting a kiss on his cheek.

He smiled back, but it didn't reach his eyes. I wondered briefly if anything ever made him *really* smile.

Once in position, we all turned on our Phera-tech. Everyone watched their bands with eagle eyes. Everyone but me. I was watching Quentin. Within a matter of seconds his M-Band registered one, then two, then three people in his immediate proximity and the colour drained from his face and his shoulders rolled forwards.

I glanced at Gus, who was also watching intently.

You see, this was never about changing Quentin's pheromone signature. Changing his signature would achieve nothing. What really made a difference was changing the way he received the *incoming* signatures.

It was called disruption.

Thanks to Dad's chemical cocktail, Quentin had just read all three of us as negatives. And because readings are mutual and a negative reading overrides any other, all of our readings had reacted the same way towards him.

'Can I get you to call out the ratings, please, as I name the pair,' Gus powered on, remaining professional. 'Please note that I may at any stage request visual verification. Miss Knight and Mr Bennett?'

Ivy, who'd also turned a ghostly shade, blurted out her response. 'Sixty per cent.'

Nathan concurred, looking pleased he'd just rated as lust-match potential with the hottest girl in school.

'Mr Bennett and Miss Stevens?' Gus asked.

'Forty per cent,' Nathan responded, sounding comfortable that this put us in the non-compatible category.

'Miss Stevens, you'll need to verify,' Gus said, barely containing his smile at the rating.

'Yes, forty per cent is correct,' I said.

Sure, I was no prize, but I could assure Nathan the feeling was mutual.

'Okay.' Gus tapped a few keys on his computer. 'Mr Bennett and Mr Mercer?'

Quentin swallowed and opened his mouth, but nothing came out.

'That's a negative response from me,' Nathan responded wearily. A neg rating was always uncomfortable. I suspected the only reason he'd said it aloud was because he'd already had the two other acceptable ratings, assuring him that he couldn't be a neg.

Ivy was looking at Quentin, who seemed to be ignoring her.

Yep. Suave had left the building.

When it became apparent Quentin wasn't in a hurry to verify, Gus used the opportunity. 'Mr Bennett, could you please bring your band over here for visual verification.'

The Privacy Act prevented ratings from being recorded on any kind of government mainframe. *Except* in the case that your Phera-tech registered four or more negative ratings in a month. If that happened, a flag was activated and privacy became non-existent. If an investigation proved the person was a neg, removal was immediate.

Technicians like Gus were authorised and expected to make random visual checks when they felt the need.

Once Gus had verified the reading and sent Nathan back to the circle, he proceeded. 'I need Miss Knight and Miss Stevens.'

'Forty-five per cent,' Ivy said, sounding distracted.

Girls tended to rate quite low with one another – unless they were gay – averaging between twenty-five and fifty per cent. Boys had higher averages, ranging between forty to sixty per cent. This reading put Ivy and me in the compatible friend category. Strange.

I verified the result.

'Thank you,' Gus said, entering some more data. 'Miss Knight and Mr Mercer?'

This time, it was Ivy who appeared to be speechless. 'I ... I ...'

Gus looked up, eyebrows raised inquisitively as if he didn't know exactly what she was about to say.

'Negative,' Quentin said, his tone low, lost.

When Ivy remained speechless, Gus took a visual verification from her before returning to his computer, entering the numbers. 'Mr Mercer and Miss Stevens?'

My M-Band gave me the exact same reading for our compatibility as it did for Quentin. He knew what the answer was just as much as I did. In my peripheral vision, I could see Ivy watching, mouth agape, and Nathan looking increasingly smug. I was glad Nathan and I were incompatible.

Quentin looked up and was about to say the word when I jumped in. 'Eighty-two per cent.'

Ivy gasped. I had to refrain from shaking my head at her. Instead of being relieved for Quentin, she looked disappointed. By rating so well with me, it meant she couldn't blame their neg result on him.

Quentin's eyes cut to mine, overflowing with fear and questions. I held his gaze, challenging him once again. He needed to corroborate the rating.

Seconds felt like an eternity as he looked at me, wondering what game I was playing. If only he knew …

Finally, and slowly, Quentin nodded and cleared his throat. 'Eighty-two per cent,' he confirmed.

My insides flipped. *Hooked*.

'Right,' Gus said quickly, entering the data into his report. 'Well, unless you want to stay behind with any questions, we're all done here.'

Nathan was out the door in a flash. While it was going to be impossible for Ivy to keep her rating with Quentin a secret, I could tell Nathan wouldn't be advertising his one neg rating.

Ivy looked longingly at the door and then back at Quentin. 'I should ... you know, get back to class,' she said, avoiding his eyes.

Quentin nodded distractedly. 'Catch you later.'

Wow, was that their way of breaking up?

When it was just Quentin, Gus and me in the room, Quentin took a nervous step in my direction. 'Can we talk, outside?'

Instead of answering him, I turned my attention to Gus. 'Mr Reynolds, could you please confirm for me – is a history of our ratings kept on file anywhere?'

'Why is that, Miss Stevens? Hoping not to leave an electronic trail of lust-matches?' Gus replied, working hard to suppress his smirk.

'Not at all. Just wondering if there is some tech-perv sitting in a room somewhere, watching over my relationship status.' I threw him a tight-lipped smile.

His eyes narrowed, but this time he stayed on script. 'There is no history recorded anywhere. The Privacy Act guarantees that your results remain your business, unless of course you trigger four or more negative readings in any one-month period. Then, well, it's a different ball game,' he replied, reminding Quentin that if he received one more neg rating this month he would be up for investigation.

Investigations didn't end well.

'Anything else, Miss Stevens?'

'No. That's it.' I made a show of adjusting my M-Band to turn off the Phera-tech and finally glanced at Quentin, who'd been listening to the exchange. 'You might want to do the same,' I said quietly.

He nodded and followed suit.

Gus glanced up at Quentin. 'Sorry about your neg ratings, man. I mean, with your girl and all. You have money riding on that?'

Quentin was still watching me as he shrugged and mumbled. 'Don't worry about it.'

Gus glanced at me one last time, his sparkling eyes saying enough. Yeah, it was a mega payday for us. I'd put almost all of my savings, plus a big contribution by Gus, against Ivy and Quentin being compatible. And the odds had definitely been in our favour.

Not wanting to delay anymore, I headed for the door. 'See ya round,' I said, smiling when I heard Quentin hurrying after me.

'Wait, we need to ... Can we talk? What you did back there ... I mean ...'

I slowed and looked at him.

'Thank you,' he rasped. 'If Thomas had been there ...' He rubbed his hand over his face as he considered the dire result. Yes, if Thomas had been there, he'd already be under investigation.

I feigned a sigh. 'Look. You're a neg,' I said, ignoring the way he flinched at the word. 'The second you turn on your Phera-tech again, you'll tip over the three limit and there's nothing you can do about it. Your flag will activate and then … you know the drill. You've got until the end of the month to register another rating. My advice, don't turn it back on until you figure out what you're going to do.'

His eyes were so wide they were mostly white. 'I can't do that.' He pressed his lips together. 'My family.'

I gave him a considering look, as if measuring him up. 'Your family will understand,' I said.

He swallowed. 'We both know that's not true.'

We did.

I pulled a stick of gum out of my pocket and popped it in my mouth. 'Sorry, not my problem.'

His eyes flashed. 'Just getting a kick out of delaying the inevitable then?' he said bitterly.

I took my time, watching as the fear and hopelessness continued to seep into him. It was all on the line and every second that passed intensified his desperation. Finally, I let out the breath I was holding. 'I might know a way I could help you.'

His eyes narrowed. 'You can't cheat the system!'

I leaned into him, just like he had done to me on the steps earlier that morning.

'If you want to be all high and mighty, go for it. Turn on your Phera-tech. Take a few ratings. It'll give you something to talk about over the dinner table tonight.' And with that I left him standing in the hall, knowing that if I hadn't covered for him in there, he would already be under neg suspicion. But then, as I stalked down the hall, I cringed. Because if it hadn't have been for me, Quentin Mercer would not have rated negative at all.

Six

Half running to work that afternoon, I wondered how long it would be before I saw Quentin again.

If he'd had enough guts to turn his Phera-tech back on, he'd know by now that the earlier readings had been bogus. The disruption chemicals he'd inhaled at school would've already stopped affecting him.

Still, I had to wait for him to come to me. If I appeared too keen, he'd know something was up.

I entered the Clarendon M-Store. Even the glaring white light and wall-to-wall light boxes couldn't suppress the feeling of darkness that came over me the moment I crossed the threshold. I hated working there, but being on staff at the M-Corp accessory and products store for the past year had served my needs. I had access to tech training, company manuals and their staff computer systems. It didn't get me access to the good stuff, but small things were helpful every now and then. The biggest thing the job had given me was Gus. He was the head M-Band programmer at the store and if I hadn't been stuck there working the register late one night, I never would've caught – or recorded – his illicit M-Band trade in the back alley.

Gus was anxiously awaiting my arrival in his back room office.

'You're late,' he said by way of greeting. He had changed out of his suit and back into his thrifty-style thigh-hugging pants, with an orange T-shirt and skinny grey tie. He was also sporting his favourite tweed fedora.

'I'm so sorry, Arlington bus and metro mustn't have received your weekly schedule,' I snarled. He knew I came straight to work from school yet he persisted in making my start times impossible.

'So?' he prompted, ignoring my comment.

I looked over my shoulder as I hung up my bag. 'So, everything is on track. He's hooked. Now we have to wait.'

'And?'

I blinked. 'And what?'

'We both know and *what*, Miss Excuse-me-while-I-beep-up-a-storm.'

I moved into the curtained excuse for a change room to put on my work clothes. 'I have no idea what you're talking about,' I called out.

I heard the creak of Gus leaning back in his chair. 'Quinny's kinda dreamy, isn't he?' he goaded.

'Leave it, Gus.'

He scoffed. 'No way in hell. You got a rating, and we both know there was only one active M-Band in that room besides yours at that time. Was that your heart-rate alert I heard go off in there?' He sounded so smug.

Bastard.

Even after seeing what we'd managed to achieve with Quentin, Gus still had faith in the system that I hated. I pushed back the curtain and stormed out, throwing my bag under the table as I settled a steely glare in his direction. 'Just do your part and stay out of the rest. I've got work to do,' I growled. Ignoring his laughter, I moved past him to the shop area where I aimlessly served customers wanting the latest M-Band accessory zips. Right now calorie counters and 3D self-hologram projectors were all the rage.

To my disappointment, I didn't hear from Quentin while I was at work. It wouldn't have been hard for him to track down my M-Band number if he'd wanted to call me. I even kept my M-band cell on active when I stopped into my local Muay Thai centre for my scheduled fight.

I smiled as I walked into the seedy gym that had come to feel like a home away from home. Like many relationships, Master Rua's and mine was not based on smooth – or welcome – beginnings. But he knew about the tunnels, which was why I'd begged, then bribed, him to train me. He even knew who I was looking for, which made him one of the few I trusted. Almost.

'You're late,' Master Rua said when he saw me. At first look he seemed like an aged, unassuming man who, apart from a couple of tribal-style tattoos on his dark skin, appeared gentle in every way. You got a different image once you copped one of his roundhouse kicks.

I looked beyond his shoulder; there was a decent crowd sitting around, clearly unimpressed.

'Weren't there any other fights tonight?' I asked.

'Three. They finished fifteen minutes ago. If you didn't bring in a good crowd I'd stop booking you, Maggie,' he said sharply.

I held my chin up even though I felt bad. This was his business and, despite what he thought, I respected that.

'I got here as soon as I could,' I said.

He shook his head, but the small lift in the corner of his mouth gave him away and I knew we were good.

'That Pre-Evo guy came in and trained here again today,' he said, walking me towards the ring. I would've liked a chance to loosen up, but I'd kept people – and their money – waiting long enough. Besides, I knew who my competitor was tonight and I didn't really need the warm-up.

'And?' I dropped my bag and started stripping off my outer layer.

He opened his mouth to respond, but then gestured to my feet. 'You're limping,' he said.

'Only a bit,' I replied with a shrug.

He shook his head again. 'He asked after you,' he explained as I pulled on my ankle supports. 'Normally I throw anyone who asks after my people out on the street, but he seems genuine. We talked for a while. He wants to meet you.'

I'd been doing the underworld circuit for a while. I wasn't happy about it, but it wasn't a major surprise the Pre-Evo guy had pulled my name from somewhere. 'I don't do team sports, you know that,' I said, stretching and noticing my opponent had taken up position in the ring. I'd beaten him the last time we'd faced off so he would be out to prove something tonight. It would help keep the fight short. A good thing, since I didn't have time to spare.

I held out my hands for Master Rua to slip on my gloves. He glanced up at me, his eyes telling a story of time and knowledge and, right then, concern. 'You should think about it. Alex is high up in their group.'

'Alex?' I asked, my interest suddenly piqued.

Master Rua nodded.

Alex was the name of the Preference Evolution's leader. Coincidence? Unlikely. 'Maybe one day, but not yet,' I said, jumping into the ring and effectively finishing the conversation.

I won the fight, and a financial boost, before the second bell. I was out of there within ten minutes of walking through the doors.

As I arrived home, I replayed the events of the day. Had I played Quentin wrong? Made a mistake? Should I have tried to be nice? Pretended to care? Had I used the disruption chemicals for nothing?

With a huff, I pushed the front door closed, having to give it my shoulder before I heard it click in place.

'Mags, is that you?' Mom called out from the kitchen.

'Yes.' I followed her voice.

'I'd been starting to wonder where you had gotten to,' she said.

'Got held up on the Metro,' I lied. The fight hadn't taken long, but I'd detoured via our local realtor to pay the additional monthly rent on our house. When we'd first moved to Arlington, there was no way I was going to let Mom live in the types of places her budget could really afford. Not that she needed to know. And the shifty realtor hadn't cared as long as he got his money.

Mom smiled and continued pressing down pastry over a bowl, creating fork imprints. 'I'm making chicken and potato pie,' she beamed.

I smiled back, noticing that Mom's pants were hanging off her waist. We both had a similar tall and lean figure. But where she was gaunt and fragile, I had more muscle. From there we were quite different. Mom's eyes were large and blue in contrast to my brown ones, and she had refined features that benefited from makeup whereas mine were just … there. Unfortunately, it had been a long time since Mom had had the opportunity to get dressed up.

She took as many shifts at the hospital as she could get, but even then, a nurse's wage wasn't great. I knew she'd secretly taken on a couple of weekend cleaning jobs as well, which made me want to scream.

Mom's extra hours weren't just about keeping up with the everyday bills. No, it was so much more. For those people who were labelled as negs and moved out of society, well, there was the problem of how to settle all of their outstanding debts and taxes. That task fell to their remaining family members.

It was a great way of ensuring families would resent their 'neg' relations rather than fight for their freedom. It had definitely worked that way for Mom – Dad's unexplainable switch from being an acceptable seventy per cent match with Mom to a full neg with everyone in just one day left her believing he had done something so unforgivable it had literally changed his chemical makeup.

Living in a small town had made it impossible to escape the rumour mill. One day Mom just started packing, changed our surname to her maiden name and told us to get in the car. It wasn't long before Sam and I figured out that her plan had not extended beyond mass exodus. I'd seized the opportunity and suggested Arlington.

Watching her load the pie into the oven, I wished yet again that she'd see past the tech and to the truth. But Mom was a true supporter of Phera-tech, always keeping hers in active mode. I knew she still held out hope that there was a long-term match out there for her. Dad's wasn't the only life that had been stolen.

'Sounds great, Mom,' I said softly, more than prepared to eat the pie I knew she was about to burn. 'Is Sam here?' I asked, even though I didn't need to.

'He left for work a few hours ago.' The moment he'd turned twenty-one, my brother had taken a job at a local club well known for its black-market trade in lust-enhancers. Sam had barely been around before, but now … he had the perfect excuse to avoid anything family-related.

Mom looked up suddenly. 'I think he might've met a girl.'

'That's hardly news,' I mumbled. Sam wasn't opposed to using lust-enhancers himself. Working like an outward aphrodisiac, they zeroed in on lust-matches and improved them for short bursts. They also sent the signal out over a wider radius, covering more ground in a nightclub atmosphere. It gave people an edge and seemed to contain some chemical that heightened … sexual needs.

'A girl who rates high,' she added.

'Huh.' That was interesting.

Mom's eyes suddenly lit up. 'I almost forgot, how did your upgrade go?'

I dug into my pocket. 'It was fine, and no, I haven't changed my mind about keeping my tech active,' I explained as I pulled out a small handful of cash. It wasn't everything I'd earned today, but it would help for a few weeks.

'Here,' I said, putting it on the bench. 'Take a few shifts off this week, Mom. Rest.'

Mom blushed and looked away. 'Oh, Mags.'

I'd wanted to distract her, not make her cry.

'Mom, please. I got a bonus at work so don't worry. I'm still putting all my other wages into my college fund,' I lied. 'Please, just take it.'

She sniffed and swiped at an escaping tear. I felt my rising anger at the state of our lives. I needed to put distance between us. 'I've got to study, Mom. Call me when dinner's ready and …' I glanced around the kitchen. Mom had used pretty much every utensil and square inch of bench space. 'I'll clean up.'

Mom focused on setting the timer on the oven. 'Okay, honey.'

I headed out the back door and towards the garage, letting my stride finally settle into a weary limp, accommodating for the pain still jarring my left butt-cheek thanks to my excursion earlier in the week. I had a bad feeling I hadn't pulled out all of the gravel.

When I was in my room, I settled in to do my homework. I had to stay on top of the workload if I planned on keeping my place at Kingly's.

But it wasn't long before my thoughts drifted back to the plan. Sometimes, despite my bravado, I felt so out of my depth. All I knew was that I wanted to find Dad more than anything. I missed him so much, everyday. He was the one person who always made me feel like I could do anything.

Now that I had started the ball in motion, I knew there was no turning back. Dad was down there somewhere and if my worst suspicions – the ones I rarely allowed myself to consider – were true, his life had become worse than any other neg's hell.

Why hadn't Quentin contacted me yet? I'd been so sure …

I snapped closed my laptop and rolled onto my back, exhaling. I had so many questions I didn't know I'd ever find the answers to. Where was Dad? Was he even alive?

Why had he suddenly turned neg? Had someone done that to him? And if so, why?

Arriving at school the next day was like walking onto Wall Street. The amount of trades and payoffs being made due to the Quentin / Ivy mismatch were huge. Arguments were in full flight with bookies out of cash. I smiled, walking through it all. I'd been smart enough to get my payout yesterday.

I could hear people murmuring out the front, whispering about what had happened in the upgrade room – that Quentin had tested neg twice. More than a few people took the time to give me a long stare: the girl who had rated over eighty per cent with the M-Corp heir. I ignored them, and kept to my normal routine – the one that usually guaranteed invisibility. Unfortunately, I suspected my days of remaining unseen were now behind me.

Head down, I took the steps to the main doors, only to be stopped in my tracks. I looked up and couldn't stop the small gasp. I'd been so anxious about seeing him that I'd forgotten to actually keep my eye out.

I quickly forced my expression back to neutral, not that Quentin seemed to notice my slip-up. His eyes were dark rimmed, probably from lack of sleep, his stance tense.

'Everyone expects me to talk to you,' he stated, barely making eye contact.

He meant because of our so-called high rating. It would be crazy for such a score to go by unexplored. Eighty-two per cent put us squarely into long-term match territory. I'd chosen the figure for that very reason – ensuring it wouldn't seem too strange if we started to spend time together.

I shifted my weight from foot to foot.

When I didn't respond, his eyes finally connected with mine and I couldn't help but notice the dark line that encircled his green irises. 'I know we're not … you know … That I'm a …' He took a deep breath, unable to say the word 'neg', and I couldn't help but feel a tightening in my chest.

Yes, guilt.

Something I just had to deal with.

'You said that you could … You might be able to …?' His voice, along with his eyes, dropped away.

'Have you turned on your Phera-tech since yesterday?' I asked, working to keep my voice unaffected.

He shook his head.

I let go of the breath I'd been holding, not entirely sure if my relief was about the plan or for myself.

'We can talk, but only if I have your word that you will never use any of this against me. You're a *Mercer* after all.' I couldn't hold back the judgement as I hissed the last words at him.

For some reason my attack seemed to settle him, as if it brought him back into familiar territory. Maybe he was used to people pigeonholing him. He threw out a sardonic grin. 'Do I look like I'm in a position to use anything against *you* of all people?'

My return smirk was equally mocking. He was so right. The upper hand was right where I had put it – with me.

'After school?' he prompted.

I shook my head. 'I've got work. Lunchtime.'

He scouted the immediate area nervously, weighing up whether he wanted to be seen with me or not. According to the rest of the school we might've rated well, but he was still an M-Corp heir and I was still … me. His desperation clearly won out because he gave a curt nod and said, 'Grass by the track.'

Arrogant bastard didn't give me a chance to agree or disagree, he just spun around and stalked down the hall, making me question yet again what I was getting myself into with Quentin Mercer.

Seven

Ivy had wasted no time, rumours already spreading like wildfire that she had rated high with one of her older brother's friends the night before. It shouldn't have surprised me when I saw her avoid Quentin in the halls between classes – neg ratings were designed to forewarn people about volatile personality combinations. But still, I was amazed. Had she forgotten so quickly that the two of them had been the perfect couple for the past year? Had she forgotten how she'd hung off his every word?

I shook my head at my naivety. Of course she had. That was the entire point of the ratings system. And Quentin was no different, barely noticing her himself – but then again, his response seemed to be more natural than premeditated.

When lunchtime rolled around, I took my time, stopping by the cafeteria to collect a hotdog topped with cheese, mustard and ketchup. I had a weakness for anything that came with ketchup. By the time I reached the grass strip beside the bleachers he was already there, reading a book.

I craned my head to read the title. 'The history of Nascar?' Not what I'd expected.

He closed the book, sliding it under his outstretched legs before he looked up, squinting into the sun. 'You know there's no real meat in that thing?' he said, gesturing to my half-eaten dog.

I shrugged, sitting down beside him, licking a smear of ketchup from the back of my hand. 'Tastes good, though.'

When I took a bite, his brow crinkled and I couldn't help but roll my eyes.

'Do you really think eating hotdogs will lower my match potential?'

With an obvious effort he relaxed his forehead and sighed. 'I guess I don't know anything anymore.'

'I guess not,' I replied, pleased that he could at least admit that.

After a few beats of uncomfortable silence, he blurted, 'Why'd you help me? You don't even know me.'

'If I had said out loud that you'd tested neg with me, they would've forced the point, asked you to take another reading, and we both know that would've tipped you over.'

'But that doesn't answer why you helped me.'

I nodded, expecting this, and swallowed a too-big mouthful. 'My father turned neg. No one knew why. One

day he was all good, rating ups and downs like normal –
then, presto, he was a full neg.' I shrugged as if it was no
biggie, but I knew my jaw had locked tight. 'There was no
explanation, no reason, and we lost everything, including
him. I know how bad it can be for an average family like
ours, I can't begin to imagine how … Anyway, it was a
spur of the moment decision I guess.' I knew that, despite
the lump in my throat, I'd done well to keep my lies as
close as possible to the truth. Best tactic for believability.

'I thought negs were supposed to be hazards or
whatever,' he rasped.

I smirked at him. 'They are.'

'So that means I'm … bad. Dangerous.' He rubbed the
back of his neck. 'Even if I haven't done awful things yet,
there's something in me that means I will.' His voice had
dropped to almost a whisper and he couldn't look at me.
I pretended not to notice.

'According to the science, but if you're asking me, I
don't really know you all that well.'

He nodded at my answer, though clearly unconvinced.
Then he glanced around, ensuring we were alone. 'You
said you could help. How?'

As I finished the last of my hotdog, I caught him
eyeing it with something new. Envy. He probably hadn't
indulged in imitation-meat products in years.

'I have a question for you first.'

'What?'

'More of a requirement really,' I added.

'Which is?'

I fixed my eyes on his, hiding my anxiousness. 'I need access to one of the M-Labs, one where control data is kept.'

Quentin's eyes narrowed. 'Why would you need that?'

'Because there's a chemical in there that can help me formulate a disruption to your pheromone rating.'

His eyebrows shot up, but his tone was dubious. 'A disruption? You mean you could change my ratings?'

I shook my head, looking right at him to make sure he understood. 'Not permanently, but maybe for a couple of hours at a time.'

He threw a hand up in the air. 'Well, how does that help?'

'Because you still need to register four minimum ratings per month. By the end of this month you will have to log at least one more rating – *a positive rating* – or you'll be found out.'

Quentin's brow furrowed and I could sense his fear.

I pushed on. 'Plus, you need to be able to prove to the people around you that you can rate like a normal person. You and I both know Quentin Mercer can't go for long with inactive Phera-tech. Too many people will start asking questions and before long you'll be forced to activate.'

He swallowed heavily and I wondered if he might actually throw up.

'*But,*' I stressed, 'if you help me, I can make it so that you can have small windows of opportunity where you can switch on and be seen interacting and registering ratings. The only catch is, you'll have to make damn sure you turn back to inactive before you clock another neg rating.'

Quentin was silent, weighing his options no doubt. He knew I was right, but still he had to know: 'What's in it for you?'

I smiled as if the question was perfectly acceptable. 'They'll have information in those labs about my father. I might be able to find him. I might be able to get him out.'

'You want to help him escape?' It was more of an accusation than a question. His steel-blue eyes narrowed. 'How convenient that I'm suddenly in your debt.'

I leaned towards him, so far into his personal space that he had to arch backwards. 'He's no different to you, Quentin. The only difference is he didn't have someone to help. As for the convenience issue, I agree. It is.' I shrugged, leaning back. 'I've learned to grab opportunities when they come around. But if you'd prefer to take your chances with your family and whatever isolation unit you're assigned to …' I held out my hand, inviting him to leave.

Quentin blinked, stunned, and I heard the small but unmistakeable beep of his M-Band registering his increased pulse. It was a satisfying sound.

'What if it doesn't work?' he asked, looking away.

I had him.

It was time to finish the conversation. I stood and looked down at him, enjoying the higher ground. 'I've got it covered. Just get me access when the lab is closed and I'll take care of the rest.'

I stared at him until he nodded.

'And if you set me up or we get caught …' I trailed off.

'Yeah, yeah, I get it!' he snapped.

Walking to work that afternoon, I couldn't deny I was pleased with myself. Years of planning had gone into this and it was all falling into place perfectly. If things kept going this way, the next time I broke into an underground hub I could be bringing my father out with me.

The thought opened up a number of other questions, but I couldn't afford to go there. I had to have faith that once my mom and brother saw Dad, once they understood that he wasn't to blame, that he hadn't done whatever horrific things they'd envisaged, everything would work itself out. Maybe we'd even move back to the countryside. Dad had been a pesticide engineer; he developed and produced tailored pesticides and plague remedies for crop farms. It would be nice to get out of the city. I imagined Dad would want nothing more than open spaces after being underground for so long.

'So, how'd it go?' Gus asked, when I made my way into the back office.

I smirked at him.

'Poor guy,' he mumbled. 'Can't wait till someone turns your world on its head and messes with you.'

They already had, but I wasn't about to sob-story with Gus. He knew I was looking for my dad, but otherwise we had a strict need-to-know relationship.

When he realised I wasn't going to respond, he went on. 'I set up a meet with that new contact tonight, if you're game?'

Actually, I was bone tired. I hadn't slept at all the previous night and I'd done a work-out early this morning that a saner person would've skipped. What I wanted to do after I finished my shift was go home, do my homework and sleep.

But providing cover for Gus was my responsibility.

Gus had the contacts to set up the meetings, but he barely knew how to throw a punch and the black-market crew were hardcore.

I clenched my teeth together. 'Sure.'

Gus nodded, looking down at his computer. He glanced back up only to say, 'We're meeting at Burn after close.'

Icing on the cake.

I hated that place – it was full of heavy gambling and lust-enhancers. It was like walking into a sensory overload. Plus I was underage, which meant I had to use the forged M-Band Gus had programmed for me. All in all, it made my head hurt.

At least I'd get to see my brother. Burn was where he worked.

'Fine, but I'll have to stop by home to get something to wear.'

Gus gave me an up-and-down look and a nasty grin. 'Completely understood.'

I alternated between stocking the shelves and running the register. I usually worked with two or three other assistants out the front, while Gus ran the programming side of things out the back. So, for the next four hours, I moved between listening to Stella – who was thirty-five and a career shop assistant – brag about her latest lust conquest, which had me somewhere between disgusted and plain embarrassed for her, and a stream of customers all looking to upgrade their M-Band software and accessories. I struggled to keep a straight face when a man who looked like he was well over seventy wanted to have his Viagra doses controlled by the M-Band medical zip. Ew.

The low point of my day hit when Stella dragged me out back and told me to feel her fake boobs. She was adamant I wouldn't be able to tell the difference. I tried to explain that I didn't need or want to be convinced, but she just grabbed my hands and thrust them to her chest, right as Gus headed past us for the back door, a huge smile on his face. His M-Band camera zip was in continuous shot mode.

I smiled grimly at Stella. 'Thanks,' I said, desperate for her to release my hands.

She nodded, and then had the audacity to start massaging my hands up and down. 'I told you,' she said, beaming.

I wondered if I should tell her that I could break both of her arms in four seconds.

'You know,' she went on, 'everyone tried to talk me out of it because of the pheromone effects, but I knew I'd come down on the right side. Honestly, girl, I've never rated better. Maybe you should try it.' She glanced pointedly at my uninspiring chest.

I'd been worried about Stella going under the knife. Plastic surgery was more of a gamble than ever because self-image could cause a chemical reaction. Even if a person seemed happy with the results, there was the chance it would feed further insecurities or encourage an addiction to surgery, which could in turn create pheromone instability. Luckily for Stella, it had boosted her esteem, causing only positive effects.

I pulled my hands free. 'No, thanks,' I said, putting some space between us before she tried to grab me again. 'I'm pretty sure there is a customer waiting.' I quickly made my way to the shopfront.

By the time I finished closing down the tills and locking up, Gus was out the front with the car running.

'Might've been faster if you'd helped,' I suggested, feeling narky.

'Or if you hadn't paused to feel Stella up,' Gus returned, smirking when I shuddered. 'I may be your bitch, but I'm not your slave,' he added, throwing his new model Audi-Glider into gear. I rolled my eyes. The sports car was much more valuable than what he should've been able to afford on his salary and had the same effect as a flashing neon sign with the words, *up to no good*. He sped down the road, drawing every passing eye.

'Are you planning on leaving me the car when you wind up in jail?' I said, purposely annoying him by putting my feet up on the dash.

To my surprise, he burst out laughing. 'Have you forgotten you are currently messing with a Mercer? Baby, if I'm on my way to jail, you're on your way to the firing squad!'

I glared at him, which only encouraged him to snort louder as he pulled up at the back of my house.

'Here,' he said, still smiling as he passed me my fake M-Band. 'Make sure you leave your true band behind.'

I rolled my eyes. 'Yes, because I never would've remembered,' I said sarcastically. The wanker at the parking garage might've been enough of an amateur to think he could get away with switching M-Bands in his car, but we knew better. Police had scanners and if they passed an unmanned M-Band in a car, they would know about it. Only someone stupid or looking for trouble risked leaving unmanned M-Bands lying around.

I ran through the house, checking to see if Mom had taken my suggestion and given herself a few shifts off. She hadn't. It meant I had another few hours until she was home. I headed for my room above the garage and changed into a pair of leather pants and a black tank top.

I tugged at the bottom of my pants, wriggling the seams into place. I didn't have time for a confused self-image. Frankly, I didn't care much about my looks, but I'll admit that when I needed to jam myself into tight-fitting clothes, it helped that I worked out a lot.

I gave my outfit a quick glance in the mirror as I tied back my dusty brown heap of hair. Discreet. Not too dressy. It would work. Despite my fake M-Band I was still underage and dressing up too much drew the wrong kind of attention, plus I was there to act as Gus's cover. Two good reasons why I needed to blend in, not stand out.

Staring down at my black work boots, I sighed. I wanted to put them back on, bad. They were perfect for moving fast and hurt like hell for the person who copped one in the head, but last time I'd worn them I'd barely made it through the club's front door. Reluctantly, I dug around in the back of my tiny wardrobe and pulled out a pair of black high heels – a re-gift from Stella once she realised they were a size too small for her.

I huffed as I squeezed into the shoes. They wouldn't kick for shit. But then I turned and studied the back of the dangerously high heel. If I didn't fall over and kill myself in them, the heels could come in handy.

Gus looked me over when I slid back into the car's black interior. I hadn't bothered with a jacket since the day had been warm. May has always been my favourite month.

'Who would've known … The hooker look actually works for you,' Gus said, pulling away from the kerb.

'I'll remember that comment if it all goes belly up tonight and you need me to save your weak ass,' I responded, shifting into a better position to put my feet back on the dash.

Gus's eyes widened as he contemplated my heels. 'Wait! Don't, you'll put a damn hole in the leather!'

I kept lifting my feet.

'Okay, okay! I'm sorry, you don't look like a hooker and I do need you to have my back in there, and I *really* need you to not put those heels on my dash!'

I smiled, putting my feet back on the floor, and turned my attention to the window. Everything was right again in the Gus–Maggie world.

Eight

Burn was aptly named.

Post Phera-tech, people were more careful. Smoking and illicit drugs – the old-fashioned kind anyway – were all but extinct and diets constantly monitored.

But alcohol was still acceptable and there were only two types of drinks served at Burn. Spirits and water. And the water was only available because it was the law.

It made serving straightforward. Waitresses simply circulated the room with trays of shots and you paid the set price for all spirits. You could run a tab or pay as you went. Either way, there was only one unspoken rule in Burn: everybody drank. And most indulged in black-market lust-enhancers.

Once through security, Gus and I were greeted by a buxom waitress holding a long rectangular tray of multicoloured shot glasses.

Gus knew the drill and didn't hesitate, taking two clear-coloured shots from the tray. He held out his

M-Band to the waitress, who flashed a digital pen at it, uploading the cost of the drinks. There was no such thing as cash anymore. Every individual was simply uplinked to a banking zip. Gus added a generous tip and thumb-printed the transfer.

Handing me one of the shots, he gave me a wink and then headed on his way to the roped-off reserved area. I rolled my eyes as Gus proceeded to detour via a table of scantily dressed girls, eyes fixed to his M-Band and his pheromone ratings. The funny part was, I knew he was doing it for my benefit. Gus wasn't interested in those girls. He just didn't want me to know he was jonesing big time for Kelsey Garner, a girl he'd started seeing a couple of months ago. He thought he'd kept her a secret, but I knew everything about Kelsey – and her brother – and if I had to, I'd use that to my advantage. For now Gus could believe he'd managed to keep his private life hidden.

The beat of the music pulsed through the floor and I glanced around at the club's patrons. The air was palpable with excitement for the night's unknown possibilities. I started towards the end of the bar and wondered if I'd ever experience that kind of thrill. I sniffed the drink and sighed. I didn't know how he picked it every damn time. I'd be okay with vodka, or even gin. But tequila tore me up from the inside. A fact Gus knew well.

I'd barely made it to the edge of the service area – a spot I knew would give me the best vantage point – before I felt a tap on my shoulder.

Spinning around, I came face to face with familiar brown eyes. Eyes like mine, sucked dry by city living.

My family belonged in the country.

'Are you trying to get me fired?' my brother hissed, his grip on my shoulder tightening to make it clear he *really* wasn't happy to see me.

I shrugged and smiled guiltily, missing the annoying but kind big brother I'd once known. 'Sam, come on. There's this guy I really like … He's meeting me here.'

Samuel's eyes narrowed. 'How old is he?'

I looked down. 'Twenty-one,' I hedged. 'He works with me. Please, Sam. We won't be here long.'

He glanced down at my shot glass, running his hand through his short, sandy blond hair. 'How many of them have you had?' he asked.

'This is my first.' I screwed up my face. 'Tequila.'

That, at least, earned me a smile. 'I'll get you a couple shots of H2O so no one bothers you. No more alcohol,' he warned.

Samuel looked around the bar, his height making it easy for him. If only he cared about himself a little more, he could be strong and useful, but Sam stopped caring about anything after Dad was taken. I'd tried to tell him my theories once. He'd simply shot me down. Sam blamed Dad. He would until I proved different.

'Mags, make sure you're out of here in half an hour.'

I nodded. 'Mom said she thought you met someone,' I said, casually looking over his shoulder to check on Gus. The contact had arrived and was sitting opposite Gus at a small table. The guy was short with slick black hair. I could see the hardness in his eyes and the bulge in his jacket that told me he was carrying. Super. Another armed baddie.

'Mom gets too excited,' Sam said, glancing around the bar again. He wasn't scoping for work to do. He was scoping the crowd. The female crowd.

'She said you rated high,' I pushed, feeling irritated that his attention was so fleeting. We lived in the same house, but we barely ever saw each other. Wasn't I worth a few minutes?

Samuel looked back at me and shrugged. 'Not looking for anything permanent. You know that.'

I sighed. I didn't want people to live by the ratings system, but I wished he'd be open to finding someone he could care about. Samuel lived by the system more than anyone I knew, but he used the ratings to ensure he never got close to anyone. He only pursued low rating lust-matches. One night was more than enough as far as he was concerned.

'You going to be home any night this week?' I asked, but he'd already caught the scent of my disapproval and stiffened.

'Mom said you're hardly around yourself. What? You got some kind of puppy love for this guy or something?'

I snorted. This conversation was on a fast track to nowhere and I needed to get back to work. 'I promise I'll be out of here in half an hour,' I snapped.

Samuel seemed to agree the chat was over because his lips pursed and then he stormed off. Another golden family moment.

Ignoring the lump in my throat, I turned my attention back to Gus's exchange. He was leaning forwards, and I watched as he glanced in my direction.

Perfect.

Gus knew better than to make eye contact.

Sure enough, the man with the slick hair turned to look in my direction. Not missing a beat, I smiled sweetly and downed my shot of tequila, fighting the gag reflex and biting down on the corner of my bottom lip. The contact smirked and looked away. Apparently I'd made myself look like enough of a party girl to lose his interest for now.

Knowing I'd need to keep a low profile from here on out, I turned my attention back to the bar, where I could just make out Gus's table in the splashback mirror.

'Never would've guessed I'd see you here,' a voice said from behind my ear. It was a voice that caused an unwelcome reaction.

I breathed in slowly, keeping my eyes down. Tonight was turning into one big cluster-f …

'I guess age doesn't matter in your world. Doors just open, right,' I said, not turning around.

Quentin leaned in and, when he spoke next, I could smell the rum on his breath. 'In yours too, it appears,' he said, surprising me by leaning even closer.

'Back off,' I warned, now turning slightly towards him.

When I got a good look at him, my breath caught, causing him to smirk. As much as I didn't want to admit it, he was a visual feast in his jeans and a fitted white shirt with the top few buttons undone. But it was the scar at his hairline that drew my eyes the most. Something about it made him seem somehow … real.

I averted my eyes when I saw his smile widening. I could hear him breathe deeply through his nose. For some inconvenient reason I was suddenly on edge. That is, until he said, 'Never would've picked you for the tequila type.'

That was when I realised his smile wasn't so much a smile as a challenge. Quentin wasn't happy about me being in his life, and he most certainly wasn't happy about me crashing his night out. And it appeared he'd acquired some liquid courage.

I glanced down the bar and spotted his two older brothers sitting in a corner booth with a pair of breasty blondes who no doubt scored off the charts in the lust department. Classy.

'Go back to your table, Quentin. I'm sure if you're a good boy, you'll get your very own Barbie for Christmas.'

He turned towards his brothers and flinched when he noticed they were looking in our direction. Out of nowhere he suddenly stumbled over his own, stationary, feet.

He righted himself and stepped towards me, swaying right into my personal space. He placed a hand on my waist and tugged me close. With barely a breath between us, I arched back. I hadn't thought he was this drunk a moment ago.

'I don't want a Barbie,' he growled. 'And it's a good thing too, since it seems the only thing I've got lately is you.'

A combination of things happened at that moment. Quentin's grip on my waist tightened, almost desperately. I felt a surge of guilt and something else in response to his touch, and I glanced at Gus's table just long enough to see his contact register the fact that I had Quentin Mercer draped over me.

Gus was talking fast, his hands raised in a placating gesture. His contact was pissed.

Quentin sighed. 'I think I'm drunk,' he confessed, unaware that his presence had just put us all in danger. The black-market world was strictly a Mercer-free zone.

I grabbed his hands off my waist and pushed him back. 'You think?' I barked, angry with him for ruining our trade. I needed to move. Fast.

He blinked, then seemed to remember where we were. 'How'd you get in here?' he asked.

'My brother works here. He snuck me in,' I answered, my attention still focused on the other table.

Gus's contact stood up and snatched the payment disk from the table. That disk had our hard-earned money on it. I waited, watching Gus and ignoring Quentin.

'My family knows about you. They want to meet you.'

That, and the flat tone of this statement, was almost enough to make me look at him. But I waited until Gus turned to me. His heated expression made me grimace. He shook his head.

'Damn it,' I said.

'Yeah, I don't like it either,' Quentin carried on. 'Why don't you just come over and sit with us for a bit. It might be enough.'

I turned cold eyes on him. 'Not tonight.' I pushed past him and started for the door, but he grabbed my wrist.

'At least come over and say hello.'

I spun back around. I really didn't have time for this so I got right up in his face. 'I'm the last thing between you and a very *unhappily* ever after. Tell me what to do again, and I'll do something that only one of us will ever regret. Now let go of me and go back to your table. Alone.'

His hand dropped to his side and I sped towards the door. I ran out the door and around to the back of the club, where I found Gus taking a right hook to the face. Anger flared. He might not be my friend, but he was mine to protect. I'd promised him that much.

Not breaking stride, I marched right up to the contact, who was lining Gus up for another jab, and grabbed his shoulder. In a split second I spun him around before I landed my own right hook in his eye. The contact stumbled, letting go of Gus who promptly slid to the ground. He was such a lightweight.

The contact grabbed at his face where I'd just hit him. 'You bitch. I'm gonna mess you up for that.'

I knew I was meant to have some witty comeback. And trust me, I'd like to have the luxury of retort time, but I was too busy shoving my elbow into his face, followed by the heel of my palm to his nose, and then moving in so that when I kneed him it hit just right. I'd work on fitting an appropriately cutting remark into the sequence next time.

As it was, it was satisfying enough to see him go to his knees, clutching at his bits.

I leaned forwards, holding onto his collar as I reached into his too-tight jeans and pulled out our money disk.

'Gus came for intel and he was happy to pay for it. I know you have it on you, and I could easily go fishing until I find it ...' The thought of poking around in his skin-tight pockets made me shudder. 'But if I have to do that, you're not getting this.' I waved our disk under his nose. 'We came for a trade. Now do you want one or not?'

I heard a loud groan and glanced at Gus, who was stumbling to his feet. I rolled my eyes.

The contact looked at Gus. 'You need a girl to be your bodyguard?' he sneered.

Gus wiped at the tiny drop of blood in the corner of his mouth. 'Jealous, Travis?'

The contact – Travis – sighed and looked back at me. 'You gonna beat the shit out of me if I hand it over?'

'Not unless you try anything else stupid.'

'I saw you with that Mercer kid. He was all over you.' He watched for my reaction suspiciously.

I crossed my arms. 'Can't help it if the guy is desperate, can I?' He held my eyes for a beat. I waited. Finally, he pressed his lips together and made his decision, reaching into his back pocket and producing a slim zip drive.

I took it from his outstretched hand.

'I trust we can move forwards from here,' I said. 'No point in us doing this deal if we can't trade again.' It was the truth. We were paying for intel we already had, just to test the waters.

Travis's ease with the current scene was enough to let me know he was a seasoned trader. And not afraid of things getting messy. Both good and bad news.

'I'd prefer you didn't beat me up every time, but my end will hold up. If yours does too, we can talk again. Expect me to bring my own bodyguards next time. And don't be having no Mercer kid hanging around again.'

Gus, apparently finished with the night's activities, started walking away. 'I'm going to get the car. And a fucking aspirin,' he said.

I passed Travis the money disk. 'Hopefully, next time you won't even see me.'

He took the disk and stood. 'Honey, I don't mind looking at you. I'd just prefer it wasn't your knee making contact with my balls next time.'

I didn't have a response for that. Frankly, I didn't want any part of my body near his balls again. Ever.

I waited a moment, to give Travis time to disappear, before heading after Gus. I wasn't in a rush. Gus was out of danger and all I had to look forward to was him bitching at me the entire drive home.

'Good trade?'

Could. This. Night. Get. Any. More. Screwed. Up?

I turned slowly.

Quentin stood just inside the alley and I instantly wondered how much he had seen or heard. Gus had been well within the alleyway's shadows but still … Had Quentin recognised him? Had I said anything that would give us away?

I put my hands on my hips and straightened my back as Quentin stalked towards me. Curiously, he wasn't stumbling now.

When he got close enough, he smirked and raised his eyebrows. 'Desperate, huh?'

Guess he'd heard quite a bit.

I shrugged. It wasn't as if he would have preferred me to give Travis the real explanation. I gestured a hand towards him. 'Did you just pull the drunk act so you could cop a feel in there?'

Quentin seemed surprised, even pleased, by my observation. He stood taller, letting go of any pretence that he wasn't in control of his actions. Oh, he'd had a drink or two, but nowhere near the amount his behaviour had indicated inside Burn.

'Just keeping up appearances.'

I assumed he meant for his brothers, given that he was supposed to be out with them. But just in case he'd had any ulterior motive, I moved into his space. This time it was him who arched back.

'Did you think you could get me to pander to your every need? That the gorgeous Quentin Mercer was so irresistible? You forget, I know the truth,' I said, leaving the 'neg' word hanging heavily between us. 'Trust me, you don't want to play with me, Mercer. I play dirty.' Oddly, I hoped he was paying attention.

His head tilted carefully, his eyes locked on mine, and I accepted his reluctant nod.

'Who are you?' This question came in a low voice coated in vulnerability and uncertainty. I couldn't help but feel a spark of protectiveness towards him. Which only pissed me off.

'Right now? I'm the difference between you having a future or not. Go home and forget about tonight because tomorrow we have work to do.'

For all my bravado, he seemed to see something different in my eyes. I watched as the corner of his mouth lifted slightly and felt how, for some crazy reason, my own lips did the same. I quickly turned my back to him and started down the alley.

'So you think I'm gorgeous, huh?' he called out after me, mischief in his voice.

I kept walking. I wasn't about to defend my slip-up. Or the traitorous smile I wasn't quite able to wipe from my face.

Nine

I made my way through classes the next day, feeling the weight of eyes following me. A target had been painted on my back since my apparent rating with Mercer, the rest of the students unsure what it might mean. I tried to ignore the stares, but it was cumbersome to have to deal with the increased male attention.

Sitting down in my English Studies class, I noticed a group of guys passing around a bottle of pills. I also noticed that Quentin – sitting in his usual seat in the back – waved them off when offered.

Celery and zinc are forms of androsterone, making them a 'natural' aid to increasing perceived attraction. Result: guys threw back zinc supplements like tic-tacs and girls drank celery juice like water.

Half of them didn't even have active Phera-tech yet. I shook my head and doodled in my notebook as I waited for class to begin. Mr Ferris was always late.

When Phera-tech started, labs went crazy, flooding the market with perfumes and sprays they claimed enhanced pheromone output, which would help people attract better partners. Most were rip-offs and the ones that did work attracted *everyone*, sending out a wide signal that responded in the same way to all recipients. The fakes were easy to spot and quickly outlawed. Following that, the tech was updated to ensure a more accurate pheromone reading.

However, even if someone used the external pheromones and doused themselves in enhancing perfumes, nothing could override a neg rating.

Dad had been interested in the way Phera-tech worked too, but his tests had been different.

His attention had been on altering the way one person *released* a pheromone signature. He had been doing similar things in his work, making pesticides for crop farms. Dad had developed a range of pesticides that 're-educated' attraction between insects. In the end, his fascination had cost him his freedom, our family, and maybe his life.

My father had been trying to make a difference. And he'd been making headway too. But he'd also had one failed experiment. One that had changed not the way a signal was *released*, but how it was received.

It was the remains of that experiment that I'd poured into Quentin's inhaler.

'You're Maggie, right?' Ryan Merit said as he took his seat beside me.

I pinched the bridge of my nose and sighed. 'You've been sitting next to me in this class all year, and *now* you want to know my name?'

He smiled sheepishly and I could tell he intended it to be charming. Ryan was 'that' guy. Correction, if Quentin wasn't already 'that' guy at school, it would've been Ryan. He was tall, dark and handsome, in that captain-of-the-rowing-team kind of way. But he didn't have the edge to him that Quentin had and, well, he wasn't a Mercer, so he simply didn't carry the same social cred. But still, he was an over achiever and the kind of guy you wouldn't be surprised to hear had set up office in the White House one day. Oval shaped.

'I've always known your name,' he said. 'I just thought maybe it was time we got to know one another a bit … better.' When I didn't respond, he cleared his throat. 'Coffee?'

Suddenly it felt as if the temperature in the room had dropped to freezing. I noticed the nervous flicker of Ryan's eyes as he looked beyond me. The combination of small gasps and wide eyes from the students sitting around me confirmed where the chill was coming from.

I took a deep breath before shaking my head and looking down at my notes. 'Not interested,' I said.

I glanced up in time to see Ryan's eyes flicker behind me again, right before he glanced at my M-Band. 'Maybe you should give the tech some more time. You might be pleasantly surprised.'

Oh, wow. I was about to tell him where to go when the screech of a chair behind us stopped me. Ryan bit his lip, as if contemplating his next move. When he glanced back at me, his sheepish smile had returned. 'Or not,' he said, turning his attention to the front of the class.

There was no need to turn around. Unlike Ryan, I knew everyone's name and where they sat. Especially Quentin Mercer.

He was playing his part. I knew that. Still, it was an impressive display of possessiveness. Quentin had just made a clear statement that I knew would travel the school halls in record time.

But had he needed to be so full on? Hadn't he wanted to avoid attention? Or was his reaction something different?

I shut my eyes tight, forcing myself not to look over my shoulder and into his eyes. I needed to *stop* thinking about him. An image of Dad flashed into my mind and I held onto it.

When I opened my eyes, it was with a fresh resolve. Tonight, I'd put Quentin to the test.

*

'Where are we going?' Quentin asked. He'd been waiting for me by my locker after the last class. I was almost surprised he'd turned up; he hadn't appeared in the two afternoon classes we shared. In fact, I hadn't seen him since English Studies.

His arms were crossed and his forehead creased. It was distracting. His buzz-short hair and olive skin lent itself well to the furrowed, solemn look. Too well.

'What's up with you?' I asked, trying to ignore his glare while I put my books away.

He waited until I was finished. 'You need to stop flirting.'

I did not see that one coming.

'I didn't think I was. It was you who was getting handsy last night from memory,' I snapped.

His nostrils flared. 'Not with *me*. With every other guy in the school!'

'Didn't peg you for the jealous type. But, again, I hadn't realised I was.' Despite having to reject a few more invitations for study dates or after-school coffees, and one offer of a lift home, which to be honest, under normal circumstances I probably would've taken just because I hated the bus, I hadn't flirted at all. 'What's your problem anyway?'

He lowered his voice. 'Everyone is going to try to move in on you now that we're a thing.'

My eyebrows nearly hit the ceiling. 'A *thing*?'

'We rated high. And as far as everyone is aware, we *both* then chose to turn off our Phera-tech. So how did you think they were all going to interpret that?'

He was right. The only acceptable reason for turning off Phera-tech was if you'd met someone you were going to be monogamous with. It was the obvious conclusion that people would draw, even if it had only happened a few days ago. I always knew I'd have to deal with this particular side effect of my scheme.

'What are you suggesting?' I said, letting him think this had all been his idea.

'That until we find a way for me to turn on my Phera-tech, you need to act as if you are mine.'

I coughed loudly. It was that, or burst into laughter.

'It's for your own protection. Do you have any idea what some people would do to take what's *maybe* mine from right under my nose?'

Actually I did. I'd done it myself when I'd taken his freedom.

'It never worried you with Ivy,' I argued. He'd seemed unfazed by all the attention she received.

'That's because Ivy was never a real match,' he said, dismissing her in a beat.

'Nor are we,' I threw back.

He shook his head. 'You know what I mean!' He took a deep breath, trying to calm down. 'Do you have any idea what it means, to be with a Mercer?'

I nodded. It meant potentially being part of the most powerful and wealthy family in the world. I had known this when I made my choice to set Quentin up, realising it would force us together in a way I needed, in a way that would give me access to M-Corp, but even so ... My mouth had suddenly gone very dry. It was possible I hadn't thought through this aspect as much as I should have.

'Stop talking to other guys,' he ordered. But when I looked up at him, I could've sworn there was something other than a warning there. Involuntarily, my stomach flipped.

'We need to make plans for tonight. My shift starts in an hour. Can you come to my work?'

He nodded stiffly. 'My car's out front.'

'Is that such a great idea?' I questioned, unsure if I should be moving around town in a Mercer vehicle.

'In future we can be more discreet. But today, having everyone watch as I take you to my car?' He smirked, leaning back into the wall. 'It's the best idea I've had all week.'

*

I couldn't help but wonder what Quentin was thinking. Sometimes he seemed so confident, then at other times, when he thought no one was watching, the façade would slip and there was sorrow there. The type that hit my chest and made it ache.

I wondered what worried him the most. If it was that he might not be the hotshot he once thought he'd be, then too bad. But I was beginning to think it was something else, something that had a lot more to do with happiness and even ... love. But that didn't make sense. He was a Mercer, and all that family cared about was money and power.

Fisting my hands so that my nails bit into my palms, I fixed my attention on the window. No more delving.

It wasn't surprising when Quentin instructed his driver to take him to the Clarendon M-Store. I was sure if he hadn't previously known where I worked, he would've done his homework on me by now. Did he find it suspicious or ironic? Had he even given it a thought?

When we pulled up, I turned my attention to him. 'There's someone I want to introduce you to inside.'

Quentin's wariness was obvious. But this was going to be a test for both of us. One – given the events of last night – I now felt was necessary.

If I'd learned anything over the past two years, it was to fix a problem before it fixed you. And I couldn't be sure that Quentin hadn't seen Gus in the alley the night before. Just because he hadn't come out and said anything … He was a smart guy. It would be foolish to underestimate him.

Eventually Quentin nodded and directed his attention to his driver. 'William, wait for me on the next corner.'

William didn't ask for how long. He was probably paid not to ask questions. He simply came out to open the door for us. The one I'd already opened and jumped out of. My bad.

Avoiding the store's front, I headed straight for the alley entrance. The last thing we needed was to broadcast our every move. Quentin followed.

When I opened the door to Gus's office, it was almost worth the apprehension just to see the look on Gus's face when he saw who I'd brought with me.

Credit where credit is due though, Gus recovered with stellar speed, turning a hateful expression on me. 'As if you haven't already caused me enough grief, now you have to bring in a ticking time bomb.' He gestured to Quentin.

I watched carefully, noting the surprise in Quentin's expression. He was either very good, or he really hadn't recognised Gus in the alley last night. Oh well, it was better to be safe than sorry. If he had seen Gus and I hadn't come clean, he never would've trusted me the way I needed him to.

Quentin cleared his throat. 'Mr Reynolds.' He put his hand out to shake, all gentlemanly, but his eyes were focused on the ugly bruise that had flowered high on Gus's left cheek.

Gus responded with a short snort. 'Maggie, you've gone too far this time. I helped you out last week, but that was where this should've ended. Don't drag me into your shit.'

Gus really should've been an actor, or an underwear designer. He covered his ass like no one.

I smiled sweetly and turned to Quentin. 'He loves me, really. Quentin, this is Gus.'

'What's going on?' Quentin asked, trying to put the pieces together.

'Yes, Maggie,' Gus deadpanned. 'What is going on?'

I dropped my backpack and pulled out a chair for Quentin and then one for myself. Quentin didn't sit.

'Gus works for me, in a sense.' I flashed a brief smile.

'You don't actually think I didn't cotton on to what went on in the testing room the other day, did you?' Gus said, now playing his part perfectly.

'You *knew*?' Quentin said, shifting uncomfortably from one foot to the other. It was a good thing to ruffle his feathers a bit, take back control of the situation. I'd realised the night before that if Quentin discovered on his own that Gus worked with me, it would only encourage suspicion. This way, I knew the surprise would catch him off guard. And it had. I could already see his focus was centred solely on whether he'd been outed as a neg.

'Apart from the fact you looked like you were going to pass out the moment you turned on your Phera-tech, I actually know Maggie and her charming personality. Not to mention her total disregard for health and highly questionable dietary choices. Frankly, I'm not sure it is possible for her to rate that high with *anyone*.'

I shrugged, comfortable with Gus's assessment of me, as I pulled out a family-sized bag of marshmallows and started popping a few.

'I don't get it. Why did you help then?' Quentin asked.

Damn it. I actually felt sorry for the guy. You could tell the pheromone rating had really screwed with him. For a guy used to always being in charge and getting what he wanted, he was now so uncertain. And while I felt low about it, there was another side of me, the one driving my actions, that found myself feeling satisfied that this uncertainty was making him play right into my hands.

'Don't flatter yourself,' I butted in. 'Gus owes me. Big time. And I'm the kinda girl who collects.'

'With interest,' Gus mumbled.

Quentin gestured to Gus's black eye. He'd taken a couple of good hits last night. Apparently I'd only arrived in time to see the finale.

'You were at Burn last night.'

Statement. But I could tell he was now only working it out.

'Yes. Getting the shit kicked out of me because you decided to show up and get in the way. Next time, do us all a favour and don't go near Maggie unless she sends you a written invitation.'

'Angsty much?' I said, holding back the smile.

Gus tilted his head. 'Apologies, mistress-of-all-that-is-bitch, were you expecting me to thank him for the beating he caused me last night? Hell, Maggie, I told you it was your thing if you wanted to help a Mercer. I covered for you in the test, but you could've done the decent thing and left me out of it.' Oh man, he was good. Sly bastard.

Not that it didn't work in nicely.

And Quentin totally fell for it. 'I won't bring you any trouble. Maggie ... she really did save me in the testing and,' he cleared his throat, 'clearly you did too. I'm not about to cause either of you any trouble.'

I glanced between them and remained silent.

Finally, Gus said, 'And what about when she helps you? Or can't? What then? You'll hand us over faster than your family tosses around six-digit money zips.'

Quentin shook his head. 'I give you my word. No matter what. I'll never be the cause of trouble in your life.'

Gus leaned back in his chair, appearing satisfied.

'Good,' he said. 'Cause Maggie's all the nightmare I can take.'

I smiled. 'Gus, I never knew you dreamed of me.'

He gave me a one-fingered salute.

My smile widened. I could see Quentin studying my interaction with Gus.

I threw my feet up onto the table, earning another scowl from Gus. 'Now that intros are done, how are we looking for tonight?' I asked, popping another marshmallow.

'What's tonight?' Quentin jumped in.

Gus chuckled. 'You poor son of a bitch. She didn't even tell you, did she?'

Quentin turned his steely blue eyes towards me and his brow did that furrowy thing it does, which in turn made my stomach do that unwelcome thing it does in response.

'I want access to one of your family labs. Not a big one, but one that might have what we need to help you and might also have intel I need.'

'Which one?' he asked, still with the furrowy.

I bit my lower lip and Quentin's eyes dropped to it suddenly. He covered the action smoothly by finally taking a seat.

'Can you get access to an M-Corp headquarters computer?' I asked.

'Yes,' he said, cautiously. 'We have a mainframe in my father's office at home which I've accessed before when helping him out. Why?'

'I need the entry code to access a lab that will be listed under the title Junction 17. Can you manage that and meet us back here at the end of my shift?'

Quentin looked baffled. 'There is no lab called Junction 17. You must have the wrong information.'

Gus tapped a pen on the table and spoke softly. 'He doesn't know anything, Maggie.'

That, or he was a very good liar.

'Have you been into the underground network?' I asked, watching for his reaction.

'What underground network?' he asked simply.

Gus snorted.

I stood up. 'You'll see tonight. I've got to start my shift. Just get the entry code from the computer. It will look like a normal file with a code attached to it. It will be long, so make sure you take down the exact sequence, including spaces. Ditch the driver and meet me back here at nine and ...' I gave him a look up and down, settling on his shoes. '... wear appropriate shoes.'

'What are appropriate shoes?' he asked, standing.

'Shoes you can run for your life in,' Gus answered helpfully. Then added, unnecessarily, 'Welcome to the Maggie-verse.'

Ten

Gus had already disappeared by the time Stella and I left the store. I'd taken the time to drop off a coffee to the night security guard as per usual and had received one of his signature bows in return. I'd made a point of keeping on Darren's good side. Never knew when it might come in handy.

'Don't suppose you want to come out with me and some of the gals for a bit of fun?' Stella said, pulling her jumper off to reveal a sequinned halter-neck.

I shook my head, smiling. Every time we worked the late shift she asked me. Every time I declined.

She rolled her eyes. 'What is it tonight. Muay Thai? Gym? Study?'

Usually it was all of the above, though I mostly did my study in the morning before school. 'Gym,' I replied, even as my eyes travelled towards the corner of the street where Quentin was leaning against the building, hands in pockets, looking straight at me.

Stella followed my eyes. 'Uh-huh, well, *enjoy* that work-out, honey,' she said with a laugh.

I shook my head at her and laughed it off, confident she couldn't make out his well-known face from under the cap he'd been smart enough to wear. 'Trust me when I say that is not the kind of work-out I'm looking for. And definitely not with him.'

She looked me over, settling on my eyes. 'You may not know it, but there's hunger in those eyes of yours. Trust me, it's a look I know well.'

Zipping up my coat, I shrugged. Stella could think whatever she wanted. In fact, it probably helped if she thought things like that.

'See you tomorrow, Stella.'

She gave me a wave and we headed in opposite directions.

Quentin had lost the dress shoes. In fact, he'd lost a lot of his previous outfit and replaced it with something … Put it this way, I hadn't realised the guy worked out. But in those faded jeans and a long-sleeved fitted charcoal T-shirt, it was all too clear that he worked out almost as much as me. I glanced down to stop from staring.

'Acceptable?' he queried, his voice soft. Low.

It was a trick question. Had to be. I swallowed.

Then he waggled his feet and I realised he was talking

about his footwear selection. I checked myself and glanced up from his well-worn blue Converse.

'Fine,' I answered. 'We should go,' I added, turning abruptly to head down the street. Quentin followed, his stride easy, some of the usual tension that radiated from him oddly absent.

'You seem different,' I blurted after a few minutes.

He shrugged. 'People don't notice me when I'm in these clothes. I always feel more like myself when I don't have to be …'

'A Mercer?'

'An … ideal,' he said, and I glimpsed that sadness I'd seen before.

'If it's any consolation, I don't see you as an ideal at all,' I said, hoping to lighten the mood.

He smiled, though his brow was back to furrow mode. 'I suppose it is, in that at least you don't just see me as the stereotype.' He glanced at me, then back to the road, before adding, 'Though I can't help but wonder what kind of person I would be if I were ideal to someone like you.'

What was I supposed to do with that? Did that mean he wanted to be ideal to me? For me? Or that he didn't want to be that type of person? I couldn't work it out. My fists clenched with frustration that I was even thinking about it.

I took the next left and headed into one of the local malls.

'Shopping?' Quentin asked as we entered.

I glanced at him wryly and made for the elevator. I pulled out my phone, pressing my auto dial.

'Old school,' Quentin commented, noting my handheld phone. No doubt, he only ever used the earpiece that connected to his M-Band.

'Dead yet?' Gus answered.

I smirked. 'Not yet, but the night's still young.'

'Here's hoping.'

'We're at the elevator. You set up?'

'Of course.'

I pressed the elevator button, ignoring Quentin's curious gaze.

The elevator on the far left dinged. 'Elevator four,' I said.

'No. It already has passengers,' Gus replied quickly.

Stepping back, I pulled Quentin with me. He raised his eyebrows. I raised mine back. He conceded and shifted away from the opening doors. We waited for the lift to open and close, and then pressed the button again.

When the next elevator arrived, I said into the phone, 'Elevator two.'

'Good to go.'

When the elevator opened, I entered and Quentin followed.

The phone cut out inside and when the doors opened at sub-level three, I redialled. 'Cameras?' I said when Gus answered.

'Down. You have two minutes to cross the garage and get into the next elevators.'

I glanced at Quentin. 'Keep up,' I said, then started to jog across the lot, moving through a small tunnel that connected the mall's parking garage with the neighbouring office buildings. When we arrived at the next set of elevators, I pressed the down button, and waited.

'Are we in a rush?' Quentin asked.

I didn't take my focus off the elevator doors, willing them to open. 'We have thirty-seven seconds till the cameras in the garage come back on. Then we're made. Thirty-two seconds.' Leaving any kind of trail was bad.

Quentin's posture stiffened beside me as he joined me in watching the doors. At twelve seconds to go, the ding came. Eight when the doors opened and two when they finally closed. Even for me, that was close, but I refused to show my relief to Quentin. If he realised how close it had been, he didn't show it either. And damn if my respect for him didn't go up a notch.

Without delay, I hoisted myself onto the railings. I pulled a small power tool from my back pocket and reached up, pressing it to the first of the four screws in the elevator's ceiling hatch, waiting as each twisted out smoothly and soundlessly. Once the hatch was open, I gestured to Quentin. He was watching in slight horror.

'Come on up. I'll give you a boost.'

His lips curled. 'You go first. I can boost you.'

I rolled my eyes, but let him hold onto his pride, placing the hatch just inside the hole before pulling myself fluidly into the dark opening and onto the elevator roof. It burned my upper arms. Just like every other time.

With a wave, Quentin followed the steps I'd taken, levering himself up and onto the ceiling. I pretended I didn't see his arms shake as they took the brunt of his weight. I didn't help him either – wouldn't want to bruise that pride of his.

Once clear of the opening, I walked to the far side of the elevator shaft. 'Stay on the support beam,' I instructed.

'Don't you need to ...?' He pointed to the open hatch.

I shook my head. 'Gus will hold the lift here for us for thirty minutes.'

'He can do that?'

'With the right contacts. Sure.' Actually, it was damn hard to do and each time it cost us more money than we had to spare. It wasn't just about hacking into the building's electrics, but also paying off the night security to be particularly lazy in their rounds, and rerouting all other lifts to compensate for one being down. But Quentin didn't need to know all of that.

'Where does that go?' he asked when he realised I'd stopped at a slim door between elevator levels.

I ignored his question and gestured to his M-Band. 'Any chance anyone could track your GPS in the next twenty minutes?'

'No, but I can put a haze on it just to be sure.' He tapped a few keys.

'You have a haze on your GPS?' Hazes were expensive stuff and required a rigorous amount of paperwork and government clearances. They sent out a frequency wave to stop your GPS giving a pinpoint location. If the police had an emergency, they could override it, but even then, it would take time. Hazes were reserved for the seriously rich and famous. Which ... he was.

He shrugged. 'It's a security precaution. The whole family has them, just in case anyone ever harasses us. Or in Zach's case, if his wife is looking for him,' he said with a grim smile, referring to his brother Zachery. 'We're not supposed to tell people we have them.'

'Your secret's safe.' But I was totally jealous. Having a haze on my GPS would come in handy. Not that anyone was often looking for me, but still ... I *was* often where I wasn't supposed to be.

'One more,' he muttered as I opened the door.

We were silent as we headed down the tunnel. I listened intently for any sign of activity. The entrance wasn't supposed to be guarded, but I'd been surprised before. I turned a corner carefully, grateful that Quentin was following my lead.

When we reached the larger tunnel network with the transit lines, Quentin was dazed, taking in the slim, flat tracks.

'What is this place?' he whispered.

I looked at him, feeling a pang of unwelcome sorrow. But he needed to be put to the test if I was going to be able to use him. And he deserved to know the truth.

'Transit tunnels. And since this main one has no patrols, it's the safest way to get around down here. The side tunnels are a different matter,' I explained. Quentin stared at me and I let out a breath. 'It was once all government property,' I said. He didn't need to know that the intricate system ran all the way to Mt Weather's main facility. '*Now*, it's a world of secrets.'

Maybe if he knew, just maybe, he could do something useful with the knowledge. If he was the guy I was starting to suspect he was.

From that point on, he was mostly silent. Just the fact that this place existed, let alone was controlled by his father's company ... It was a lot to take in and I didn't push.

Walking briskly, I heard a familiar whirr and froze.

'What's wr—' Quentin started to say. But he never had a chance to finish because, without a second thought, I fisted my hands in his shirt and pushed him into the shadows of the wall. I pressed into his body hard, willing us to melt into the wall, as the transit pod approached then whizzed by us at top speed. I didn't dare glance behind me to see if there were any passengers aboard. I just waited. Listening for any sign that the pod was slowing or stopping. If it did, we were toast.

'What the hell was that?' Quentin breathed.

His chest was moving up and down in time with mine and I concentrated on it, using the distraction to calm myself down. I wasn't sure if either one of our heart rates had beeped off. If they had, it would've been covered by the noise of the pod.

'Transit pod,' I said tightly. 'That's why there are no foot patrols in this tunnel.'

'A bit of warning might've been nice,' he said dryly.

A few moments passed and I kept concentrating on my breathing.

'Um, Maggie?' Quentin said.

'Yeah?' I replied, still distracted.

'As nice as this is, I … I can't breathe.'

It was then I realised I still had my body, head to toe, pressed flush against his. I jumped back. 'Sorry,'

I said, quickly starting forwards again to cover my embarrassment.

Why the hell had I been so panicked? I'd done this how many times now? Why was tonight any different?

I glanced at Quentin. 'Hurry up,' I snapped.

Two junctions down we arrived at the doorway we needed.

'Junction 17,' Quentin said, reading the painted sign.

I put out my hand, still annoyed with myself. And him by default. 'Code?'

Quentin read out the sequence, including spaces, and I entered it, wondering if this was it. If he'd set me up. Any moment sirens could sound and guards with more weapons than they knew what to do with could be on top of me. But this was part of the gamble. There was no way forwards without it.

The screen beeped, causing me to flinch, then required an M-Band verification barcode. I was grateful yet again for having Gus in my pocket. I reached into my backpack, pulled out the black-market band he'd programmed earlier and held it up for scanning. Like the others, it was untraceable and had been uploaded with a mid-level M-Corp scientist's credentials. Ones that we'd anonymously extorted from him after I secured pictures of him downing lust-enhancers at Burn one night. It wasn't just girlfriend concerns – though they'd definitely helped – it was highly frowned upon in M-Corp to alter Phera-tech. Although when you knew where those alterations actually come from, it was ironic.

Another thing Quentin probably didn't need to know.

The door opened and we slipped in.

The lab was dimly lit, but there was enough light to see where we were going. I left Quentin to his wide-eyed explorations and headed straight for the main office, knowing that if there was any intel, it would be in the main computer.

I jumped right into my usual routine, pulling up the access files I needed while I called Gus again.

'In?' he answered.

'Like Flynn.'

'Give me the IP address?'

I rattled it off and then a series of other numbers Gus demanded, until he was satisfied. 'Okay, plug it in.'

The data transmitter looked like an ordinary USB stick and was a much smarter option than trying to use any M-Corp tech to hack into their system. The transmitter was old school, like our phones, but Gus had also tweaked it so it would send him a mirror image of any computer we plugged it into. I glanced up to see Quentin moving around the stainless-steel lab silently, picking up paper files and glancing at them in horror. I could imagine what he was seeing on those files was as simple as transport orders, experimentation approvals and behavioural reports, but even that was enough for him to realise the face M-Corp showed the world was not the same as the truth underground. Not to mention the sterile environment, and the fact that it wasn't supposed to exist. It was eye-opening stuff. And this was one of the small labs.

Quentin stopped dead in his tracks when he reached the far wall, and I strained my eyes in the low light to see what he was looking towards.

'Streaming,' I told Gus. Anxiously, I waited while he uploaded what he could. His hacking systems were incredible and nearly undetectable. As long as we got out of there unseen they would never know we'd been there. While I waited, I pulled out the small vial I'd brought with me and palmed it, ignoring the all-too-frequent twinge in my gut.

'I can only access the files that guy's ID was cleared for,' Gus mumbled. Uploads were never a sure thing, and there was always a two-minute time limit before we had to pull the plug, just in case. 'Okay, pull it,' he said, and a second later the plug was out of the computer and I was closing all of the screens I'd opened, carefully ensuring I left the computer exactly as I'd found it, including the angle of the keyboard and mouse.

'Anything?' I asked Gus.

'I'm looking, looking … maybe,' he muttered. I started to move back into the main room, phone still to my ear, seeing now why Quentin was stock-still. He was staring at a wall of empty glass cages.

Human-sized.

'Oh shit, Maggie,' came Gus's voice.

'What?' I asked, now alert.

'Get out of there. It's a cleaning day.'

I felt the blood drain from my face. 'A cleaning day,' I repeated, my voice dropping to a whisper. Quentin, as if sensing the problem, turned to me.

'At Junction 18. You're too close. Haul ass,' Gus insisted. He almost sounded worried about me, but I knew better. I had tech on me that, in the right hands, could be traced back to him. He was in danger too.

I didn't respond. Silence surrounded me, but inside my mind was screaming out orders to do something. Quentin was watching me intently, wondering what the hell was happening. I stared back at him briefly, wondering the same thing.

'Damn it, Maggie. I can hear your mind thinking something very, very bad,' Gus said.

'How long left on the elevator?' I asked.

'Seventeen minutes. You don't have time!'

'We'll be back in time.' And then I hung up the phone as Quentin stepped closer.

I opened my palm, showing him the vial. 'It's for your disruption. It was all I could find, but it's enough to make a few doses.' He eyed the vial and watched carefully as I placed it in my backpack.

'What's a cleaning day?' Quentin asked.

I huffed, angry that he could be so naive. 'Where do you think they all go, Quentin? The negs?'

He wet his lips, feeling my anger. 'Rehabilitation farms,' he answered, trying to stand tall, but already wavering.

I started walking back the way we'd come, careful to make sure everything was as we found it.

'And how many farms have you visited?' I hissed as we exited the lab and returned to the tunnels.

'A few. Three, maybe four. There is one in every state.'

I couldn't stop the bitter laugh that bubbled out. 'Gus was right. You really have no idea. Do you honestly think all the negs go to *rehab*?' Before he could answer, I walked on, in the opposite direction to the one that led us back to the elevator and out of here. 'Let me ask you this, Quentin Mercer.' His name fell harshly from my lips. 'How many negs do you know who have been reintroduced to society?'

Keeping pace, he answered, 'We're not *supposed* to know them. They're given new identities and places to live so that they can start fresh. That's how we protect them, *Maggie*,' he said my name with the same vehemence that I'd just delivered to him.

Moving faster now, increasing to a run, I could feel myself beginning to shake with fury.

'Where are we going?' he snapped.

Not slowing, I looked over my shoulder at him. 'You'll never believe it until you see it.'

'What else is down here?'

I slowed when I saw the opening that signalled we were at Junction 18 and blew out a breath before meeting his eyes, keeping my voice low. 'Down here is where M-Corp plays God.'

Eleven

Junction 18 had been scheduled for cleaning. That meant it was crawling with security – the kind who had really big guns and weren't opposed to using them. But I had one thing going for me: Junction 18 had been one of the first communities I'd visited underground and I knew how to stay unnoticed.

There were dozens of soldiers near the main entrance, taking orders and generally milling about in case there was any excitement. They were all big men, dressed in intimidating combat uniforms and laden with weapons. But that wasn't why they frightened me. It was their hardened eyes. They were in this place because they were the best. Or rather, the worst. Soldiers in the underground were all negs. This was about as much rehabilitation as any neg could hope for – the chance to become a soldier for hire. And M-Corp had the cream of the crop. For the soldiers, the alternative was final and all the motivation they needed. They killed in a blink and followed orders without question. Without fail.

I noticed the pod we'd seen zoom by earlier was parked at the entrance, probably on standby.

Staying in the shadows, I led Quentin down a narrow, unused tunnel to the side. He stayed close enough that I heard the muted beep of his M-Band go off. I wondered fleetingly why he didn't have a vibrate accessory on his heart-rate zip. Even I could afford one of those. I bit my lip, my thoughts going one step further to consider the possibility he might simply prefer to beat the heart-rate beep. Like me. Whatever the reason, I was impressed he'd had the foresight to keep it covered. No one else would've heard it.

Finally, we came to a small opening. It wasn't much, just a ventilation hole and emergency exit. No one would use this tunnel unless they didn't want to be seen.

I crouched down on all fours and crawled to the edge. Quentin followed my lead wordlessly. The ground was hard-packed dirt, rough with gravel, and we had to be careful not to stir up a dust cloud and draw attention to ourselves.

Nearing the edge, I dropped onto my stomach and levered up onto my elbows. Quentin mimicked my movements, shuffling commando style behind me.

The community below was similar to the last one I'd visited. Like a salad bowl carved out of granite. And within the bowl, a small group of buildings that I knew were dorm-style prisons.

Security and other uniformed personnel were moving between the buildings quickly, making short time of a messy job.

There were dump piles outside each of the buildings. And they were growing larger as more and more items were tossed onto them.

'What is all that stuff?' Quentin whispered.

I glanced at him. His face was a multitude of questions.

'Clothes, sheets, anything else they can find.'

I pointed to the far side of the community, where a large truck had been driven in through an aqueduct. People in plain grey uniforms were being loaded into the truck.

'Who are they?'

'Negs,' I answered.

I cast my eye over them carefully, out of habit more than anything else. I'd already checked this community. I knew Dad wasn't down there, but I couldn't stop myself.

'Where are they going?' he asked.

I didn't answer.

'Maggie, tell me!' he ordered.

We were running low on time. But he needed to see this.

'There are so many more negs than they ever told you or anyone else about. They're herded up and locked away. There are dozens of cell communities like this down here. Dozens.'

Quentin listened to me, glancing between me and the community.

'But still, there isn't enough room to fit all the negs,' I went on. 'Eventually they need to clear a space and start again.'

'Where do the people go?' His voice was lower now, filled with a new dread.

I began to shuffle back from the opening and into the dark tunnel. Quentin followed, watching me closely. My phone vibrated and I glanced at Gus's message.

When my eyes connected with Quentin's, I answered the only way I knew how. 'Down here, they're not people. They're negs.' I let the word hang for a moment. 'We have to go,' I added with a little more force.

Quentin shadowed me, moving at a quick pace. Just as we rounded the corner to get back into the main transit tunnel, Quentin grabbed me, pulling me back into the narrow side tunnel. Eyes wide, I watched as he put his finger to his lips, guarding me with his body as I had done for him earlier. Instinctively I wanted to push him off and take charge, but he held my eyes knowingly, holding me in place. A few seconds later, two guards walked by.

Quentin stuck his head around the corner. 'They've gone down a side tunnel,' he whispered, releasing me.

Stunned by the close call, I licked my dry lips and nodded. 'Thanks,' I said.

He shrugged. 'Glad to be of use.'

Carefully, I led us through the transit tunnel until we were well clear of Junction 18. Then we started to run.

'How much time do we have?' Quentin asked. He was starting to run out of steam and I didn't blame him.

'Seven minutes.' When Gus had messaged me, it had been ten and I'd been keeping count since then.

Quentin baulked. 'It's at least a fifteen-minute trip back.'

He was right and I didn't know of any closer exit points. But I had one card left to play.

When we arrived back at Junction 17, I grabbed the public phone by the wall to the entrance. 'Stay over there,' I ordered Quentin.

He was getting frustrated. And scared. It was a good sign that his self-preservation was still intact.

I glanced up at the tunnel camera. It would come on, since I was using the phone. These ones only activated when they knew they had activity, so I kept close to the wall where all it would catch was the top of my head.

'Transit request, press star,' the automated message said. I did as instructed.

'Transit destination?'

I pressed the number six, sending it far beyond where we needed to go, so as not to leave a trail.

'Transit deployed. Arrival in … forty-five seconds,' the computer responded.

I hung up and positioned us out of the oncoming pod's line of sight, making sure I kept clear of the camera as well. If the camera wasn't off by the time the pod came by, it would be more difficult. But I was out of options.

'Maggie,' Quentin began, but I cut him off.

'Stay back against the wall. When the transit pod arrives, wait until I signal for you.' I narrowed my eyes at him and pressed a hand to his chest, pushing him further towards the wall. 'I mean it. Not until I signal, no matter what. Do you understand?'

He swallowed and nodded.

It was only moments until we heard the sound of the approaching pod. I sighed when I saw there was a passenger already onboard. I knew there had been a good chance, but still, it would've been nice if there hadn't been.

The door opened and the security guard stepped out, looking for whoever had called the pod. I waited until he paced a few steps towards us, and when he turned to pace in the other direction, I moved fast, coming up behind the pod, raising my hand that was already holding the tranq gun. When I was sure I had a good aim, I fired.

The dart went straight to his neck, and though he spun around and his hand flew to the dart, he was down in three seconds tops.

I blew out the breath I'd been holding and leaned back against the pod for a second, checking with relief to see the camera light had gone off. Then I got moving, waving to Quentin.

He joined me as I leaned over the security guy. 'Help me load him in,' I said after I pulled the dart, pocketing the evidence.

'Is he …?'

'He's asleep, and hopefully won't remember this when he wakes up.' The propranolol mixed into a sedative caused minor amnesia, but it wasn't guaranteed; some people took to it more than others. Either way, the guard hadn't seen us.

'How long will he be out?'

'Only a few minutes, so we need to hurry.' I started pulling at the guard's legs and Quentin dutifully gripped under his arms. We heaved him into the pod and sat him on the bench seat. I arranged his head so he looked like he'd simply drifted off.

Quentin watched in horror as I brushed the dirt off the guard, cleaning him up. Details mattered.

'Jump on the back. There's a small ledge and a handhold at the top. Get a good grip. I'll follow you.'

He blinked. 'Aren't we going in the pod?'

I shook my head. 'It won't stop where we need to go. Hurry up.'

He did as ordered. And when he was in position, I pressed the door button and jumped out and onto the back just in time.

The pod jerked forwards and sped through the junction tunnel. It would only take a minute to get where we needed to go, which was a good thing, since we only had four left.

And we still had to get back into the elevator.

When we passed Junction 16, I nudged Quentin. 'When I nod, you jump! Don't hesitate!' I yelled.

He nodded nervously.

I nudged him again. 'Jump and run, or jump and roll!'

He nodded again.

I saw the approaching junction and timed it to the second, nudging Quentin one last time and giving him a sharp nod.

He jumped immediately and I followed. I chose to jump and run, since my last jump and roll had resulted in a gravel-filled ass. I wasn't sure what Quentin chose exactly, since he ended up on his back, but in all honesty, he'd done a lot better than I had my first go. I'd ended up in a wall.

With no time to lose, I was running and yelling at him to hurry up. We sprinted down the narrow side tunnel that led to the elevator shaft and through the door. I was so relieved to find the elevator still there, I actually let out a small giggle.

Quentin stared at me in dismay as he climbed through the hatch, which only made me laugh outright.

I followed him through the hatch, resting my feet on the railing so I could quickly put the screws back in place. It was one of those times I felt like forgetting about the damn details and just getting the hell out of there, but I'd already left a guard drugged in a pod. I couldn't leave any other clues behind.

Each screw took a small eternity, but my hand remained steady and I got the job done. Then I grabbed my phone.

'Tell me you're back,' Gus said.

I jumped down from the railing, rolling my ankle as I did. Quentin grabbed my waist to steady me. My eyes shot to his, and I flashed back to having my entire body pressed against his in the tunnel.

'Open the doors,' I said to Gus, stepping back from Quentin.

'Move it, Maggie. Cameras come back up in thirty seconds. Take the mall parking exit.'

I hung up as the doors opened. I glanced at Quentin, who was watching me intently. 'Run,' I said.

We sprinted and made it out the pedestrian exit

back onto the street. I abruptly slowed to a brisk walk, grabbing Quentin's arm to indicate he do the same.

Panting for air, we kept moving until we saw a bus pull up across the road. I tugged on his sleeve and jogged over to it, jumping aboard.

When we sat down and the bus pulled out, we both breathed a sigh of relief.

'Where are we going?' Quentin asked, tugging his hat down so no one recognised him.

I watched him, this time focusing on the cuts and scrapes on his face and body. It wasn't so much the small wounds on the outside though. It was the look in his eyes. I knew that look.

It was the one that signalled the end of the world as you knew it. The one that meant your new reality was unfamiliar and unkind.

I blew out a breath, mad at myself, both for caring and for not caring enough. 'We're going to get you cleaned up,' I responded.

Mom wasn't home. Tonight was one of those nights where we didn't overlap with one another. I had work until nine and she started work the same time. It was why it was one of my preferred nights for breaking and entering.

There was a note and a plate of lasagne near the oven. I wasn't hungry, but I grabbed it, and detoured by the laundry before heading to the garage.

When I walked into my room, Quentin was sitting at my desk. His shoulders were slumped, his head hanging. When he heard me, he looked around but didn't say a word. He hadn't spoken since we'd first got on the bus.

He turned back to my desk and I couldn't help noticing the blood seeping thought his shirt on his shoulder blade.

I headed to my bathroom and grabbed the supplies I'd so often needed. When I came back out, he was still in the same position. I put the first-aid kit on the bed and sat on the edge, trying to suppress the urge to just throw him out. My life was not about sharing and caring. I didn't know the first thing about how to tackle this. And I most certainly didn't need to feed my guilt. That was something I'd have the rest of my life for. But not now.

'They're dead,' he said, breaking the silence.

I swallowed audibly. 'Not all of them, but enough,' I responded, wondering yet again, what I had been thinking, taking him to the clean-up.

When he didn't say anything else, I stood and moved towards him. 'Take your shirt off and I'll clean your wounds.' I tried to make it an order, but it was a pathetic attempt. Whether I wanted to or not, I felt bad.

He shrugged out of his T-shirt and I was glad he wasn't facing me when I got a good look at his exposed back. He was so defined, his olive skin making every muscle look that much more …

I felt the air hiss into my mouth.

He heard it and stiffened.

Suddenly, the atmosphere in the room changed dramatically. For the first time that night, my hands shook as I picked up the sponge and started to clean away the blood from his shoulder. Not at all noticing the few drops of water that escaped down the deep groove of his spine.

After I dried his wound and applied some antiseptic cream, I put a square bandage on it. Neither of us spoke, and all my traitorous mind could conjure were thoughts that involved my hands exploring the details of his back.

Well, shit. I closed my eyes briefly and stepped away. 'All done. I'm sure you can clean up the small grazes on your arms,' I said.

He turned towards me in the chair and I had to work very hard to keep my eyes focused on his.

'Is my father a murderer?' he asked suddenly.

I thought about the question and, strangely, what the answer would mean to him. I grabbed the fresh clothes I'd got from the laundry and handed them to him, not sure I had a response he'd be happy with. 'They're my brother's.'

Seeing through my pathetic attempt at diversion, he snatched the clothes, his eyes flashing with disappointment, and headed towards the bathroom.

I looked at my feet, but gave him the best answer I could. 'I don't think he pulls the trigger, if that's what you meant,' I said.

Just before he closed the door, I caught his quiet response. 'No, that's not what I meant.'

It was a while before he reappeared. When he did, he left without another word.

Twelve

I don't know how I'd let myself be suckered into this field trip. I had things to do, intel from last night that needed to be sifted through. But when Quentin had called me first thing in the morning, insisting we visit one of the rehabilitation farms so widely advertised on television and city billboards, I'd caved.

We were changing onto the orange line at Rosslyn Metro station, where I'd caused a delay by running above ground to grab a breakfast burrito.

'Did you have any trouble ditching your babysitter?' I asked.

Quentin's brow lifted in question.

'Your driver,' I elaborated.

He put a hand in his pocket and leaned against the wall, looking completely at ease. 'Security is important to my family, but my brothers and I learned a long time ago that staff all have a price.'

'You're paying off your driver?'

He shrugged. 'More like, sending him on some other errands for the day.'

'With compensation.'

He grinned. 'With compensation.' His eyes dropped to my hands. 'Is that chilli?'

I took another large bite, shifting my feet apart to accommodate for the drips, and nodded. Okay, so it wasn't technically a 'breakfast' burrito as much as an extremely tasty way to start the day.

'That's disgusting,' he mumbled, even as he kept eyeing it.

'Want some?' I asked.

He shook his head.

I rolled my eyes and looked away.

'You don't think much of me,' he said, breaking my study of the waffled cement ceiling. Since it wasn't really a question, I didn't answer. He nodded slowly, my silence apparently enough, and reached to pull a bottle of water out of his bag. As he did his arm grazed mine, his hand skimming my forearm. Goosebumps shot across my arm and down my back.

I clenched my jaw and threw the last bite of my burrito into a nearby bin.

'You're angry?' Quentin said, his tone unnervingly intrigued. 'At me?'

I was. Working to control my damn heart rate around

him was becoming a constant task. It was infuriating. I kept my gaze averted. 'It's going to be a long day, that's all. Why do you even want to do this?'

He pondered my question, letting go of his own for now. He was a Mercer and that meant almost everything was accessible. In his world, desires were simply there to be met by others, so the level of consideration he seemed to be giving my question was intriguing.

'I've only visited the farms on official tours. You know, with media and liaisons. I want to see one of them when no one knows I'm there. I need to do this.'

He needed more proof. This, I understood.

'Okay.'

He raised his eyebrows. 'Okay? You're not going to try to tell me I'm being stupid?'

I stubbed my booted toe into the subway station floor. 'Nope. But be prepared to be disappointed.'

Seeing the truth of the rehabilitation farms would open Quentin's eyes once and for all. In fact, it was even a good idea, as long as we could get close enough and remain undetected.

'Right now, disappointment would be little surprise,' he said, watching pensively as the red lights flashed along the platform edge, signalling our train's arrival. I wondered if he was remembering what had happened last month. The image of the desperate man as he broke free of the M-Corp guards and leaped in front of that train had most certainly imprinted on my mind.

We rode the first half of the trip to Fairfax in silence. A group of girls had boarded the train after us, and it was soon obvious they'd recognised the Mercer heir. Quentin kept his attention on the floor as the group shuffled closer to us, continuing their whispers until they disembarked at East Falls.

Once we were moving again, Quentin turned to me. 'Are you scared of the negs?'

I understood the question and why he was asking it. But the answer was not so simple. I looked out the window. 'Some negs are frightening,' I admitted. 'Especially those who've been locked underground for a long time. You only have to study how insane coal miners get after being trapped underground to understand what it could do to someone. I can't imagine anyone being okay with having their freedom stolen from them.'

'You're avoiding the question, even though I agree with you.'

I let out a deep breath. 'What do you want me to say? Yes, they … Some of them are dangerous, the type you hope you never run into in a dark alley. But others … I don't know, maybe they're destined to do or become something horrible like they say, but they haven't become that yet. They seem normal. Lost. Desperate.' I huffed, struggling to communicate my jumbled thoughts. 'I don't know the answer exactly. But people should have the right to become whatever they're going to be *before* they are judged and sentenced.'

After a few minutes, he simply looked back at me and said, 'I agree.'

I blinked, surprised by his assessment of my opinion.

'Tell me about your father,' he tacked on, again catching me off guard.

I swallowed the fast-forming lump in my throat. Just thinking of Dad …

'He was …' I caught myself. 'He *is* a good person.'

'I'm not surprised,' Quentin said softly.

When I didn't respond, he elaborated. 'To do what you're doing, to risk everything the way you are. He must be an amazing man. He's lucky to have you.'

The compliment only triggered all of my feelings of failure. All of my fruitless trips into the tunnels. I shook my head sharply. 'I've done nothing to help him.'

'But you will, won't you?' he said, as if he was already certain.

I blushed, but my reply was firm. 'Whatever it takes.'

He nodded, as if he were pleased with my response. 'I have no doubt.'

Good to hear, I suppose. Considering he was the 'whatever' it was going to take.

*

Fairfax County is vast. Once we arrived at Vienna Metro, we hailed a taxi. Though Quentin knew the location of one of the rehabilitation farms near Manassas, we asked the driver to instead take us to a prestigious golf course that neighboured the facility.

The rehabilitation farm was hidden in plain sight, like so many things M-Corp. It was almost as if Garrett Mercer took pride in laughing at the world's blindness.

We paid the taxi driver and crossed through the back paddocks of the golf course. I was grateful we didn't come across any roaming golfers.

'We'll have to cross through the forest. It'll take about half an hour,' Quentin instructed. I'd had a close look at the map this morning and the location of the farm was nestled within the bushlands of Hemlock Overlook Park. I'd expected we'd have to walk, but it felt odd not being the one making the decisions. Nonetheless, I nodded and let Quentin set the pace.

It was refreshing to be outdoors. I seemed to spend all of my time now entrenched in urban landscapes. Or below ground. The clean air, the sounds of rustling tree leaves and nearby birds calling, reminded me how much I missed country life. It also served as an affirmation of what I was doing. If I could get Dad back, I knew he'd make things right and get us out of the city.

We made good time. Both of us were fit and capable of taking the most direct route, even if we did have to push through some dense forest along the way. Before long we came to a large barbed-wire fence, most of it blacked out by a dark tarpaulin. We travelled the perimeter until we found a gap that we could look through. Beyond, we could see a farm site. It was a large plantation-style home, and there were a number of people outside, in what looked like lines. But we were too far away to see much.

'We could cut the wire. I brought cutters,' Quentin suggested.

Well, wasn't he nifty?

But I shook my head, pointing to the electrical wires. 'Cut them and it will set off an alarm instantly.'

'What then?' he asked.

I smiled. It was good to be back in the driver's seat.

I reached into my backpack and pulled out a piece of my own black tarpaulin along with two pairs of gloves.

'Sometimes the old-fashioned way is the one they forget,' I said slyly, unfolding the tarp.

Quentin watched me dubiously. 'Will the tarp protect us from the barbs?'

'Not completely, hence the gloves and ...' I looked him up and down. He was in jeans and a distractingly well-fitted navy T-shirt. 'It will protect the important bits,' I said with a smirk.

'Maybe this wasn't such a great idea,' he mumbled while I laughed.

The tarp would do its job. It wasn't the strongest material, but it matched what was already surrounding the perimeter. If a guard was to look up and see it flapping in the wind, he would just think it had come loose from the fence. Anything else would entice unwanted interest.

'Put these on,' I instructed, handing him a pair of thickly padded garden gloves. 'Use them to hold down the barbs when you go over. And be quick. We have no idea what the security's like here. They could have eyes on the perimeter at any time.' It wasn't how I liked to do things, but from everything Gus had been able to pull up this morning, it didn't seem like there was much more than hourly sweeps by guards on foot.

Quentin shoved his hands in the gloves and reached for the fence, only to snatch his arm back.

I bit down on the inside of my lip to stop my smile. 'Oh, by the way, there's probably an electrical current running through the fence to keep wildlife away.'

He threw me a sharp look. I gave up trying to suppress my amusement. 'I'm sorry,' I laughed, holding up my hands in surrender. 'It's only a little current to frighten them away. It won't do any lasting damage.'

He grunted and we both began to climb. I quickly realised the little current wasn't quite as *little* as I'd thought. Without trying to look obvious, I powered to the top first and pushed down the barbed wire, hauling myself over it, not worrying about the tears in my jeans or incisions being made along my forearms. I just kept moving down the other side, jumping the last portion to escape the electrical jolts shocking my body.

Quentin landed beside me, sporting similar tears in his jeans and T-shirt. Once we'd both finished shaking the ghost tremors from our arms and legs, he raised his eyebrows. 'For just a little current, you seemed to have a big reaction,' he teased.

'Bite me,' I snapped, adjusting my backpack and walking towards the trees while he chuckled away behind me.

We moved as close as we dared, taking up position behind a large boulder. Quentin pulled out a pair of binoculars. I didn't need to look. This wasn't my first visit to a rehabilitation farm. I'd staked one out in the exclusive area of Middleburg over a year ago. Nothing good came of it.

'When I came here with my father six months ago, it looked so different,' Quentin said, the binoculars fixed to his eyes. 'There were animals grazing in the paddocks over there.' He pointed to an area that now served as a parking space for transport buses. 'Tables and chairs were scattered in that area out front,' he went on in a daze.

I looked over the fields now. It was a sombre sight; lines of negs were being herded and numbered. As far as I could tell the rehabilitation farms – when not on show to the world – were simply processing camps where negs were interviewed, then stripped of their identities and personal items.

He pointed to the far corner of the property. 'They had a meditation centre set up there when I visited. It was … Oh God, there's smoke … Is that?' He nudged me. 'Down there, is that what I think it is?'

I just nodded, even though he wasn't looking at me. His eyes were fixed on the chair that a neg was strapped to, and on the silver cylinder being lowered just above the neg's right hip. This was where the negs were branded. By the time they were taken below ground, they were nothing but a number.

'What are they doing there?' he asked, gesturing to a line of waiting negs on the veranda, all headed to a large desk where a number of guards were seated.

I couldn't make out everything he was seeing without the binoculars, but I'd seen it before and knew enough to explain. 'Collecting records, employment history, lists of assets, debts, everything. Family members and all of their details too. They download and record everything from the negs' M-Bands, then they interview the neg's family. It's how they control the family's reactions. For some, they recount the events that led to the neg's detainment. Sometimes that's enough. But when it isn't, they threaten the future of other family members or the loss of social or financial status. Whatever they have to do to make people co-operate. They always find some angle.'

'Does it always work?' he asked, watching in horror as a guard started to brutally beat one of the negs in front of all the others. Shows like this were common practice below ground too. It was disheartening to know I was used to them.

'Most of the time. But I suspect many of the Preference Evolution members have some stories to tell. There are people who still want to fight the system, they just have no way of doing it and no idea what they are really dealing with.'

Quentin put down the binoculars and we both moved behind the cover of the boulder. 'But you know, don't you? You see everything.'

'I don't know what you're talking about,' I said, adjusting my cap to shield myself from the now glaring sun.

'I saw you documenting things as we went last night. You took photos or video of anything you thought was worthwhile. When you thought I wasn't watching, you'd log them. My guess is you've been doing the same thing for a while now and somewhere out there you have a stash of information that could make a real difference.'

I was surprised by his observation. And annoyed. I prided myself on being discreet and I'd never told anyone about my stash, not even Gus. It was my quiet backup. I'd carefully catalogued and hidden all of the intel as I'd gone along.

'I'm not in this to change the world, Quentin. I just want to find my dad,' I said, because it was true.

'Come on, you can't be serious. Look at those people down there, Maggie. Are you really just going to get your dad out and then walk away from the rest of them, knowing you could make a difference?'

'Yes,' I said, my voice flat, my expression neutral. I wasn't going to have this discussion, or admit that I'd kept all of that data in the hope that maybe someday I might be able to do the right thing for a change. That there might be a chance for some kind of redemption after all this.

'You're a liar,' he said, his own voice just as flat.

I was too unnerved to respond. Before I had a chance to gather my thoughts, a loud gunshot echoed from below. Quentin jolted, and looked over the boulder. I closed my eyes and briefly pressed my lips together before joining him.

We didn't need the binoculars to see. The man who had just been roughed up by a guard was now motionless on the ground.

Just. Another. Demonstration.

Quentin swallowed repeatedly, probably trying to stop himself from retching. He slumped back behind the rock. There were frightened cries from the negs below, and soon others were being hit with the blunt ends of the guard's weapons.

'They just … They killed him,' Quentin stammered, his face sapped of colour, his eyes brimming with remorse.

I pulled on my gloves, angry at yet another life being stolen as I'd stood by and watched, still unnerved by our entire conversation. I threw a dispassionate look in Quentin's direction. 'Have you seen enough?'

Thirteen

Later that night, I sat in Gus's apartment staring at the new tunnel map, just one of the handy scores from our data upload yesterday. Unfortunately, the upload hadn't given me the one thing I really wanted. But on the bright side – we'd managed to compile enough saleable intel to get some more money flowing in.

'There was a flag on his name,' Gus said out of nowhere.

I flinched and darted a look at him. He was staring down at some papers, avoiding my eyes. 'You said there was nothing,' I said.

He shrugged nonchalantly, but I saw his jaw tense at the implied accusation. 'Easy, tiger. It was just a flag, nothing we can really work with. It's years old, probably from around the time he was first brought in. It's unreliable at best. You know how often negs get moved around. You'd have more chance finding him in Afghanistan and you know it.'

He wasn't exaggerating. My hands fisted tightly.

'Where, Gus?'

He leaned back in his armchair, looking towards the ceiling as he sighed. 'You're not going to find him, Maggie. But you *are* going to get us both killed, or locked up.'

'Where?' I repeated.

He didn't look back at me as he answered. 'His name pops up in relation to a core junction. Possibly a testing facility he was taken to briefly. But we are talking about the *core* here, Maggie.' He paused to meet my eyes. We'd both heard the rumours of what went on in the core – horrific and invasive experiments on negs, brainwashing, torture, execution chambers.

I schooled my features back to neutral, but Gus had already seen my reaction. As if reading my mind, he gave a small nod.

'And even for me,' he said softly, 'it's impossible to get you physically in and out of there without being caught.'

I just stared at him.

And waited.

I knew that the 'core' was the headquarters of the once-government site originally designed to withstand nuclear attack. And *he* knew what I was going to do. He knew I had no choice. And more importantly, he knew *he* had no choice.

'We'll need maps and passcodes,' he said finally, still not looking at me, still not happy. 'The kind that don't come easy and cost a lot of money. Money we don't have.' He paused before adding, 'And fresh DNA, Mags. DNA is the only thing that will open up those labs.'

I swallowed and nodded calmly even as my stomach flipped. This could be it. This could be my way to finding Dad.

And we both knew who could likely gain us access to a high-level clearance door.

The question was, would Quentin let things go that far?

Saturdays were a routine, like every other day. When Quentin strolled into the garage, I was well into the work-out portion of the day. Working out didn't just keep me fit, it always helped me sweat the nightmares – filled with the unnamed faces of all the people I'd left to rot in those tunnels – out of my system. The advantage of belonging to a family too poor to own a car was that the garage was an open space. I'd taken full advantage, setting up a boxing bag and a number of weights I'd collected along the way.

'Hey,' Quentin said over the music. I stopped kicking the bag and wondered briefly if he'd been watching for long. I went into a world of my own when I was training.

I turned down the music, using the time to catch my breath. 'Hey.'

He gestured to my hands. 'You're supposed to wrap them.'

Sure, they were red and would be bruised and grazed tomorrow, but they almost always were. I shrugged. 'Don't get time to wrap them when I need to fight, see no point when I'm training.'

He gave a slight nod. 'What discipline do you study?'

'The type that doesn't get me dead,' I said, turning back to the floor mats with a bottle of water in hand.

He leaned against the wall and crossed his arms, waiting.

I sighed. 'Muay Thai.'

He gave a low whistle. 'Intense.'

'It's clean, it's upright, and as street smart as they get.' Most of the other martial arts spent too much time rolling around on the ground for my liking.

Quentin nodded, looking down and stepping out of his leather shoes.

'What are you doing?' I asked, taking a gulp of water.

He gave me a small smile as he unbuttoned his shirt cuffs and began to roll up his sleeves. 'Seeing how it holds up against karate.'

I raised my eyebrows. 'You know karate?'

He shrugged. 'A bit.'

I smiled at that; he was clearly trying to downplay it. 'Okay, but you're about to get your ass kicked.'

He returned my smile and walked past me to turn the music back up.

We danced around each other. I could see he was trying to make me comfortable. He was clearly worried I'd be too chicken to kick the shit out of him. He really didn't know me.

'Rules?' he asked. Then I kicked him in the stomach.

'Okay, no rules,' he grunted, spinning to return the favour.

Men are stronger. It's just a fact of life. It wouldn't matter how much I trained or how strong I was, they had more weight to throw around and, judging by the stinging pain making its way up my side, Quentin knew what to do with that weight.

I moved in close and struck his chin with my elbow.

'Cheat,' he said, shifting his jaw from side to side.

I stepped back and shook my head. 'Not in Muay Thai. We get all eight points, including knees and elbows.'

'Interesting,' he said.

'What colour belt?' I asked, though I already knew. He moved with such precision. Another Quentin surprise.

'A dark one,' he answered slyly.

Then we moved in again, blocking and dodging kicks, taking a shin here and there. It was fun. And even if I was impressed, after a short while I had his measure. When he moved in with a round kick that should've taken me down, I crouched low and spun fast, coming up behind him and grabbing his arm as I did.

Men might have the strength, but girls have the speed.

With his arm now locked hard around his back, all I had to do was squeeze and he'd be in a world of pain. 'Give,' I said.

He chuckled. 'Give.'

After a quick shower, I returned to my room. Quentin was back in position at my desk. It wasn't like he had much choice. It was either the desk or my bed.

I towel-dried my hair and caught him watching me when I looked up. I raised my eyebrows mockingly to cover my blush. He looked away.

'So, what's the deal with your family? You go gallivanting around at all hours of the night and your mom is completely oblivious?' He shook his head. 'At least my parents pay attention,' he mumbled.

I moved so fast, the sound of my sharp slap across his face shocked us both. All I saw was red. 'Don't go there,' I warned. 'My mother is not oblivious. She doesn't have the time to be oblivious, between working nine shifts a week at the hospital and all weekend as a cleaner for rich bastards like you. She barely has time to eat.' I stepped back, some of my anger fading to sadness with my words. 'And even so, she leaves dinner for me almost every night and makes time to speak with me every day, even if it is just on the phone. And why does my mother have to do all of that?'

He stared at me.

'Because her husband is a neg, and she was left with all of his debts, a family to feed and now the new Poverty Tax on top of it.' I stepped towards him. 'All thanks to M-Corp.'

The silence lingered, but Quentin surprised me. He didn't look away. He held my eyes and finally gave a nod. A forfeit.

'I was out of line.' He swallowed. 'Of all people, I should know how easy it is to look at a family from the outside and make assumptions that aren't correct.' He half laughed. 'Or in my case, from the inside.'

I slumped down on the edge of my bed reeling from my emotions. 'Forget about it. It's not your fault.'

He nodded, but his eyes said he wasn't entirely sure of that. After a few beats of awkward silence, Quentin spoke. 'There's a party tonight.'

I was grateful for the subject change. 'And you want to go and be Mr Phera?'

He seemed irritated by the question. 'I have to go. My mother has already started to become suspicious, asking why I haven't turned on my tech in social situations.' He glanced quickly at me, then back at his feet. 'They want to meet you.'

I chose to ignore that comment for now and reached into my drawer to pull out one of the vials I'd put aside for him. 'I was able to make enough for four doses. It is a basic mix of synthetic pheromones – your usual epiandrosterone and androsterone mixes. But unlike enhancers, this changes the way your signal reacts with each person's individual signal, so that you don't just have one broad signature.'

'So it will seem like …'

I nodded. 'Like you're completely normal, reacting better with some than others. But it won't last all night, Quentin. You'll be safe for two hours, but don't risk it beyond that.'

Quentin stared at the vial as he repeated, 'Two hours.' He looked up. 'Will you test it with me?'

'No,' I said, too quickly. I had to turn away from him to close my eyes and steady my heart rate. 'I refuse to be any part of the system.'

'Why? It's not real anyway.'

I shook my head. 'I turned on my Phera-tech on the test day because I had no choice. That is the only reason I will ever turn it on.'

'Fine,' he snapped. 'Then you'll just have to come with me then.'

I blinked. 'Sorry. Can't.' Even if I wanted to, which I didn't, I still had to clean the house for Mom and I had a load of study to get through.

His eyes narrowed and I instinctively crossed my arms. 'How do I know you're not setting me up?' he said. 'That you didn't just need my help to get in that lab the other night and now you're going to take me down?' He leaned back in my chair. 'I want you nearby in case anything goes wrong and, since I went underground for you, you can come to a party with me.' He finished with a satisfied grin while I settled for a scowl.

'Fine. I'll be the designated driver.'

He scoffed. 'You don't have a car.'

I looked out my grimy window at his shiny black BMW and smiled. 'Yours will do.'

I had no idea what to wear to one of these things and I was most certainly not up-to-date on the latest fashion trends – the last magazine I downloaded was *Tasers and Other Defensive Tools*. I avoided the school party scene like a disease, and even if I hadn't, I'd never have been included in this particular clique. My total net worth was way too low.

I perused my wardrobe options. It took about three seconds. There really wasn't much to choose from, so I grabbed the cleanest of the two outfits I wore when I had to play the vixen part in a trade – I hoped it would help me remain inconspicuous. Finally, after messing around with some colours, I wiped my face clean and settled for a heavy dose of mascara and dark grey eye shadow, smudging it around my eyes. I knew that colours were currently the rage, but pink and I just don't mesh.

Looking at myself in the mirror, I shook my head. I looked okay and, though I probably wasn't Quentin's cup of tea, my outfit had its appeal. It isn't that hard to put on fitted clothes and make the most of what you had. But still … I looked longingly at my sweats and T-shirt handing off the edge of my bed.

Quentin was standing by his car when I walked out. His eyes dropped to my feet and I suddenly felt nervous. Why? I couldn't say. I'd worn Stella's damn heels before, and my black jeans and black singlet were hardly daring, just tight and more … exposing than my usual clothes.

He raised his eyebrows. 'Should've brought the bike,' he murmured.

'Sorry, I was all out of wannabe Barbie clothes,' I snapped, unusually defensive.

He watched me, his mouth slightly ajar at first, then lifting at the edges.

'Car access!' I said, holding my arm out and contemplating turning tail and storming back into my house. I knew I didn't look like he wanted me to, but the way he kept looking at me made me self-conscious. It was annoying.

Quentin tapped his M-Band a few times and then held his band close to mine as he transferred driver privileges to his car. Car keys were a thing of the past. 'Do me a favour and never *ever* change your wardrobe,' he said, keeping his eyes on me throughout the transfer.

I glared at him.

He shook his head slightly, as if confused by me. 'You really don't get it, do you?'

'Get what?' I said, already exhausted with the conversation and missing my sweat pants again.

He opened his mouth as if to respond, but then he took a small step back, speaking softly. Now it was him who seemed awkward. 'I'm a neg, Maggie. What I think doesn't matter.' He half laughed and opened the car door. 'You'll see for yourself when we walk into the party tonight and every pair of male eyes fixes on you.'

*

Out of all the insanely rich kids from school, Morris Delaware was one of the few I could actually stand, so I was relieved to discover the party was at his house – which just happened to look out over sprawling lawns equipped with terraced, Tuscan-styled gardens and an indoor pool. Naturally.

Morris was the son of a popular senator, a star on the athletics track, a solid grade getter, and came from ridiculous wealth. Rumours circulated that, since his Phera-tech was fitted a couple of months ago, he'd rated impressively on a number of occasions.

By the time we arrived, the party was already in full swing. A bunch of people were hanging out on the front veranda, which looked like it swept all the way around the house.

It didn't take long for people to recognise Quentin's car and start waving in our direction. It was at this point I noticed just how nervous he was.

'Stop,' I ordered, holding down his bouncing knee. 'You'll be fine. I promise this will work. Just remember –'

'Two hours,' he cut me off.

I nodded, looking down.

He opened the vial. 'Just swallow?'

'Yep.'

And he did, both of us taking note of the time. He had until 11 p.m.

Quentin punched a few keys on his M-Band and an activation beep sounded. His Phera-tech was live. The next person he walked by with active tech – everyone inside that house over eighteen – would rate with him.

My mouth was suddenly dry.

He glanced at my M-Band, which remained silent. I couldn't give him what he wanted at that moment. Turning on my tech was not an option. So instead, I put my hand on his forearm and squeezed. 'I promise it will work.'

He grabbed my hand and closed it in his, meeting my eyes. 'I trust you.'

I forced a smile, even though at that moment the only thing I really wanted to do was leap out of his car and run as far away as I could.

When we walked up the steps, there were a few random whistles, which I ignored.

'Hey, man,' Morris said, pushing through the people milling about on the veranda. He shook hands with Quentin and the two of them seemed to be genuinely pleased to see one another. Quentin glanced down at his M-Band, prompting Morris to do the same.

If I judged a person purely on his wardrobe, I'd never have tolerated someone like Morris. He had the whole wealthy-but-casual look mastered, wearing khaki pants, a navy button-down shirt and tasselled loafers. Morris was just lucky he had kind eyes and a nice laugh, which was in full swing. 'Good to know we can still be mates.'

Quentin nodded, glancing at me shyly. He'd had his first non-neg rating. His first *real* rating, given that the vial he'd just swallowed was nothing more than saline and bitter flavouring.

Morris nodded to me. 'Hey, Maggie. About time you started to make the circuit.'

I couldn't help but smile back at him. Then he looked me up and down, turning his attention back to Quentin.

'Dude, you should've brought the bike.'

Quentin started laughing beside me. My defences kicked in and I glared at Morris.

He put his hands up in mock surrender. 'Sorry, babe. But come on, who wouldn't want to see you on the back of a bike. You look kinda saucy!'

My eyes darted between Morris and Quentin, who seemed to be sharing a look I couldn't decipher. Then, saving me from the awkwardness of the moment, Quentin grabbed my hand and started to lead me inside. 'See you later on, man,' he said over his shoulder to Morris.

I followed, feeling out of my depth and still uncomfortable with the 'saucy' comment. When I had to play the part out with Gus at the clubs, it was different ...

Anonymous. This was the school crowd. The people I'd made sure I remained invisible to.

We stepped into the entry foyer, which also gave us a good view of the massive open-plan living area. Morris didn't do parties by halves. And with the kind of money he had at his disposal, he'd never have to.

My eyes perused the dozen red-felted rectangular tables that bordered the room, each manned by a dressed-to-the-nines attendant. In the centre of the room, high round tables with white linen and stools took up one half while the dance floor, equipped with a lounge band I'd seen flyers for around town, occupied the other half.

Although drinking was still in vogue, nobody wanted to do it in excess anymore. Too risky for your pheromone ratings. But that had also left a hole to be filled and Morris, who ran one of Kingly's largest gambling rings, always came through. He had staged a cross between a 1920s prohibition bar in Paris and all the glitz of a Las Vegas high-roller room.

In short, he'd built a casino in his house.

I was instantly jealous as I considered the profits he would reap from this night and the intel that money could buy.

The majority of the girls were familiar faces from school. They were dressed as I'd expected: short skirts, bouncing boobs and too much – colourful – makeup, but

I figured they knew what they were doing since they worked so hard at it.

One of the positive side effects of Phera-tech was that underage sex was now uncommon. No point rushing into sex with a non-viable partner at sixteen when at eighteen you may rate with an ideal partner – one who may not see you as so ideal if you couldn't hold out for them. STDs were also a dying concern; M-Bands provided a zip accessory to authorise a 'partner-check' for any red flags before getting it on.

On the flip side, once people were finally fitted with their Phera-tech, well … Let's just say pants didn't stay on for long. If it wasn't with long-term matches, lust-matches – which basically translated to 'consensual random hook-ups' – often proved too hard to resist.

Looking around the room, it was obvious to distinguish who was and wasn't over eighteen. Mostly due to the R-rated behaviour.

Quentin led me to the far side of the room, stopping in front of me and putting his hands on my upper arms.

'You don't have to babysit me,' I said. As much as I'd been taking in the room and the girls, my main focus had been on him. He hadn't glanced at his M-Band again.

'I know that, but I have a point to prove.'

I narrowed my eyes. 'What's that?' I asked, my attention drifting towards a game of Phera-bet. It was a stupid tradition for those not yet eligible for Phera-tech. Guys or girls would throw their tops on the table and then a person would be chosen to basically 'sniff the shirt'. The person sniffing would then choose the one they liked the smell of most. Punters would bet on the outcome and results were often embarrassing.

It was stupid. Most traditions were.

'Do me a favour and turn around,' Quentin said. 'When you do, tell me if I was right about all those eyes.'

He was talking about what he'd said earlier. Fine. If he wanted to make fun of me, he could do his worst.

I turned around slowly and, as I did, I felt the fast onset of heat in my cheeks. More than a handful of guys' eyes had followed me. Not just creepy bar-guys, but guys I went to school with, guys I'd made a point of staying under the radar around. Quentin stood close beside me and I noticed he tilted his head, but when I looked in his direction, he wasn't looking at me. His jaw was locked and he was glaring back at every pair of eyes turned in our direction.

I crossed my arms. 'You do realise the only reason they are all checking me out is because I walked in here with you?'

He gave me a no-holds-barred smile and, hell, the shock of it almost took me to my knees. I'd never seen him smile like that. It changed his face completely, freeing him somehow. And yet, something in his eyes, the something darker that had been spearing guys around the room a moment ago, remained.

Before I could ask what was going on, we were joined by a group of his buddies and he was quickly submerged in the latest sport and school gossip. I noticed every now and then that he would glance at his M-Band – obviously picking up more readings that he was satisfied with. It wasn't a surprise to me that his true ratings were consistently strong.

There were two girls standing in the group from school, Olivia and Avery. They were both over eighteen, which meant they had active Phera-tech and, by the way they were eyeing off Quentin, they wanted to be first in range, and fast.

'You want me to grab you a drink?' Quentin whispered in my ear, his hand lightly touching the small of my back, catching me by surprise. For some reason it seemed so intimate. He could've just yelled over the music. God, what was I thinking? *Why* was I thinking?

I shook my head and leaned back. 'I'm going to grab some fresh air. I'll catch up with you in a bit.' He studied me for a moment, then nodded. I stepped away, leaving a gap beside him; I wondered who would fill it first. As I headed for the doors, I glanced back. Olivia.

I smiled when I saw the disappointment on her face.

I walked around the crowded front veranda until I found the more deserted back half. I sat down on a swinging chair and watched the party inside the house.

Eventually Quentin moved into my line of sight. He was smiling and looking relaxed. In control. Like his old self. He glanced out the window and caught my eye, giving me a wave. He made a drinking motion. I shook my head. He was there to get ratings and be happy and normal, not to look after me. He shrugged and stayed where he was. I saw him wave at someone and then Morris joined him. Whatever they were talking about seemed serious and private. Morris nodded and shook Quentin's hand, glancing over his shoulder in my direction as he did. It made me nervous. Maybe he'd told Morris to throw me out of the party now he knew his Phera-tech was working.

But more time cruised by and nothing interesting happened on my deserted section of the veranda. Settling in for the final hour, I picked up a magazine that was on the chair beside me, the cover advertising a debate on the recently introduced Poverty Tax. I didn't look at the article, knowing it would only infuriate me. The new tax would take another four per cent of Mom's salary to subsidise the costs of microchipping and M-Bands in countries that couldn't afford the outlay. It was crazy. Why was it suddenly so important every single person in the world had this tech? I was sure the people of

Zimbabwe would prefer the money went towards food and housing if they were asked.

I flipped through the pages, stopping at an article that caught my attention.

It was about a 43-year-old man who'd been so adamant about finding his true match, he'd taken to walking the world. He believed if he walked for long enough, eventually he'd pass her and get the rating he'd been waiting for.

I shook my head, imagining how many ratings he must have had along the way. He'd probably amassed a number of long-term matches and turned his back on them in favour of an ideal he may never find. Would he walk his entire life? Waste it all for the one thing he may never find? Was his true match just like him, dedicated to the cause so much that she would walk the world? Was *she* reading the article right now, feeling some kind of connection with this man?

All because of a stupid rating.

Reading on, the article speculated on his motivations, stating it was likely that he was after the riches and fame that accompanied a true match. I wondered if that were the case. True matches were treated like uber-celebrities, and money and power accompanied the position, but still … I looked at the picture of the man's face and saw only desperation in his eyes. The kind of desperation that comes from knowing you won't settle until you have your answer. Even if it kills you.

The article made me feel sick. Was I just like that man? Walking the world trying to find my father? To prove his innocence? Would I walk on and on until there was nothing left?

I knew I would.

I glanced back through the window. Girls surrounded Quentin, shoulders back, boobs out, basically lining up to get a reading with him. Some looked disgustingly ecstatic with their results. I rolled my eyes, more at the grin plastered on Quentin's face than the ones on theirs.

A door clicked open and I turned back to the veranda to see Ryan Merit walk out. He was smiling at me as if he'd found exactly who he was looking for.

'Why out here all alone?' he asked, taking the liberty of settling himself in the chair beside me.

I shrugged. 'Not really my thing.'

He nodded, as if he understood. I wondered how a guy like him could.

He held out one of the two drinks he was holding. I didn't need to taste it to know it was alcoholic. I shook my head. 'Designated driver.' The car wouldn't even start if my M-Chip registered alcohol in my blood.

He put the drink on the ground by his foot. 'You came with Mercer?'

'I did,' I answered.

He glanced towards the window. 'He seems otherwise occupied.'

I didn't need to look to know he was referring to the girl-horde.

I raised an eyebrow. 'Are you trying to make me cry and cause a scene?'

He laughed. Not a small chuckle, but a full-out laugh. It sounded kind of sleazy. 'I heard you rated high with him?'

I nodded.

'And now you keep your tech off?'

'Ryan, what do you want?' I asked, cutting to the chase.

But before he could answer, Morris was standing by the open door. 'Merit, yo, this area is closed, man.'

Ryan gave Morris a harsh look, but he stood. Then he leaned over me, actually putting his hands on the sides of my chair as he whispered, 'If you were here with me, I wouldn't have let you out of my sight.'

Seriously? I tilted my head to the side. 'That's impossible, Ryan.'

He smiled, moving a centimetre closer to getting my fist in his face. 'Why is that?' he asked, swaying just enough that his arm grazed my shoulder.

I returned his smile. 'Because there is no way in hell I would ever be here with you in the first place.'

I heard Morris's snicker and watched Ryan's smile disappear. His nostrils flared and, right before he straightened and walked back into the party, I felt his M-Band buzz where it was touching my shoulder. He had his pulse rate zip on mute, but I still felt it. It was perfect.

I started to stand, but Morris put up a hand and swallowed his chuckle. 'You're right, Mags. Sorry about that, I just stepped away for a bit. No one else will bother you.'

I did a double take at his words. 'What do you mean, no one else will bother me?'

'Nothing,' Morris said quickly. 'Just … relax. Quin said you weren't feeling well and wanted … Ah, don't worry about it.' He tried to wave the conversation off, before slipping back inside.

I looked back through the window, beginning to fume. Quentin was still surrounded by girls, all still giggling and casually touching him on his arms. But he wasn't paying any attention to them. No. He was glaring right back at me.

Turns out I wasn't the only one fuming.

Well, good.

Fourteen

The drive home was hell. Actually, the *drive* was heaven. Quentin's car was freaking amazing and I was tempted to really open her up, but I held back. Quentin spent most of the trip glaring straight ahead. This guy could do moody and then some. And he didn't even have a reason to be!

Finally, when we pulled into my street, I'd had enough. I gritted my teeth. 'Do that again and the deal is off.'

'Do *what* again?'

I inhaled deeply, resisting the urge to resort to violence. 'I know you made Morris keep people away from me at the party. I'm not a leper. You can't stop me from talking to people.' When he didn't respond, I felt like screaming. Instead I huffed, 'God, am I that much of an embarrassment?'

His eyes flashed towards me. 'Is that what you think?'

'Tell me you didn't ask Morris to make sure no one talked to me?'

I bit down on the inside of my cheek as I waited.

It took a long time for him to finally answer. 'I apologise,' he said tightly. 'I thought you didn't want to be there and was trying to make the night easy on you, instead of you having to spend the entire time fending off sleazebags.' His eyes cut to me accusingly. 'Morris barely stepped away to take a piss and Merit was in there like a flash. Slick bastard.' He ran a hand through his barely there hair and my hand twitched on the steering wheel. 'I thought …'

I sighed. 'You were keeping up appearances, making sure no one went near what's supposed to be yours,' I said, starting to calm down and understand. He still needed people to believe he was entertaining the idea of going out with me since he still had to have his Phera-tech inactive for the majority of the time. Even if he *was* tallying up Phera-ratings at the same time.

'It was stupid, but I get it. Just … tell me next time.'

He opened his mouth, but then closed it just as quickly. Finally he nodded. 'Thanks for understanding. I'll discuss it with you next time.'

Why was I sure that wasn't what he'd been about to say?

I nodded in return, hoping to move on. 'So your ratings went well. You must be happy.'

He shrugged, leaning his head back. 'Do you think it would've lasted much longer?'

My dry mouth returned. 'No. Maybe a few minutes, but hardly worth the risk,' I lied. 'You're not in a position to test the theory at this stage anyway,' I added, looking away.

'There is that,' he answered. After a few beats of silence, he said, 'The, um, annual Mercer Ball is on next week at my home.'

'That's nice,' I responded, still distracted by my guilt.

'And my family expect that you will be my date.'

My eyes widened. 'No. Take one of the girls who rated well with you tonight.'

'No,' he replied, sounding somewhat disgusted by the prospect. 'None of them rated well enough to justify not bringing you, and anyway … I can't go through a whole night …'

'Being nice?' I jabbed.

He didn't laugh. 'Lying to someone like that.'

'How else is it going to be, Quentin? Even once we get you enough supply of the disruption, you'll still question it.' Would he really never let himself get close to someone because he believed he was giving off fake ratings? My stomach churned as I realised just how much damage I was doing to this guy.

He shrugged. 'I've thought of that. I won't lure someone into a false relationship. Using the synthetic chems is one thing, but that's to protect my family and keep me out of one of those communities. I won't lie to someone I'm supposed to love.'

I bit down on my lip and blinked back the sting in my eyes. Was he saying he'd never have a real relationship again? Because of what I'd done?

'Maggie.' His voice softened, causing me to look up at him just as his shoulders dropped. 'Like it or not, you're the only one in the world who knows the true me.' His nose crinkled with a thought. 'Well, you and Gus, and I'm not taking him.'

I forced a small laugh, trying to pull myself together. 'Gus loves a ball, you should ask him.'

When he didn't respond, I felt myself sigh. Then something else occurred to me, something selfish and awful, but something that also helped to clear my head. 'You said there was a mainframe computer at your house?'

He nodded. 'There is.'

I made a quick decision. Even though I wasn't a hundred per cent sure it was for the reason I told myself it was. 'Okay. I'll go with you, as long as you get me five minutes on that computer.'

If I could get Gus to hack that computer, we might be able to get a lot of the codes and passwords we'd need to break into the core junctions. It would save us a small fortune. Plus, if my father's location was recorded anywhere … I might just hit gold.

'Deal,' Quentin replied.

Since I didn't have a suitable dress, or any dress for that matter, Quentin insisted that part of the deal included a trip to the mall.

It seemed strange to go to the mall for any other reason than breaking into the underground. Not to mention, it was very unsettling to be ball-gown shopping with Quentin Mercer. To start with, you couldn't be inconspicuous with him anywhere. The moment we entered a shop, the assistants were all over him, offering him refreshments – basically laying themselves out on the table for him to peruse.

To his credit, he didn't. And, after hearing his words last night, I gathered that was part of the reason why. The worst thing was, I didn't know if I was more proud of him for his morality, or ashamed of myself for my lack of it.

'Mr Mercer, are you buying a suit?' one shop assistant crooned at him.

He shook his head. 'My friend Maggie will be my guest next week at out annual ball. She needs a gown.'

'Any requirements?' the assistant asked him, not me.

He glanced at me. 'She can have any gown she chooses and whatever else she needs.'

I pulled him aside. 'As much as I appreciate your help,' I pulled one of the vials out of my pocket, 'maybe you should take this and go catch up with your friends. We could meet up in an hour or so.'

He eyed the vial and took it in his hand. 'You don't want me around?'

'I'm not a shopper at the best of times and having you here feels a little –'

He put up his hand, cutting me off. 'Call me when you're done. I have an account here so just put whatever you get on that.'

'Of course you do,' I mumbled.

He was already walking out, tipping the vial into his mouth discreetly.

'Wow, he's like the catch of the century,' the shop assistant said, returning to my side.

I turned to glare at her, but then I realised I needed this girl to help me find something that wouldn't make me the social laughing stock of forever, so I smiled slyly instead. 'Balls do seem to be the theme of the day. His, in particular.'

She giggled and I held back an eye roll. Whatever made her happy, I guess. 'So, dresses?' I pushed on, desperate to get this torture over and done with.

It turns out that big is back, in terms of gown skirts. And colour is key. I've never had so much colourful material lugged out and shrugged on top of me. It was a wonder I didn't fall under some of them. I had a new appreciation for my shopping trips to Target where I could dash in and out, collecting four pairs of the same jeans and a few black T-shirts to last me until they were either ripped or stained irreparably.

Finally, I'd had enough. 'Mia,' – because half an hour ago we'd crossed the first name threshold – 'I can't wear any of these dresses. They're beautiful, really, but I'm just not one of these girls. If you send me home with one of these, I'm going to embarrass myself by falling over it, or knocking someone out when I turn around, or worse, suffocating them by simply sitting in their vicinity. Please tell me there are dresses that won't look out-dated and embarrass Quentin, but that don't have skirts as large as a small house.'

Mia gnawed on her lip for a while, looking me up and down. Finally she smiled conspiratorially. 'How brave are you?'

I straightened. 'Depends what you mean by brave. I'm not afraid of much, if that helps.'

'How do you feel about black?' I could tell she was worried, since everything currently fashionable seemed to be dripping with colour.

I overlapped two fingers. 'Black and I are like that.'

She smiled. 'Be warned, it might cause a bit of a stir, but I think I have a dress you're going to love.'

I gotta give it to Mia. She was right.

By the time shoes and bag were taken care of, and I'd finally made Mia accept that I wouldn't be adding to the Mercer tab by buying jewellery to go with the dress, an hour and a half had gone by.

I lugged the large bag with me and headed for the escalators down to the ground floor. I decided not to call Quentin, as I didn't want to intrude on his time. But when I stepped off the escalator I saw him sitting around a table with friends. They were laughing at something. I couldn't help but stare at the way his legs were stretched out and crossed at the ankle, so casually, as he tossed his head back and laughed. He seemed so relaxed. He was never like that around me. I'd made sure of that.

I dropped my head and stepped towards a nearby shop window. What had I done? I could feel the panic building up in me. The worst part was, knowing him the way I did now, how decent he was, how … uniquely Quentin he was, I couldn't even say with certainty I wouldn't do it again. The drive to find my father had been all that had powered me through the past couple of years. It was a terrible reality to regret my choices and yet at the same time know I was the kind of person who'd probably do it all again.

'Find a dress?' his smooth voice said from beside me.

I didn't flinch, but he'd snuck up on me all the same. I hadn't even realised he'd noticed me.

He gently wrapped his hand around my arm. 'Come and sit with us for a minute,' he said, already tugging me towards their table.

I sat beside him, nodding my head in greeting to his friends. Morris was there and gave me a warm smile, which helped me to pull myself together. It wasn't that I couldn't get my game face on. It was more that, after shopping for ball gowns, I couldn't have felt less like myself. It just took an extra moment. Or two.

Two girls approached the table around the same time. They were both carrying trays with drinks and proceeded to hand them out.

'Oh, hi, um …'

'Maggie,' I jumped in. 'And you're Nerida. We have English together.'

She looked at me blankly. 'Really?'

'Really,' I deadpanned.

The other girl, Holly, put her drinks on the table and grabbed a nearby chair, wedging it in on the other side of Quentin, taking the time to register her rating with him before sitting. I could sense Quentin's surprise and couldn't help but steal a glance at his M-Band.

Seventy-three per cent *was* high.

Holly, looking smug, leaned forwards to talk to me, and to give Quentin a good look down her top. She was beautiful, of course, and had plenty more than I had to flash. Not that I wanted to flash anything anyway. Not that I even cared.

'I heard you don't keep your tech on?'

I shook my head. 'No need.'

'Why?'

I knew she was expecting me to say it was because of Quentin, that I was dedicated to him or something. While there he was using his tech whenever he liked. So I shrugged and leaned forwards, taking a sip of Quentin's drink, just to show I could.

'I don't believe in it,' I said when I leaned back.

The entire table stared at me in shock. 'Why?' she shrieked. 'Aren't you the one who rated high with Quinny?'

I narrowed my eyes. 'According to a gland that I cannot see or feel and that cannot talk on my behalf, *Quinny* and I show the world of potential.' I held back the gag reflex at calling him that. 'I'm not interested in a match.'

'Then what *are* you interested in, Maggie?' This question came from across the table; Morris had jumped into the fray.

I was about to open my mouth and tell them the truth, but I felt Quentin's eyes on me, burning a hole right through all my bravado. Instead of blurting out that I wasn't the relationship type, I remembered the façade we were supposed to be keeping up. I smiled. 'I just prefer to make my own decisions.' I stood then, desperate for escape. 'I gotta get going. Nice to … see you all.' I glanced at Quentin quickly and mumbled, 'I'll catch you later,' before I spun around and started powering out of there. Give me a real fight any day, but girls? Girls, I could do without.

The worst thing was, there was a part of me that wanted to march right back and tell her to get her fake orange claws away from him. A thought that just infuriated me even more. It was none of my business. His love life was *not* my concern. Now or ever.

I headed for the exit, for once resenting my deactivated Phera-tech. Maybe I should just turn it on. Yeah, right. I picked up the pace, more desperate than ever to get out of there, but Quentin surprised me for the second time by simply appearing by my side, keeping easy pace with me.

Neither one of us spoke. I couldn't look at him, scared that I wouldn't be able to hide the elation trying to break free. Not even when he reached down and took the heavy shopping bag from my hand.

I really hoped he wasn't looking at me.

But my surge of happiness was quickly squashed beneath the heavy realisation that Quentin would *never* have been by my side if he actually knew the truth. He'd walked with me because he believed he was a neg. I was just his way out of it.

Fifteen

On Monday night I hit the tunnels again, desperate to eliminate the possibility of Dad being held in a community we'd discovered was scheduled for a 'clean-up' in the coming week. I knew there was only a tiny chance, but as with every other community I'd checked, if there was any chance at all, I had to do what I could.

This time though, the failed trip stung.

What I wanted to do more than anything was have it out with my kicking bag in the garage, but it was Monday and that meant Mom would be expecting us to have a family meal, and I was already late.

I raced into my room, dumping all of my gear and slipping into a pair of comfy jeans and an old football jersey before I headed into the house.

'Hi, darling. I was wondering if you'd gotten caught up.'

I smiled at Mom and let her pull me into an embrace. 'No, just lost track of time,' I said, hoping not to have to elaborate further. The lies were starting to leave an increasingly bitter taste in my mouth.

She brushed the hair back from my face. 'I forget you're still so young,' she said.

I stepped away from her awkwardly. 'I don't feel very young. Haven't for a while.'

She sighed and started dishing up the casserole. 'I know, Maggie. You do so much, it's like you're on this mission to prove something.'

I froze, unsure what she was saying.

She continued, heaping rice onto the plates. 'You study so hard and work such long hours and when you aren't doing that you're at the gym. You don't stop and I'm worried you're going to burn out and affect your Phera-ratings.'

My stomach turned. It always came back to the ratings for Mom. 'I'm fine, really.'

She passed me my plate and we settled into our chairs at the small dining table. 'I know you are, it's just … I'd like to see you going out with friends and having a bit of fun. See you smile more. Maybe then you would consider turning on your tech.' The silence felt heavy. I leaned against the back of my chair, watching Mom load rice onto our plates.

When she put down my plate and sighed, I bit down on the inside of my cheek. 'I know what happened with your father was … it was terrible. He wasn't the man we thought he was, but Maggie, you're nothing like him. You won't have the same problem that he did. Negative ratings are not hereditary.'

She'd given me this spiel before and I wasn't up to it after the evening's failure below ground. I forced the corners of my mouth up. 'I'm going to a ball this weekend, if that helps,' I offered, hoping to placate her.

Mom's eyes lit up. 'A ball? Where?'

I dug into my dinner, realising I hadn't actually eaten all day. Well, unless you counted the doughnut I'd had for breakfast, but that was mostly chocolate icing.

'The Mercer Estate,' I answered around a mouthful of food.

Mom dropped her fork.

'*The* Mercer Ball? Who are you going with?' Her eyes were still alight, but now they were also ridiculously wide.

I shovelled another mouthful of casserole in. It was bland, and way too healthy, but after a good slathering of salt, it was really hitting the spot.

'Maggie!'

I groaned and took a gulp of water to wash down my food.

'Quentin Mercer,' I said quickly.

'I'm sorry, say that again. It sounded like you said Quentin *Mercer*.' Mom laughed.

'I did.'

I waited patiently as her jaw basically hit the floor. Her reaction was no surprise.

Wide-eyed, she finally snapped out of her stupor. 'Is it Friday or Saturday? I'll get the night off so I can be here when he picks you up. Oh my God, Maggie. The house. What are we going to do?' Her rambling halted with a sharp gasp. 'Maybe we could rent a house for the weekend and you could give him that address.'

'Mom, stop. Seriously, he doesn't care about the house.'

'Oh, I know, darling. I'm sure his sole focus is on you, but you know ...' Then her eyes narrowed in on me. 'Why is the Mercer heir taking you to a ball hosted by his family?'

'Mom,' I pleaded.

She gasped again and threw in some kind of all-body jolt. 'You rated with him, didn't you? You must have for him to justify it.'

'Justify it?' I said, raising a brow.

'Oh, come on, Maggie, look around. His family aren't the type to ever let the likes of us near them. The only way into that world is through the rating system.'

Sadly, this was true.

I picked up my fork, keen to get back to dinner.

'Just tell me yes or no?' she pushed.

I suppressed another groan, knowing she wouldn't let it go. 'Yes,' I said.

'High?'

'Yes,' I answered.

'Maggie, high enough?' I knew what she was asking. Was the rating high enough that if Quentin chose me, the rating would support the match? If the rating supported the match that was all society cared about.

'Mom, drop it.'

'Come on, Maggie. It's my last question, I promise.' Her voice was getting pitchy and she was all but bouncing out of her seat.

I stared into Mom's eyes, the one person I always hated lying to the most – until recently. 'High enough.'

Tired as I was, my night was hardly over. Back in the garage, I changed into a pair of work-out clothes and got to it, grateful that I had my makeshift gym area, which saved me from crossing town to the Muay Thai centre every time I needed a work-out. I still had to go there for sparring – although memories of my work-out with Quentin reminded me that there were now some alternatives … much nicer than Master Rua.

I made my way through a long list of drills, working up a decent sweat before noticing it was past midnight and I still had study to do.

It was after 2 a.m. by the time I allowed my head to hit the pillow.

I was at Mitchell's Diner. Dad and I sat at the back in what had become our usual booth. Thursdays were now my favourite day of the week.

I watched myself, this time from a bird's-eye view. I took a moment to marvel at how innocent I looked in my flannel shirt and jean shorts, but my attention quickly fixed on Dad.

He seemed distracted, not joining in like he normally did, and I watched as he quietly excused himself from the table and headed in the direction of the bathroom. Just before he reached the bathroom doors, he paused at the cash register and quickly tipped something into a glass of iced tea. When he glanced over his shoulder and caught my eye, he simply winked and carried on to the bathroom.

When he returned, I leaned over the table and whispered, 'What did you put in her drink?'

Dad just put a finger to his lips, motioning towards the unpopular waitress, Beth, who was now drinking from the glass. When I looked back at Dad, he smiled. 'Just a little experiment, Maggie.'

I watched the waitress carefully. Dad was no doubt trying to help her and his enthusiasm was contagious, but I also worried something might go wrong. As time passed and nothing happened, my concerns drifted away.

Dad seemed contemplative as we left the diner and got back into his car. I watched on as sixteen-year-old me buckled up, pondering what Dad had been trying to achieve. 'Wasn't that kind of risky?' I asked him.

He chuckled. 'You're a good kid for worrying about her, Maggie. I promise I'm trying to do something good. It might take some time to iron out the kinks though. Our little secret, okay?'

I smiled and nodded, loving that Dad and I had our Thursday nights.

After a tired day at school, I found myself going through the motions in the stockroom at work. Gus had decided to shadow me. He wouldn't let up, adamant that this time the risk was too high. He tried warning me with catchy phrases like 'playing with fire' and 'bit off more than you can chew' and, my personal favourite, 'you're beating a dead horse'.

He was just sour that while I'd been stuck on the late shift, I'd forced him to meet with our particularly unfriendly new contact, Travis, to buy tonight's intel. Not only had it drained the last of our funds, Gus had also been required to endure a fairly rough pat down.

'Stop being such a baby. You were one block away and I was connected to your phone the entire time.' Not that I was about to admit it to Gus, but I had stayed right next to the door the entire time, ready to run the distance if he'd had any major trouble.

Gus gave a dubious grunt. 'Travis said he wouldn't deal with me again unless you're there,' he explained. 'And frankly, I couldn't agree with him more on this one. He creeps me out.'

I shrugged, concentrating on loading my backpack with all the essentials. Money, check. Rope, check. Tranq gun, check.

'Maggie, this is crazy. You can't go back down there tonight. It was reckless enough going down there last night on such short notice, but at least it was a zone we'd worked in before. Junction 47 is completely new territory and you know preparation is everything. You'll have to go out to Falls Church and the only entry way I've found is through the basement of an old homeless shelter.'

It was a mystery how an entry way had ended up there, but we guessed it had to do with the previous businesses on the site before it became a shelter. I continued to unpack stock, knowing I'd be stuck working late if I didn't. 'At least I won't have to worry about what I wear.'

He didn't see the humour.

Gus just didn't get it. If Dad was in that community and I didn't go there, I'd have lost my one chance. Everything else we'd done, all the rules we'd broken, people we'd hurt and left behind, the ones we'd stolen from, and the ones we'd deceived – it would've all been for nothing.

I checked the time. My shift was finished. 'I'm going in.' I didn't look back at him as I slung my pack over my shoulder. 'You know what to do. I'll call you from the shelter.'

'You're losing it, Maggie,' he called out, stopping me before I left the storeroom. 'How are you even going to get there?'

I'd been planning on catching the Metro, but he'd pushed too far. 'Good point,' I said, turning back and holding out my arm. 'Mind if I borrow your car?' It wasn't a request and by the scowl on his face he knew it.

'I really do,' he replied, his voice thick with hate. But he held out his arm and transferred driving privileges to my M-Band.

I smiled sweetly. 'Promise I'll treat her better than you do.'

'Yeah? Well, I hope she wraps you around a pole.'

'That's the spirit,' I said with a wink as I walked out the door.

Getting in through the homeless shelter was so easy it was almost funny. There were so many people in the shelter, so many people fighting for survival in this society, that no one paid much attention to me. Once I was in, however, my task became more difficult. The maze of tunnels was disorienting. I lost my way on a number of occasions, and questioned whether Gus might've been right this time.

When I realised I was just feeling sorry for myself, I sucked in a few deep breaths and got back to work.

Eventually I found the community. It was the largest I'd seen. That alone should have encouraged second thoughts, but I was determined to continue so I pushed on. I surveyed the point I'd selected on the map carefully, ensuring it was the best spot to drop rope.

When I couldn't see anywhere better, I got on with it, sailing down the black rope on a relatively short drop and onto the roof of one of a handful of interconnected buildings. I jogged straight to the far side of the structure. I knew from the blueprints that this building had high windows and, given that the air vents were too small, they were my best option.

Finding a spot to anchor another rope, I tied myself in and edged over the roof, positioning my feet on the wall.

I inched towards the first window only to find it was locked. On the third one, I hit the jackpot. I squinted through the glass before I carefully slid it open.

I found myself in a sparse kitchen attached to a dining area where the tables and chairs were bolted to the cement floor.

Given the time, I imagined most of the negs were heading towards their dorms to meet their 10 p.m. curfew. I waited patiently just inside the door until I saw a young girl walking down the hall. She didn't look much older than me and she was alone.

As she passed me, I opened the door and pulled her into the kitchen.

'What the hell –' she started, attempting unsuccessfully to yank her arm free.

Urgently, I put a finger to my lips. She was smart enough to stop talking and I was glad. I didn't want to have to put her down.

The girl's eyes went straight to my clothes, pausing at my waist. Slowly, I released my hand and lifted the edge of my T-shirt, exposing my bare hip and proving that I wasn't a neg.

'You broke in,' she deduced.

It seemed an obvious thing to say, but most negs never dare to consider the possibility. They are taught there is no escape, so how could anyone break in?

I nodded then passed her a picture of my dad. 'Have you seen this guy? Is he in this community?'

She glanced at me, then at the photo, before nodding slowly.

My stomach flipped.

'He's not here, but I've seen him,' she said quietly. The way she seemed so timid and restrained made me relax a little.

'Where? Where have you seen him? Please! Is he still alive?'

She passed me back the photo. 'He was alive when I saw him.'

My anxiety skyrocketed. 'Where is he?'

She shook her head. 'I'll tell you as soon as you get me out of here.'

I had my hand fisting her shirt before she blinked. I pushed her into the wall, my face close to hers. 'You'll tell me now before I seriously hurt you.'

The girl just smiled. 'I heard the guards talking. This site is scheduled for cleaning next week. I know enough to know the word "cleaning" means a whole lot of bad. You get me out of here and I'll tell you everything I know. Or you can beat me up and leave with nothing.'

Damn it, damn it!

I released her. She was fearless, I'd give her that. I could probably push her, force her to tell me more, but there was something about her that made me want to help her. Save one. Just once.

'What's your name?'

'Sarah,' she responded.

'Can you climb a rope, Sarah?'

'I can do whatever it takes to get free of this hell.'

I nodded. 'If you fall behind, I won't come back for you.'

She licked her lips, excited. 'I get it.'

'You know if they catch us …' I eyed her.

'Not like I'm ever going to actually regret this choice.'

I understood what she was saying. Her only other option was to stay. And she was right, if she wasn't skilled and couldn't be of use, things would be coming to an abrupt end for her soon.

It was definitely a mistake. Nonetheless, I justified it in my mind quickly. She had information about Dad. But it was more than that. I *needed* to do this. Needed to give the whole damn system the finger and set at least one person free. I gave her a nod, which caused her features to soften and eyes to fill with guarded hope, and then we were at the window. I went first so that I could get into position to help her up.

She was surprisingly strong, and very determined; we made it off the roof and up to the tunnels in good time. I sprinted down the tunnel, Sarah panting at my heels. Everything might've gone smoothly, except when we turned into the main transit tunnel and started the run through the maze that would take us back to the shelter, I took a wrong turn.

Right into an area where two guards were stationed.

I drew to a skidding halt. Sarah took a few more steps past me before she saw what was in front of her and stopped too.

It felt like slow motion.

The guards looked up and saw her.

'Hey!' they screamed, raising their guns.

'There's someone behind her too!' one of them yelled, but I was shadowed enough that they couldn't see my face in the darkness of the tunnel.

'Sarah, run,' I hissed at her.

She didn't hesitate, turning back and lifting her feet. I spun around and started to move. Maybe we would make it.

The shots were deafening in the tunnel, the sound rebounding off the walls. I turned in time to see her head rock forwards as it took the force of the second bullet. She went down hard. Motionless.

My speeding pulse set my M-Band off with a string of

wild beeps. My body jerked forwards. I had to check her. Even though I was sure. I wanted to check she wasn't breathing.

But then I heard the footsteps and I was running again. Another shot rang out and I felt the bullet puncture my side. I kept moving, my legs and arms pumping harder than ever before. I focused ahead, paying attention to the tunnels, making my way back the way I'd come and then eventually to the tunnel that led me to the homeless shelter's basement door. It was concealed within their cool room.

I burst into the cold space and then through the outer door I'd left wedged ajar. Trembling and clutching at my side, I cried out in pain and stared at my blood-covered hand. Every step was agony but I was certain if I stopped now, I would never make it.

When I stumbled up the steps, I saw a dirty grey blanket hanging from the railing and I grabbed it, wrapping it around my shoulders to hide the blood.

Head down, I walked through the shelter, my M-Band finally beginning to quieten.

I was surrounded by people who had lost so much – homes, families, friends, jobs. Love. I staggered through the room and knew the haunted look in their eyes was eerily similar to the one that would now remain with me forever.

'Miss,' a voice said. 'Miss, are you okay? Do you need help?'

The man looked at me kindly, his eyes free of judgement. A freedom I did not deserve.

I shook my head and kept going, dragging my feet out the door.

'Miss?' he called after me. But his duty of care had a perimeter and he didn't follow beyond the door.

Sixteen

I banged on Gus's door, leaning against the wall. I couldn't remember the drive. Or parking. I could barely remember taking the steps to his apartment. Somehow the blanket was still half wrapped around me and I was clinging to it with a shaking and bloodied hand.

I was starting to slide down the wall when the door opened and a hand caught me under the arm.

'Jesus Christ, Maggie,' he said, helping me into the apartment. He put me down on his couch.

'Where are you hurt?' He was breathing fast, his eyes panicked.

I let the blanket fall away as a round of curse words fell from his lips. And then again, when he pulled up my shirt and the bullet wound gushed more blood.

He ran to his bathroom and returned with a pile of towels. Beads of sweat were forming on his forehead. 'We're going to have to get you to the hospital.'

But we both knew we couldn't do that.

'Maggie ...' He let out a weighted breath and tried to mop up the blood. 'This looks really bad. I don't think we have a choice.'

I shook my head. It didn't matter how bad it was, hospital was not an option.

He cursed some more, disappeared, and returned with a glass of water and a handful of pills. He put them in my hand and held me up while I swallowed them. There were more than should be right, but I didn't argue.

'I need to see if there's an exit wound,' he said, gently pushing me up further and pulling my top up. I was fairly sure his answer was in the affirmative when he blew out a heavy breath. 'Jesus, Maggie. There's blood everywhere.' He positioned a towel at my back before laying me down again.

On the bright side, an exit wound was good news. At least he wouldn't have to go fishing for a bullet. The sag in his shoulders told me he was feeling a similar wave of relief.

He took a few more steadying breaths and looked again. 'Okay,' he said, trying to sound in control. 'The blood's bright so hopefully it hasn't hit anything important. But we have to treat this. It's going to hurt.'

I nodded tightly. 'Just do it.'

He disappeared again and came back with a bottle of vodka. When he poured it onto the wound, I could feel it burn its way through as if it had set my soul alight. It was what I deserved.

Tears sprang from my eyes.

I didn't make a sound.

Once satisfied the wound was clean, Gus wrapped gauze around my belly, pulling it as tight as he dared.

'This is only going to hold it for a bit, Maggie,' he said.

'It'll do,' I responded. 'Can you drop me home?'

'You're staying here,' Gus replied, distracted now by his phone.

I rolled my eyes. 'Can't. Mom will check on me in the morning before she heads to work. Need to be there.' I couldn't handle her launching an inquiry at the moment. Plus, I needed to be back. My place. My bed. My nightmare.

'Can you sit up?' Gus asked, as he typed something into his phone.

Whatever Gus had given me had started to kick in. I nodded and moved to get up. But when I couldn't hide the wince, Gus was there with his arm under my shoulder.

'You might want to bring a few towels,' I suggested.

He narrowed his eyes, glancing at the wound.

I made a pathetic attempt at a smile. 'Not for me. There's blood all over your driver's seat.'

He grabbed the towels and cursed all the way down to his car.

*

When I opened my eyes, I was back in my garage, lying on my bed.

I swallowed, my throat paper dry. 'Did I fall asleep?'

'Passed out,' Gus responded.

'Oh.' Had Gus carried me upstairs?

He was sitting on the edge of my bed, looking at his phone again. 'Mags, I gotta go,' he said.

I'd already figured he had something going down. Right then, I didn't want to know what it was. I just couldn't take anymore, so I nodded.

'Thanks,' I rasped, my eyelids now heavy.

He looked down guiltily.

'Don't worry. I'll be fine,' I said.

He shook his head. 'That's not it.'

My eyes opened a fraction. 'Then what?' I asked, now suspicious.

'Don't kill me, okay, but you can't be left alone right now.' As he spoke I saw the lights of an approaching car light up my window. The car stopped and the engine was switched off.

'Gus, what have you done?' I whispered, dreading the answer. If he'd called my mom or Samuel, I was going to be extremely unhappy.

He stood up. 'I really have to go. I called Quentin.'

I couldn't stop myself. 'How the hell could you do that?' I yelled, my words slurring thanks to Gus's painkiller cocktail. 'After all your warnings! He's the worst person to … Do you *want* us to get caught? Do you want to go to prison? How can you bring him into this now!'

He smiled sadly. 'You left me no choice.'

'I swear to God, Gus, you are going to pay for this!'

'What's new, Maggie?' He headed for the door, pausing to look back at me. 'And why do I think you're more worried about him being involved than anything he could actually *do* to us?' With a shrug, he left.

My head fell back on the pillow. Perfect. Now Quentin was going to see me all messed up and weak. That was the last thing I needed. The entire plan depended on him knowing he could rely on me to help *him*.

A couple of minutes later, I was trying pathetically to reach my blanket. I'd given up on reaching for my shoes, which wouldn't come off until I untied them, but at least if I could cover myself with the blanket he wouldn't see the whole dramatic scene.

Of course, I was sweating like a pig in my futile attempts only to look up and see him standing in my doorway. Livid.

'What the hell have you done now?' Quentin boomed.

'Great to see you too,' I said, wincing as I eased back on the bed.

Quentin continued to glare at me, a fierceness in his eyes that was pretty darn intimidating.

'Sorry Gus bothered you.'

He ignored my comment and said, in a low and threatening voice, 'Who did this to you?'

I knew he was worried about me, but his tone startled me so much that I shivered. One day that fierceness would be directed at me, and what frightened me the most was that the emotion I was feeling was one I hadn't expected to feel for anyone other than my father. One I didn't want to feel ever again. But invited or not, there it was. Regret.

'You should go,' I mumbled, turning my head away from him as I once again reached forwards to try to grab the damn blanket.

'Stop!' he growled, and then he was moving forwards and snatching the blanket further away.

'That was just mean,' I grumbled. 'Please go.'

But when my head finally turned to his, our eyes locked and I saw an intensity in his that told me he wasn't going anywhere. He looked away quickly. And it seemed as if it was with a kind of shame, not dissimilar to my own. Had I done that to him?

'I'm sorry,' I whispered. I couldn't stop the words. They had to be said.

'For what?' He still wasn't looking at me.

I swallowed. I wanted to be good enough, to fess up, but I wasn't. 'For … making you come here in the middle of the night. I'm sure you had something better to do or, you know, sleep.'

'I don't sleep,' he said bluntly, looking back to me briefly before turning to my chest of drawers. Without asking, he started to rummage through my stuff, pulling out a few items before returning to me. I saw he had a pair of sweats and a large T-shirt in his hands.

He sat gingerly at the end of the bed and, wordlessly, began to untie my boots before gently sliding them off. Each action seemed to take away a little of his anger. When he was finished, he glanced up at me, gently lifting the blanket to my waist. 'I'm going to take off your jeans, okay?'

Things were already beyond humiliating, what would a little more hurt? And God knows they had to come off, I could smell the blood drying on them already. I unbuttoned my fly and zip and pushed them down, but when I winced he put his hands on mine, stopping me.

'Hold this,' he said, giving me the edge of the blanket.

Quentin put his hands underneath and gripped the waistband of my jeans, slowly moving them down, as I remained covered beneath the blanket. It was all very chaste. But I felt his knuckles on the inside of my pants as they moved down my legs. I received a repeat performance when he pulled on my sweats and though I wanted to look at him, to see if it was affecting him at all, I didn't dare.

When he was done, I could feel my breathing quicken and I had to concentrate to avoid a beep-off. Hell, if I wasn't getting the mute upgrade next chance I got.

Quentin gestured to my top. 'You're covered in blood. Maggie ... I want to help, but I don't want to –' He swallowed. 'If you can manage alone, I'll turn around.'

But we both knew I couldn't even reach for the blanket. I nodded rigidly and bristled a little too. 'I'm not afraid of you, Quentin,' I said, falling back into my reliable bravado.

He smiled weakly. 'I'm well aware of that, Maggie. I'm a neg,' he said, causing a crack at the edge of my resolve.

I've done this.

I thought back to the testing day – if only I'd known him. If only I'd known that never before had a more dangerous person crossed my path. And never would again.

He swiped at the tear that slipped down my cheek.

'Are you in pain?' he whispered.

I shook my head. The painkillers were really doing their stuff and I was starting to feel increasingly groggy. No doubt that was also the reason for my runaway thoughts.

'Will you let me do this?' he asked.

I nodded, and when he pulled my body up, instead of just taking off my top, he pulled me to his chest and held me while – for the first time in two years – I cried.

'They killed her,' I sobbed into his chest.

'What's that? I can't hear you,' he soothed.

'I'm so sorry, Quentin,' I whispered. 'I'm so sorry I brought you into this.'

'Shh,' he comforted, brushing down my hair. 'I don't want to be anywhere else, Maggie. For the first time in my life, I'm right where I'm supposed to be.'

His words made it worse.

Eventually he eased back from me, lifting my arms above my head. Then, not taking his eyes from mine, he lifted my top, leaving me in nothing but a see-through white bra. But he didn't look down. Not once. He kept his gaze locked on mine, even as he lowered the T-shirt over my arms and head.

And God help me if I didn't wonder what it might be like to kiss him.

Dad and I were in our booth. Weeks had gone by and Dad had been perfecting the small concoction that he slipped into the waitress's drink each Thursday night.

So far nothing had happened, but Dad's interest never waned and, as a result, nor did mine. Our meals had arrived and we ate silently as we observed Beth drinking her iced tea.

It happened almost instantly, with the next customer she passed. You could see Beth's surprise as she stared at her M-Band. I glanced back at Dad to see a small grin forming on his face. Beth was moving around the room slowly, eyes fixed to her wrist.

A rosy flush made its way into her cheeks and one of the customers approached her up at the counter. Dad and I listened on as he asked Beth if she might be interested in getting a coffee after her shift. Beth, still seeming to be in a state of shock, nodded shyly.

'Dad, oh my God, did you ... Did you do that? Did you change her ratings?' I couldn't even believe I was asking the question.

'It's not so different to treating insects, Maggie.'

I shook my head. 'But I don't understand. Aren't the lower ratings supposed to be the dominant signatures? How can you make her take higher readings?'

Dad's eyes glittered with excitement and he leaned in. 'I'm not. That's the beauty of it. I've simply altered her signal output, just enough to create positive results when her signature is received by others. Like insects, alter the output signal for positive results. Alter the inward receptors for a negative.' Dad gave a humble smile.

I stared, open-mouthed. I didn't fully understand what he was saying, but I knew it was huge.

Dad gave me one of his signature winks and pulled out his wallet, dropping a few bills on the table before leaning towards me and speaking softly. 'Imagine all the good we could do.'

That was the day he became my hero.

When I opened my eyes, I was still in bed. It was barely dawn and there was a quiet murmuring nearby. I looked towards the sound to see Gus and Quentin talking in hushed tones.

'I'm awake,' I slurred, the night's events coming back to me.

'Oh, joy,' Gus retorted.

I smiled.

I glanced at Quentin. 'Did I pass out?'

He looked like he was biting back a grin. 'After you started slurring about some … things you were wondering about.'

The smile slipped from my face. The last thing I remembered thinking about was kissing him. No … no way. Please don't let me have said that out loud.

He chuckled. 'It was all very sweet, but entirely incoherent.'

Was he saving me? Either way, I took it.

'Hmm,' I said. 'I can't remember any of it.'

'Understandably,' he said, his own smile fading.

Gus chose that moment to sit on the bed beside me, reminding me of the pain down the right-hand side of my body. I pulled the blanket down and lifted my shirt to see the blood had soaked through the bandage.

'Awesome,' I groaned.

Gus, still wearing the same clothes as yesterday, pulled a tube out of the brown bag he was carrying. I raised my eyebrows when he started to deftly undo my bandages.

'What is it?' I asked.

'Just let me concentrate for a minute, Mags,' he answered.

I waited, watching as he passed the bandages to Quentin, instructing him there were fresh ones in the bag by the door. Once he'd cleaned the wound for a second time, he pressed the tip of the pressurised tube at the opening of the wound and a towel at the opening in my back.

'This might hurt,' he said.

'Guess it's your lucky day,' I slurred.

'Damn straight,' he replied, pressing down the top of the tube like it was a syringe. The contents moved through my insides, at first cold and then just uncomfortable.

'Glutaraldehyde?' I asked.

He nodded, not looking at me.

'Who?' I asked.

Gus didn't answer.

When Gus finished, he motioned for Quentin to pass him the bag by the door. He pulled out what looked suspiciously like a staple gun.

'Tell me you didn't get that from the hardware store.'

He gave me a toothy grin. 'I'd recommend looking away.' Then without another word, he pinched together the skin of the wound, causing me to cry out. I stopped when Quentin grabbed my hand tightly in his. He crouched down beside me, his other hand bracing my shoulder, his eyes holding mine.

Gus stapled me together three times on the front and four on the back before bandaging me back up and leaving with barely a 'See you later'.

'Was that strange?' Quentin asked after Gus had disappeared.

'No. I get stapled all the time.' I made him laugh, which was a good thing. Especially since I didn't want to give him the real answer.

Gus had just used the last of whatever money we had stashed plus, I was sure, a large chunk of his personal loot to buy black-market medi-supplies. Glutaraldehyde was what they used to patch up soldiers in the field. It was top of the line, expensive and damn hard to come by without having to answer a lot of unwanted questions.

Gus, who wanted to see the back of me more than anything else in this world, had just saved my ass. No wonder he wasn't in a chatty mood.

Seventeen

Quentin roused me and made it safely into the bathroom just before Mom let herself into my room.

'Maggie, are you okay? Why aren't you up?'

I fiddled with the blankets, still groggy from all of the drugs. 'Not feeling the best,' I rasped. Understatement of the century.

Mom moved forwards to put a hand to my forehead. 'You don't feel hot, but you're white as a ghost and all clammy.'

While she leaned over me I glanced around the room nervously, looking for bloody clothes or telltale signs of what had gone on last night. Quentin had taken care of everything.

'I think it's a stomach bug. There's been one going around at school.'

Mom smoothed the hair back from my forehead. 'Maybe you should come in and get checked out?'

I relaxed my facial muscles and did my best to make my smile convincing. It's not easy when your body is screaming in pain and your mind is freaking out. 'Mom, I'm fine. I'll call you if I need anything. I just need a day or two of rest.'

She pursed her lips. 'I told you you've been pushing things too hard.'

I nodded. 'Guess you were right.'

Her expression softened. 'Okay, darling. You rest. We need to get you right by the weekend. Last thing you want is to be looking green at the ball!' she said with a giggle. 'Oh, you know I saw a picture of him in the social pages yesterday. He's ...' She shook her head, smiling. 'I mean Maggie, even you have to admit he's –'

'I get it, Mom,' I cut her off quickly, knowing Quentin was listening in the bathroom. 'I really just want to go back to sleep.'

Her face softened. 'Okay, okay. Call me if you need me.'

I waited until she had gone downstairs and I'd heard the door close behind her. 'You can come out,' I said.

He strolled out of the bathroom, his expression blank.

'Thanks for tidying up.'

He shrugged.

'And for staying all night.'

'You should get some sleep.'

I nodded and closed my eyes, only to reopen them an instant later. 'Aren't you going to gloat?' He hadn't said anything about my mother's comments.

Quentin put his hands in his pockets and looked out the window with his back to me. 'I told you before, Maggie. People see an ideal. It's nothing to gloat about.'

I didn't go to school for the rest of the week. But by Thursday afternoon I was starting to move around a little more, much to Quentin's frustration. He insisted I shouldn't move for at least a few more days. I explained that he wasn't a doctor and that not only did I need to get moving to get strong again, but that I still had every intention of going with him to the ball on Saturday.

Sarah had recognised Dad. She'd known enough to point me in the right direction. Then I'd gone and let her die before I'd even discovered what she knew. I'd failed them both.

I *had* to believe Dad was still alive. Had to believe this was all worth it. Maybe, just maybe, when I got him out of there and back to us, it would all be okay.

Images of Sarah were with me constantly, every little sound causing me to spin around. And every time, for just a moment, I was there again, watching as the bullet … I knew that until I did something good, something worthwhile, I had no chance of stopping them from haunting me.

On Friday I tried to get ready for work so I could at least earn some money, only to end in a pathetic fail, calling in sick yet again. But since I'd at least managed to get a pair of shoes on, an hour later, I decided to attempt a walk around the block.

At about the halfway point, Quentin rolled up in his BMW and pulled to the kerb.

In trademark alpha fashion, he jumped out of the car, slamming the door. 'What are you doing?' he growled, stalking towards me. He grabbed my arm, halting me in my tracks. 'Don't be stupid, Maggie. You need to rest.'

But the concern in his eyes didn't help. I yanked my arm free of his, angry at the world. 'You don't tell me what to do! You don't get to act like you care! That we're *something*! I have a job to do and no one is going to get in the way. Do you hear me! Not Gus, not that stupid girl, and most certainly *not* you!'

He blinked, watching me like I'd just sprouted horns. 'What girl?'

I shook my head, losing my fight and feeling increasingly faint. 'It doesn't matter. She's dead. Your father's army killed her,' I bit out. 'And I helped them.'

He flinched.

I walked to his car and slid in.

He joined me and we drove back in silence.

Quentin sat at my desk in front of a white paper bag, looking over at me as I resettled into bed. At least I could sit up now. He was in grey pants and a white shirt. His sleeves were rolled up and his tie hung around his neck, undone. As if that weren't enough of a distraction, he hadn't shaved in a couple of days. At least I'd finally applied a mute zip to my M-Band. It was worth enduring Gus's laughing fit when he delivered it to know I didn't have to muster the energy right now to control my pulse rate.

'The company. My father. That's what they do. Kill negs,' Quentin said. Each sentence broken and heavy. Each conclusion a step away from the world as he knew it.

This is what I'd wanted him to see and understand. But now, listening to him say those words, how with each one his head hung a little lower, I wanted to take it all back.

'That's what I thought too. The first time I saw a clean-up I thought they were all dead, but then I really thought about it and it didn't add up.'

He nodded. 'Why feed them and keep them alive for years at a time to just kill them? It has to be some kind of investment. My father wouldn't … He's astute.'

I preferred the word 'cold-blooded', but was impressed he'd deduced so much.

His head shot up. 'So why do they keep them alive?'

I took a deep breath and let it out. 'What's in the bag?' I asked, stalling for thinking time.

He picked up the paper bag and rolled on the chair towards me. When I looked inside, my mouth began to water.

'I thought I could smell something delicious and bad.' I pulled out the hotdog, covered in sauce, and took a huge bite, savouring the flavour hit. 'I think this is the nicest thing anyone has ever done for me,' I said around my full mouth.

When I looked up, he was smiling proudly.

'Want a bite?'

He shook his head.

'Liar.' I held it out to him.

After a moment's hesitation, he took the hotdog and bit into it.

His face lit up when he started chewing. I burst out laughing, which hurt, but not enough to stop.

'What?' he asked.

'You groaned!' I spluttered, still laughing.

He laughed too. 'Okay, they're good.'

I raised my eyebrows.

'Very good,' he corrected, taking another large bite.

'Hey!' I said, reaching out and yanking back my hotdog. 'Next time bring two.'

He smiled as he chewed. It was a nice view.

I held onto the hotdog and took another deep breath. It was time to tell him. 'They strip them of everything – family, friends, independence, a future – then they train them. Some are used for factory work, some of the skilled are relocated into research facilities and most of the physically able are assigned to the military. Haven't you noticed how the need to recruit army personnel is no longer an issue, and yet we have more armed forces than ever? And it's not just the government forces, it's privately funded armies as well. Soldiers who know beyond a doubt that they serve or they will be killed. It's their one chance at survival. And let's face it, as far as they are concerned, they're negs with nothing else waiting for them, so many of them gladly take up the positions.'

I handed him the last bite of the hotdog. I knew he was using the time it took to finish it to absorb this new information. When he looked up, there was a kind of hope in his eyes.

'Maybe it's a step towards rehabilitation, like they say. Negs aren't designed to be a part of society, but maybe giving them something to fight for – a country to honour – maybe that is a good thing.'

'Is that what you believe *you* need? Is that the future you deserve?' Even as I said the words I knew it wasn't a solid argument since Quentin wasn't technically a neg. But I was sure he wasn't the only one being led to believe he was something he was not.

'Maybe it is,' he replied, his words a whisper.

'You're really willing to accept that? That your life should be defined by some rating?'

He ran a hand over his scalp. 'It's what I've been raised to believe. A technology that can provide society with acceptable and peaceful boundaries.'

'That is such bullshit!'

His sad eyes met mine. 'I'm a neg, Maggie. There is something in me that makes me that way. On some level … I'm wrong. Maybe I should just accept that …' He swallowed roughly. 'Come clean.'

I wanted to scream at him. Tell him he wasn't a damn neg at all. But I couldn't. So instead I decided to give him as much as I could right then.

I leaned back against my headboard, knowing this was going to take a little explaining.

'When I was sixteen, my father used to take me to this little diner not far from where we lived. Mom used to work on Thursday nights and Samuel was old enough by then to avoid family time. Dad liked junk food, like me, it was one of the only things we really had in common.'

I blew out a breath. 'Anyway, Dad designed pesticides for local farms and he enjoyed the development side and experimenting. He used to joke about how the M-Chip was a disease. How people would flock to it until it destroyed them all.'

Quentin kept his head down, listening intently.

'But he was fascinated by the pheromone tech. He started to apply some of the science from his pesticides, and one Thursday night I caught him slip something into our waitress's drink on his way back from the bathroom. She always kept her drink by the register. When Dad realised I'd seen him, he just winked. And it became our secret.'

My hands started to tremble as I relived the memories of my dad. 'The first few times, nothing happened. But each Thursday we'd go there and each Thursday he'd slip another concoction into the same waitress's drink. I asked him once if it could hurt her. He smiled and told me how proud he was that I had asked such an important question.' I smiled at the memory. 'Then he assured me it was all very safe.' I paused, swallowing a few times before going on. 'Finally, one night, something happened.'

Quentin looked up, his interest growing.

'Moments after taking a sip of her water, the waitress – who'd consistently scored below average in her phera-ratings – was suddenly scoring higher than ever before, with one or two customers in particular. She was completely baffled.' I smirked. 'But when I looked at Dad, he just winked, paid the bill, and drove us home.'

I remembered the feeling of awe I'd felt towards my father that day.

'He altered her ratings?'

I nodded. 'It went on like that each week. Dad worked tirelessly at perfecting the formula, trying to increase the waitress's appeal and also the limited period of time it seemed to work for. He didn't discuss it much with me, but when I asked a big enough question, he'd always put down his pen and explain it in the same way. He'd say, "Margaret, just imagine all the good that we could do."'

I stared blankly into the room, lost in my memories. 'He was my hero.'

'What happened?'

I shook my head, coming back to the present. I couldn't tell him everything, as much as I wanted to at that moment. 'One day he came home from work frantic, grabbing things and throwing papers everywhere. Mom arrived home, calling out for him. She was … crying. I remember sitting in the kitchen doing my homework. Mom came in and grabbed a glass of water. Her hands were shaking and the water spilled everywhere. Dad came in a minute later. He looked at me and said, "Sorry, kiddo." Then Mom took his phera-rating.'

Quentin didn't say a word.

I stared at the wall. 'Apparently he just started registering negative ratings that day. He never had before, and definitely not with Mom. They'd been a steady seventy per cent from the beginning.' Not perfect, but good enough to be happy together.

I shook my head. 'Mom couldn't take it. She screamed at him, threw the glass at the wall and accused him of doing something unforgivable. She couldn't see any other way for a man to suddenly go from completely normal to full negative. Even now I think she suspects he cheated on her and contracted some deadly disease. Dad just sat down opposite me and took Mom's anger until the patrol cars arrived. They said they were taking him in for an interview. We never saw him again.'

'Wow,' Quentin said, taking it all in.

'He was a good person, Quin. He was, *is*, my dad. And out of nowhere everything was taken from us. Now he's gone and Mom works every day to pay off his debts. Samuel doesn't care about anyone, least of all himself. And I –'

'You spend your life hidden in the shadows, risking everything, trying to rescue all of them.'

It stung that he somehow knew me better than anyone. 'Someone has to believe there's another way. The system is flawed. My father was no more a neg than you are.'

Slowly, Quentin nodded, but I could see he still wasn't convinced that anything I'd said meant anything good for him. And after a while of staring down at his feet, he stood up. 'I'd better get going. Are you sure you want to do this thing tomorrow night? I really think you should keep resting.'

'Pick me up at seven,' I said.

'Okay, Maggie,' he said, as if he wanted to argue, but wouldn't at the same time. When he reached the door, he looked at me over his shoulder. 'We only have two doses left of the disruption.'

I pressed my lips together and dredged out a small smile. 'I'll find the permanent disruption before you run out.'

His forehead furrowed in that way it did. 'I didn't think there was a permanent disruption.'

'Yeah, well, turns out there is. Gus found something in that data we lifted from the lab last week. I'll get it for you. I promise.'

He watched me, hesitating. I could see a question in his eyes that he wasn't going to ask. I didn't know what it was. After a moment, he gave a slight nod and left.

Eighteen

I'd never been to a ball. Hell, I'd never been to a school dance. Once I was old enough to take part, my life had already taken a very sharp turn in a non-dance-conducive direction.

Bottom line, I felt like a fool getting all dressed up. I had no idea where to start and, as I grappled with my hair, I was fast regretting telling Mom that Quentin would be picking me up from work. If I'd let her, she would've stayed home to help me get ready. She probably knew some uses for a bobby pin that didn't include break and enter.

After another failed attempt at doing some sort of up-do, I threw the brush at the wall and growled. One, I sucked at styling hair. Two, it hurt like a bitch to keep my arms raised for so long. Three, it was stupid that I even cared.

Giving up on the brush, I settled for a good finger combing and left my hair out. I already had my shoes on, so when I stepped into the dress I was careful not to catch the fabric with my heel. One little catch and I imagined the entire dress could fall to pieces. The bottom half anyway.

Sliding it up and over my bandages proved painful, but once I'd tucked my head through the halter and very slowly eased up the side zipper, I was glad for the boning in the corset. It would help hold me together.

I studied the dress in the mirror. The dark grey corset was the thinnest and softest leather I'd ever laid eyes on and it fit snugly around my torso, softened only by an edging of intricate black lace that followed my chest line up and around the halter. It was the shape at the top that made me fall in love with it so much in the store – the way the halter material spread out to cup the tops of my shoulders, allowing for just the smallest trim of lace to skim my upper arm. It felt feminine but also strong.

It was the bottom half that had me second guessing my choice.

I started swishing around the metres of soft black tulle – interlaced with layers of dusty grey. It hung with body but not flare. I twisted as much as I could bear in order to catch the light.

'Is *that* see-through?' I said to myself, squinting as I tried to figure it out in my poorly lit room.

'Entirely,' came a voice from the doorway.

My head snapped towards the voice. I cringed at Quentin. 'Really?'

He was leaning against the door jamb, wearing a tux. All black – suit, shirt and bowtie. He looked … I swallowed and held back the whimper that seemed to want to escape.

'Can you see everything?' I said, glancing down again when he didn't answer. I couldn't bend properly due to both my injury and the corset.

He looked down the length of me slowly, and back up. Then he opened his mouth, pausing before any words came out. He ran a hand over his scalp, back and forth as if trying to rub a thought away.

I contemplated bailing on the whole thing.

Quentin cleared his throat. 'There's an inbuilt slip. Um, just at the top. It covers … the important parts.'

Okay. I do not have these kinds of conversations. Ever. But since I still had the whole night ahead of me, I had to make a decision there and then.

Either be a girl, or man up.

I could cope with a little leg showing as long as my main attraction wasn't flashing for everyone to see.

Once I pulled the fabric back and confirmed the additional opaque material travelled a few inches below where was absolutely necessary, I grabbed my clutch bag and headed for the door.

Quentin held the door open for me. I glanced up at him from beneath lowered – and determined – lids. 'Don't even think of starting with bullshit compliments,' I warned.

He chuckled, seeming to relax. 'What would they matter anyway?' He patted his chest. 'Neg, remember?'

I shook my head, angry at his conclusion since it judged me just as much as it did himself.

'It doesn't, but not because you're a neg. That doesn't even come in to play. I've told you, I don't believe in a system that listens to our glands and not our brains.'

'What about our hearts?'

'Hearts are overrated.'

I could feel him staring at me all the way to the car. When he opened the door, I finally looked back in exasperation. 'What?'

'You really want to mean it, don't you?' he asked.

I looked at my feet. I *really* did. The tech was controlling too many lives. And I wasn't about to let it control me.

When I didn't answer, Quentin filled the silence. 'Well, in the spirit of your sentiment, while you do look … stunning, in a way that is probably burned in my memory forever, I much prefer you in jeans and a dash of blood.' He shrugged nonchalantly. 'Just seems more you.'

It hurt my side, but I laughed out loud, more flattered by his comment than if he'd said anything else. As soon as I stopped laughing, my mouth ran away with me.

'You, on the other hand, wear that suit like you were born for it.'

He lifted a shoulder. 'I always thought I was. Funny thing is, on some level, I also thought I was meant for something more. Egotistical, right? Especially since it turns out I was only ever meant for something considerably less.'

'A rating doesn't define a person, Quentin,' I said, looking at my fingers as they twisted the strap on my bag.

Again, I felt him staring at me like some kind of puzzle. It frustrated me so I moved to open the car door, but he stepped closer to me instead, one hand entwining with mine, the other wrapping around my unwounded side. It was close. Intimately so. And when he spoke, it was in a low quiet voice.

'Do you really mean that? *Really* believe it?'

I nodded, but a part of me realised that for the first time I was actually questioning the statement. Questioning my sureness. My heart pounded, dangerously close to overload. Because looking into Quentin Mercer's eyes, I couldn't help but wonder if the rating system wasn't spot on.

My band vibrated against my wrist. If he hadn't been holding my hand he'd never have known.

Before I could say anything, his hands dropped from me, staring in disbelief. His own band beeped but he didn't even seem to notice, he just stared back at me, mouth ajar.

I stumbled back a step, realising my mistake. I'd let my thoughts run away from me and given up too much of myself. Too much that could be used against me later. He was Quentin Mercer. *Mercer* being the operative word. And *I* was Maggie Stevens. I had a plan and I couldn't forget what I was doing and *who* I was doing it for.

I dropped my expression to neutral. Concentrated on my breathing, then looked up. 'We should go,' I said.

He nodded but didn't move. It was obvious he was attempting to dismiss the thought. He believed he was a neg. And negs were incompatible. Undeserving. Unlovable. Yet his confused expression remained and I could tell he was sifting through all the possibilities as to why my band had beeped. He knew I wasn't afraid of him. I had no obvious reason to have such a strong reaction to the conversation. Not unless I was thinking the kinds of things that could rattle a person standing within shared breathing space of someone they found …

I pushed past him and slid into the passenger seat, dreading to think what kind of outrageous conclusions he was drawing.

Mine were crazy enough.

*

When people use the words 'estate' and 'mansion', you expect big, but the Mercer estate was the biggest damn home I'd ever seen. The building was bigger than our entire block, and that wasn't including the estate's surrounding gardens and river – not river as in one everyone shares and visits, river as in their *own* river – running right through the middle of their land with bridges and a small boat.

'Big, huh?' Quentin said, gauging my reaction.

I snorted. 'Seems like it might be over-compensating for some other … insecurities.'

He chuckled and some of the tension from our awkwardly silent drive seemed to dissipate.

Burning torches lined the long driveway and suited waiters holding trays of champagne flagged the grand sandstone stairs leading to the massive double doors where the entry line of guests slowly moved in.

The who's who of not only Arlington, but also Washington DC and further afield were no doubt in attendance. Mia had been right. It seemed the bigger the dress and brighter in colour, the better. A fact that made my dress stand out rather than blend in.

Quentin grabbed my hand and whisked us up the stairs and straight past where all the guests were greeting a number of waiting hosts. From the corner of my eye,

I spotted Garrett and Eliza Mercer. I'd never met them, but their faces were easy to recognise given the amount of press time they received.

I was grateful I didn't have to suffer formalities I'd probably get all wrong anyway. I let Quentin lead me through the groups of guests and tried not to gasp at the grandeur of the entry hall. As we made our way towards the sound of music I noticed a man and woman being stopped at the base of the broad marble staircase by a security officer in M-Corp uniform.

'Apologies but upstairs is restricted to family members,' the guard instructed, turning the guests around and pointing them down the hall.

Quentin squeezed my hand, which surprisingly I hadn't realised he was holding, and we entered the ballroom. The sheer expanse of the stately hall was breathtaking. Teardrop chandeliers rained down, making the ceiling appear more opulent than any manmade structure should.

'This place is …' But I just didn't have the words.

'Yeah. Mom is fanatical about the house. She redecorates every couple of years from top to bottom. It's very annoying. I think she does it as some kind of substitute for not having a daughter.'

I accepted the mineral water he deftly lifted from a passing tray. 'Raising three boys would've been challenging.'

'I suppose,' he replied.

We settled into a corner. Quentin stood close, pointing out all the important people. It was hard for me to not glare at some of them or call out murderous intentions. Not that I hadn't expected so many of the heavy hitters of M-Corp to be present. But having them so close, unprotected, and watching how they laughed and drank champagne while they so easily ruined other people's lives was hard to take.

'It was always fake, but now it all seems sinister too,' Quentin said, his jaw clenching as he looked out over the mingling high rollers.

I took a sip of my drink, deciding it would be wiser not to risk opening my mouth.

'How are you holding up?' he asked, turning towards me.

'Fine,' I lied. The ache in my side was fast becoming a burning pain. 'Where's the office?'

'Upstairs.'

A man approached, heading in our direction. He was wearing a service uniform and an earpiece.

'Excuse me, Mr Mercer, your father requested you join him in the front sitting room for a moment.'

Quentin disregarded the man quickly. 'Tell him I have a guest.'

The man nodded, but remained where he was. 'I apologise, sir,' he glanced at me, 'and to Miss Stevens, however your father said to tell you it will only take a moment.' I wondered if the man knew everyone's name in the ballroom, or if I was just special.

Quentin glared at the man. He didn't like being ordered around and I wondered if this was a new development in light of his recent education about his father.

'It's fine. I'll wait here,' I offered.

'You'll wait right here?' Quentin asked.

I smiled. He was worried I would head off in search of his father's office without him. He knew me well. I probably would've.

'Right here,' I promised.

He nodded. 'I'll be back as soon as I can.' He pointed to the other side of the room. 'The food is over there. I'm sure you'll be able to find something terribly unhealthy. My mother always likes to put out a tray of temptation for fun,' he said.

'Sounds promising.'

He hesitated, but then followed the man towards the front of the house.

My first thought was to do exactly what Quentin had *not* wanted me to and go in search of his father's office. But I'd seen the guards at the stairs and ... well, I'd promised. For some reason I liked the thought of keeping this promise. So I made my way over to the food area, enjoying the idea of the perfect guests seeing me dive into Eliza Mercer's honey trap.

I was just reaching for the miniature pots of what looked suspiciously like chocolate mousse, when a voice murmured in my ear.

'Beware, an alarm may go off if you touch those.'

I straightened, still managing to snag one of the pots on the way and turned to see a slightly familiar face. Familiar in that I'd mostly seen it in the social pages. But also in that he shared the same eyes as his brother.

He put out his hand. 'Sebastian.'

I shook his hand, then picked up a spoon and scooped a mouthful of chocolate into my mouth while he scanned his M-Band. At least it was a delicious honey trap.

'I take it you like to live on the edge,' he said, watching me with open fascination.

'Because I eat what I like?'

He looked me over. 'Something tells me it's more than that.'

I gave a slow, condescending nod. It was my best attempt at blowing him off. He didn't take the hint.

'You don't have your Phera-tech on. May I ask why?'

'You may,' I replied, leaving it at that.

He smiled as if intrigued by me, but his interest came second to his blatant determination.

'Would you be interested in a dance?' he said, glancing towards a dozen or so couples who were already dancing. I heard a few nearby girls gasp with what I was fairly certain was envy and almost rolled my eyes.

I shook my head. 'I don't dance.'

He was almost as surprised by the decline as the girls panting behind him were. I held back a smile. Most annoyingly, he still didn't go away. He actually moved in closer to speak in my ear. 'You have absolutely no interest in me, do you?'

I stepped back. 'Should I apologise?'

He laughed. It was a nice sound and made me think I might've been able to like him. Slightly. When a waiter passed by, he reached out to take a glass of champagne. The expensive stuff. A tall blonde wearing a sunflower-yellow dress swept by, brushing against Sebastian's shoulder, and I noted he glanced down to register their Phera-rating on his M-Band. His eyebrows lifted in response before he looked back at me.

He put out his hand again. I took it, hoping this might encourage his goodbye.

'Never apologise.' He smiled and leaned in. This time it didn't seem so awkward. 'No wonder my little brother seems so smitten. Goodnight, Maggie,' he said. I'd never given him my name and he delivered a wink before simply sauntering away. No surprises he bee-lined for the blonde in yellow.

I helped myself to another spoonful of chocolate while replaying the conversation. The biggest question was, had Quentin been a part of the set-up to see if I would fall all over Sebastian Mercer because I was just a power-hungry Barbie like every other girl in that place, or had he not known about it at all?

Either way, I had to admit that I admired his big brother for looking out for him.

I was contemplating whether Sebastian had ever pulled a similar stunt with Ivy, and imagining exactly how that would've turned out, when Quentin reappeared at my side. Sometimes he was impressively stealthy.

'I see you found the jackpot.'

I dug in to scrape out the last spoonful and held it out for him cheekily.

He beamed, leaning forwards and smoothly cleaning the spoon. 'Never dare a Mercer, Maggie.'

'I'll bear that in mind.'

'And so you should, it is good advice,' added a new voice.

I turned, surprised to see Eliza Mercer standing right behind me.

'Mrs Mercer,' I said.

Instead of taking the hand I offered, she kissed me on each cheek. 'Please, everyone calls me Eliza, Maggie. Quentin has been very intent on keeping you hidden away from us. It is so nice to finally meet you, and in such a divine and daring dress. I love it.'

I wasn't exactly sure that was true, but I plastered a smile on my face. 'I think black is mostly the boring option these days.'

Eliza gave the dress another look over, smiling not unkindly, but knowingly. 'Perhaps, but wearing a black *wedding* dress to a ball is certainly taking a risk.'

My throat closed in. 'Wedding dress?'

'Yes, dear. That's a signature vintage Vera Wang. One that very few people are able to do such justice.'

The air had become so thick, my chest heaved for breath. Perfect. Mia had asked me if I was brave, but this … I wasn't equipped for this shit.

And yet, I had to be. Tonight was too important. So what if I'd chosen a wedding dress? It was black for chrissake! Oh, hell. Even I'd heard of the world-renowned designer and I lived under a fashion rock. I hadn't even bothered to look at the labels, and when Mia had brought it out to me I'd thought she'd referred to it as 'Avira' not 'A Vera' as in: The. Vera. Wang.

Seconds were ticking by and I needed to say something. I straightened and glanced pointedly around the room – it looked like a fluorescent material shop had exploded in it.

'Well, then,' I said, giving my full attention back to Eliza, noting that her admittedly stunning azure dress looked like it had become lost on its way to a fairy ball. 'I guess wedding dresses are now the more understated fashion,' I said, glancing around the colourful room.

'But still the most memorable,' Quentin said, placing a gentle hand on the small of my back and serving a piercing look in his mother's direction. 'Wouldn't you agree, Mother?'

Eliza's growing smile seemed curious and yet genuine as she glanced between Quentin and me. But her response was drowned out by the siren-like sounds coming from the centre of the room. Everyone's attention shot towards the sound.

Guests were stepping back, removing themselves from the source, and our view cleared to a young pregnant woman who appeared to be in shock backing away from a man.

The man, not much older than her, mirrored her expression.

The atmosphere in the room was palpable, as if not one person dared to breathe.

The man took a small step towards her, but she held up a trembling hand, just as another man rushed to her side, pulling her into his arms possessively, one hand on her swollen belly.

The guests attempted some pretence of looking away and restarting their conversations, but it was clear everyone's attention was focused solely on this odd event.

Everyone knew what an M-Band siren alert meant and how incredibly rare it was. Adjusting the factory settings was one of the first things people did when they received their Phera-tech, resetting the standard beeps so that if they ever crossed paths with their true match an alarm would sound.

And fuel to the fire … the woman was heavily pregnant. I could already hear the word 'scandalous' being whispered.

The man holding the woman, who I presumed was her husband and the father of her unborn child, ushered her across the hallway and into an adjacent room. But it was the look of growing intent coming off the other man that had my full attention. He was standing stock still, watching the woman being dragged away.

As I watched, Garrett Mercer appeared by the man's side, saying something in his ear and then escorting him in the opposite direction.

'Wow. I don't think I've ever seen anything like that happen before,' Quentin said.

Eliza nodded. 'Garrett will settle them down for now.' She watched as her husband disappeared with the mystery man.

'Who is he?' Quentin asked.

'If memory serves me correctly, he's an M-Corp representative from our New York offices. He's here in place of the Head of Operations who was unable to attend at the last minute.'

'I wonder what the guy is going to do,' Quentin said.

'What do you mean?' I asked.

Eliza spoke first. 'They're a true match, Maggie. The very positioning defines their relationship to one another as finite. To put that person above all else. To be with that person at any cost. It is irrefutable.'

'I don't believe that,' I replied. 'Nothing is finite, and *everything* is refutable.'

'Are you really so sure about that?' she asked, raising an eyebrow and giving me a smile that felt eerily knowing.

'Are *you* really so sure that if a couple doesn't receive a Phera-tech true match rating then they are not capable of feeling that depth of love and devotion to each other?'

It probably wasn't advisable to have this discussion, but it was already too late.

'Certainly not. It's just not a guarantee.' Her smile ended the conversation and she turned her attention to Quentin. 'That's going to be the talk of the town for months to come.' She handed him a napkin. 'Just as well, since otherwise all they would've had to talk about is you,' her eyes briefly flashed in my direction, '… indulging your sweet tooth.'

'Well, I'd hate for a spoonful of chocolate to irreparably harm the Mercer reputation,' he answered dryly.

'I'll take that as my cue.' Eliza turned to me, kissing me on each cheek again. 'My son must think very highly of you,' she said, dropping her voice so only I could hear.

I followed her eyes to my M-Band. She thought it was a sign of commitment that we both currently had our Phera-tech off at such a social event.

'Quin, be a darling and save me a dance,' she said, giving his arm a squeeze. 'And please do what your father asks. I'm sure Maggie will understand the responsibilities that come with your family name.'

Quentin nodded. 'I'll think about it.'

She smiled as if the concession meant it all. 'Thank you.'

She took a step before pausing to glance at me one more time. 'Your family name is Stevens?'

I swallowed, suddenly sure she knew it hadn't always been. Did she know my father was a neg? Did she know where he was?

'That's right,' I said, holding her gaze.

She nodded once, but unsaid words remained in her expression.

I watched her glide away as people tried to get her attention. She acknowledged everyone in some way or another. She seemed kind, motherly and well liked, but she was undoubtedly strong and there was another side to her, I was sure of it. She was a Mercer. She couldn't have stayed for as long as she had by Garrett Mercer's side and not known what really went on. But the fact she played her part so convincingly was an unnerving reminder I was now mixing in a new league.

Nineteen

Using the distraction, Quentin ushered me away from the crowds and, with a nod to the security guard, guided me upstairs. His hand stayed on my lower back, steering me as we moved down a long corridor lined with dark mahogany doors.

'Your mom seems nice,' I said.

'You sound surprised.'

'I am. I mean, I expected her to be different.'

'What? Wicked witch kind of stuff?'

'With lots of power and money,' I added with a shrug. 'No offence.'

He nodded sadly. 'Mom is ... In some ways she is what makes this whole thing so hard to accept,' he said, looking away briefly to hide the emotion I could hear in his voice. I gave him his moment.

At the end of the hall, Quentin paused briefly to look over his shoulder before he opened the double doors, swiftly ushering me in.

'Does he always leave it unlocked?' I asked the moment he closed the doors. It seemed sloppy.

Quentin turned on the light. 'We don't often have people here and Mom has a thing about locked doors.' Maybe because she knew enough to know whatever happens behind them is usually not good.

I glanced to the right of the large office space and noted a door.

'Panic room,' Quentin said instantly, reading my thoughts.

I looked to the left, spotting another door.

'Bathroom. Only one door in and out,' he pre-empted.

From over my shoulder I gave him a dry smile, which he returned.

Wasting no time, I jumped behind the gigantic desk – honestly, it was the size of a car. 'Any booby traps you know of?' I asked.

'No. But then again, it turns out I don't know much about my father, or what he does.' He came to stand beside me, so close his shoulder touched mine and he leaned over me and began typing on the keyboard. 'This password is the only one I have. I've seen him use the same one so it *should* open everything you need.'

'Only one way to find out, I suppose,' I said, once again embracing my 'chance favours the bold' approach. I pulled out my phone, dialling Gus.

'Just so you know,' Gus answered. 'I seriously considered getting in my car and disappearing this afternoon so I would never have to see your face again.'

I smiled, even though he couldn't see me. 'You say the sweetest things, Gus. But you know just as well as I do, thanks to the M-Chip, no amount of distance could keep us apart if the right people were looking for you.' As in the police, if I handed over the evidence I had on him.

'Hence why I stayed by my phone waiting for your call, even as I hoped you fell into a deep dark abyss.'

'Jesus, Gus. Is it that time of the month?'

I heard him snort sarcastically. 'I really wish you were only a once-a-month occurrence.'

I waited.

'I take it you're at the computer,' he said eventually, accepting his role.

'Bingo,' I replied.

'Plug in the transmitter. Only sixty seconds on this one, Maggie.' It was a warning and, though I could've pushed him, I knew he was right.

'Sixty seconds,' I repeated, plugging it in. 'Starting now.' I started a timer.

I could hear Gus typing away on his end, trying to drain as much as he could through the transmitter. I kept my eyes glued to the screen as different documents and images flashed by. Then, causing both Quentin – who'd been watching over my shoulder – and me to gasp, we watched as blueprint plans started spilling onto the screen, the small print in the bottom corner saying M-Corp Headquarters, then a number of documents, entitled in bold red print: 'Food Resources at Critical'. And finally, before Gus shut it all down, one that we only glimpsed, but saw enough – 'Population Control Solutions Successful'.

'Pull it, Maggie,' Gus said. 'Christ, Maggie!' he yelled. 'Pull it now!'

I did, even as I felt the confusion at what we'd just seen.

'Maggie,' Gus said, his voice low. 'Listen to me very carefully. That computer was a full access. If anyone finds out you … You need to get out of there now. Leave, go home, go anywhere, just get the fuck out of there.' After a brief pause, he added, 'And don't call me again tonight.' Then he hung up.

It wasn't like it should be a huge surprise. Garrett Mercer was the Head of M-Corp, of course his computer would have full access. But Gus and I were so used to only finding dead-ends rather than real intel that I think we'd both presumed the same would happen tonight.

'Maggie?' Quentin whispered from behind me. I was still frozen, the transmitter wrapped in my hand.

'Tell me what that was?' His voice was shaking. Probably because it didn't take a genius to work out population control was most likely a bad thing. I was on autopilot, Gus's words replaying in my mind, and I started to put everything back where it had been, closing the computer down carefully, ensuring I didn't leave a trace. Just as I was finishing, Quentin grabbed my arm and pulled me back from the desk.

'Maggie, talk to me.'

I shook my head. I didn't know the answers, or where to start with my crazy suspicions. There were too many things running through my mind. Possibilities that I'd never …

'Maggie, what's wrong? You're so pale,' he whispered, his hand coming up to the side of my face.

My eyes went to his and I could see his concern, see that he cared and it only made everything worse.

Quentin glanced down and air hissed in through his teeth. 'Oh, Christ, you should've told me,' he accused, prompting me to look down and see the blood that had started to seep through my dress's dark grey bodice.

I looked back into his eyes and felt my world begin to swim. I was not a normal person. Nothing I did was simple. Nothing was easy. Nothing was particularly kind. But it had all been for a reason, all the sacrifices for something good. I had to keep believing it would all be okay in the end.

Quentin kept studying me, his hand still on my face. Time seemed to slow down around me, so many thoughts washing through my mind in a matter of seconds. For some reason the oddest thought was the one that I verbalised.

'Did you love Ivy? I mean, did you think you two would be a good match?'

He shook his head. 'Why are you asking me that? We need to get you out of here before someone sees this.' He gestured to my dress. It actually wasn't that bad, the red wasn't that visible from a distance on the dark grey.

'I can't feel it anyway,' I said.

'Why?'

I swallowed the lump in my throat. 'Everything is numb.'

His hand moved around my neck, his fingers into my hair, making it clear to me that everything was in fact *not* numb.

'No,' he said quietly. 'I never loved Ivy. I thought we'd match okay, but nothing amazing. What about you and Gus?'

His question made me blink. 'What *about* me and Gus?'

Quentin shrugged, keeping his hand on me, moving his fingers slowly, brushing loose strands of hair back from my face. 'I've seen the way you two can be around each other. Things get pretty intense. I guess I just assumed there was a history ... Or a present.'

I would've cracked up laughing if I wasn't feeling so hollowed. 'I'm blackmailing him.'

'*What?*'

'I'm. Blackmailing. Gus. He does what I ask him to because if he doesn't I'll turn over what I have on him and he'll go down – for a very long time.'

'But he's your friend.'

I shook my head and took a step back from his touch. 'Haven't you worked it out yet, Quin? I don't have friends. I don't have anyone.' I turned to head for the door, but Quentin was faster. He took one large step and spun me back, into his arms.

His hand slid behind my neck and, just before his lips touched mine, he whispered, 'You have me.' He kissed me with a knowledge that would suggest our lips were not meeting for the first time, or at very least, were meant for one another.

My mind turned inside out, not knowing how to deal with this kind of overload and choosing instead to shut down completely. My hands went to his shoulders, somehow pulling him closer with my fingers while pushing him away with the heels of my palms. I could feel the tightness in his body, even in his face, as if he was holding back too. Afraid to let go.

I'd kissed guys before. But it was always for a reason and I'd controlled the situation. I'd instigated it for some benefit to my cause, and then walked away without a second thought. No one had even gotten close enough to actually be the one who kissed me. But there was no doubt about it, something in me was thawing fast and, just as I feared I might truly melt, the sound of a throat clearing had the two of us jumping back from one another.

Before I got very far, however, Quentin's arm around me tightened as he – quite forcefully – pulled my chest towards the side of his body, even as he turned to face his father. My heartbeat was racing and I was well aware of the fact that both Quentin and I had just let off a few rounds of pulse alerts.

Seeing Garrett Mercer standing right there, knowing I'd just broken into his mainframe computer and then hung around to make out with his son ... I was damn glad Gus had sorted me out with the heart-rate muter.

Quentin ran a hand through his hair. 'Dad,' he said, his voice uneven.

I had no idea what to do. This man was responsible for so many terrible things. He was beyond cruel, beyond dangerous. Quentin kept a tight arm around my waist, holding my front to his side. I realised he was making sure the seeping blood was covered. He'd been so fast to cover it. Cover for me.

'Quentin, what are you doing in here?' Garrett Mercer said. His tone was level, untroubled. I glanced towards him; his eyes were on me, one hand in his pocket, the other on his hip. He was a good-looking man. Sure didn't hurt that his tailor-made suit probably cost more than most people's mortgages.

My instinct was to be fierce. To stare him down and show no fear. But I couldn't quite move past the fact that I'd just been in a lip-lock with his son, and a blush crept up my neck.

'We were taking a tour and got … waylaid. Sorry,' Quentin replied sheepishly.

That was when I began to truly panic. Had I put everything back where it was supposed to be?

Garrett Mercer walked towards us, keeping his eyes on me. There was no warmth in them. He had taken an instant dislike to me. Yeah, well, the feeling was mutual. He put out his hand to shake mine and I was grateful it was my right hand that was free.

'You must be Maggie,' he said. It wasn't a question, more like a disappointed fact. I dropped his hand as fast as possible.

He walked over to the desk and I started to do a mental check.

'What do your parents do, Maggie?'

I pressed my lips together briefly then met his eyes. 'My mother is a nurse at St Catherine's Hospital,' I replied, hoping to leave it there, but the look in Mr Mercer's eyes said he expected the rest of the answer. I cleared my throat, my hatred for this man and everything he stood for seething beneath the surface of my skin. 'My father isn't around anymore.'

Garrett Mercer lifted his chin slowly, digesting my words and clearly settling on his conclusion. I clenched my fists.

He leaned a hip against the desk and I was relieved to see in the window's reflection that the computer screen had gone back to sleep. At least I was sure I'd done that right. But then I looked down to the table and saw something I'd missed. Shit. The mouse was off centre.

I wanted to slap Quentin for his stupid kiss. It could've cost us everything. Not *us*. Me. There *was* no us. And it didn't matter how nice or mind-destroying that kiss was, it had been crazy to think –

'Dad, we're going to keep having a look around. I promised Maggie I would show her the lake.'

Garrett ignored Quentin.

'Maggie, I'm sure you understand, Quentin has responsibilities. You are entitled to your views,' he gave me an unflattering once-over, 'whatever they may be, but Phera-tech is an important part of the image of the Mercer brand and therefore one I need the world to see my family embracing.'

I bristled at his blatant attack on my choice to keep my Phera-tech inactive. 'I don't want to activate the tech,' I said simply. 'Quentin and I decided we would explore our high rating and he chose to support me in my wishes and has kept his tech off. But he's turned it on from time to time and shown that he has nothing against it,' I explained, hoping to steer Garrett's attention away from asking Quentin to turn on his tech. Quentin gave my side a discreet squeeze of thanks.

'Clearly,' Garrett deadpanned. 'So, Maggie, tell me more about your family. Where are you from?'

I still considered my real home as the property back in the countryside of Charlottesville. It hadn't been much, but it had been a home and I'd loved living among the farming community. But I wasn't about to give any of that away to Garrett Mercer. Nor was I about to offer my real name. My father's name had disappeared the moment we'd moved into Arlington.

'We're just on the outskirts of town, sir. Have been for as long as I can remember,' I answered. He raised his eyebrows at my evasiveness. 'You have a beautiful home,' I said, hoping to wrap up question time.

'Dad, we should really get back downstairs. Mom has probably sent out a search party,' Quentin said.

Garrett kept his eyes on me, breaking his gaze only to glance down and readjust the angle of his computer mouse. I stopped breathing. Was it a message? His way of telling me he knew I'd been on his computer and had forgotten to put the mouse back in place? Or was he just moving it?

'Can you waltz, Maggie?' Garrett asked.

'Ah, no,' I said.

'Quentin, you really should have prepared your date better for the ball. Especially as she's your guest.' He made a *tsking* sound.

Quentin stiffened beside me. 'I thought I could be Mom's partner and give the rest a miss.'

Garrett seemed to consider this for a moment. 'That would have been fine, but I already took the liberty of requesting Genevieve be on standby in case your ... date wasn't skilled.' He looked at me condescendingly. 'Though I am sure you are certainly skilled in other areas.'

There were so many ways I could take that comment. None good.

'Dad,' Quentin said in a warning tone that Garrett completely ignored.

'The dance commences in a few minutes. I expect to see you there with Genevieve. There is little point in the entire room watching you stumble through the steps, Maggie, and I'm sure you'd rather not endure the embarrassment.'

I didn't respond.

'Quentin?' Garrett waited.

After a few beats, Quentin responded, his tone stiff. 'Of course, Dad. We'll head downstairs now.'

Garrett nodded and a sly smile formed on his lips that I was quite certain was intended for me.

Quentin turned me carefully, his body shielding mine.

We made it to the door and paused when Garrett spoke again. 'I expect your Phera-tech to be active when I come downstairs. We are a family, Quentin. A united front. The world needs to see us that way, always.'

Quentin didn't turn around to face his father, he just nodded and we walked out.

Twenty

'What the hell was that?' I hissed as Quentin ushered me down the hall and into another room. A bathroom. The size of my entire garage room.

'Which part?' he hissed back.

Excellent question.

I felt like my lips were still burning from his kiss, not to mention the whole getting-caught-in-the-office part, the mouse or the damn dance.

Quentin ran the tap and filled a glass with water, gulping it down before refilling the glass and passing it to me. I took a sip, but put it down before he noticed my trembling hand.

He shrugged out of his jacket, quickly putting it over my shoulders, covering the blood that had now seeped out to the size of a fist. Charming.

Taking a deep breath, I reminded myself that this was just like any other job and that I had to look at things practically. As in, getting whatever needed to be done,

done, so that I could get the hell out of there. I reached into my small clutch, jostled aside my taser gun and pulled out one of Quentin's small vials. I handed it to him, lost for what else to do at this stage.

He took it, his fingers brushing mine in the transfer.

'Thank you,' he said, quickly downing the contents and slipping the empty vial into his pants pocket.

I nodded. 'We should go.'

We headed back out to the hallway and took the stairs. Halfway down I stumbled. He caught me by the elbow and kept me on my feet. 'How are you holding up?' he whispered.

'Not so great,' I admitted. Each step felt like torture and I was starting to lose perspective. My orientation was slipping and my vision had dark spots in it.

He nodded, his brow furrowed in concern. 'I have to get through this dance, or it will cause too many questions. Can you last?'

No. 'Yes. Just put me near a wall.'

He hesitated. 'Maybe we should just get you into my car.'

'No. That will look like I can't hack it – you dancing with someone else. I'm not doing that.' He rolled his eyes, but I could tell he also agreed.

We re-entered the ballroom. Quentin's parents, along with his brothers and their partners, were already gathered on the dance floor. Given that the only person without a partner was a very attractive, tall blonde resembling Ivy Knight, I gathered that was Genevieve. I wondered fleetingly if she was Quentin's typical type. Quentin stopped with me just near a pylon, giving me a good spot to stand while having some support to lean against.

He put his hands on my shoulders as I looked anywhere but at him.

'You should wear your jacket,' I suggested, moving to take it off.

He shook his head, and his hands encircled my wrists, bringing them back down to my sides. 'Keep it,' he said. Then he leaned closer, speaking into my ear. 'If I didn't know better, I'd say you might be jealous.'

I bit my lip and looked him in the eye. 'Good thing you know better.'

His smile was small and twisted as he glanced down, activating his Phera-tech. Then he walked towards the dance floor. When he came into Genevieve's range, I noticed they both glanced at their M-Bands. It was obvious by the look of pure delight on Genevieve's face that they had rated very well. She all but started humming 'Here Comes the Bride'. I couldn't see Quentin's face, so I didn't know if he was smiling too. But when he took her hand in his, and spun her out away from him, he took the opportunity to glance in my direction and roll his eyes. I couldn't help smiling, even if my happiness did fade just as quickly.

He didn't take his rating with her seriously because he believed it wasn't real, that the disruption had fabricated it. He believed he was a neg. What would he think if he knew he wasn't? That he actually did rate well quite often. And with the likes of Genevieve?

And why wouldn't he? He really was the complete package. And he could seriously dance.

Beads of sweat started to form on my forehead. It was mostly from the pain, but I knew a part of it was from the knowledge that everything was coming to an end. One way or another, I would find my dad and set Quentin up with a fake dosage that he would believe permanently released him from his neg status. Then we'd go our separate ways. Simple.

So why did the thought rip me in two?

Finding my dad had been everything. Even now ... I still had to get to him. I needed answers and I was going to get them. But that didn't stop me from wishing that I had taken a damn moment somewhere along the line to learn the freaking waltz.

My hands started to shake and I leaned more of my weight against the pylon, my thoughts drifting in and out as my vision played tricks on me. But the instant I heard the gunshot, I was bolt upright, my eyes darting straight to Quentin, my breath returning to me only when I saw he was unharmed. His eyes had found me too, and I watched as his chest deflated, mirroring my own.

The guests panicked. Screams echoed through the large space, music screeched to a halt, ridiculous bundles of wide colourful skirts pushed towards the Mercer Estate front doors.

I moved to the side and slid along the wall towards the sound of screaming coming from the end of the hall. I reached the open door in time to see the man who'd rated as a true match with the pregnant woman drop the gun in his hand and stagger back. The pregnant woman was sitting on the ground, cradling her motionless husband in her arms, a large patch of red spreading over his white dinner shirt.

Garrett Mercer flew into the room, closely followed by Sebastian, Zachery and Quentin, an impressive number of security flooding in behind them.

'What happened?' Garrett demanded.

The pregnant woman looked up, her eyes moving from Garrett to the man who'd just dropped the gun. 'I … I … don't know. I didn't see,' she sobbed.

Bullshit.

Garrett looked at the man, who was now standing in the corner. 'Did you just arrive here?'

The man swallowed, his petrified eyes still on the woman. He was frozen.

The woman glanced up again, tears streaming down her face. 'He just ran in a second ago!' she blurted. She started sobbing and I wondered if her tears were more about her husband or her awful deception.

I couldn't believe it. A three-year-old could work out what had happened.

Garrett nodded to the woman, some kind of understanding passing between them. He turned to one of his security team. 'Call the police and let them know we had an intruder. Zachery and Sebastian, could you please help Mrs Henley out of the room and settle her in one of the front sitting rooms.'

The brothers nodded, moving forwards.

'Wait! What?' I said, earning myself every set of eyes in the room.

'She shouldn't be in here,' Zachary said, casting a stern look in Quentin's direction.

I held up my hand in disbelief. 'Are you seriously going to just let this happen? *He*,' I pointed to the man standing statue-still in the corner, 'just killed that woman's husband. I walked in here in time to see him standing over the body, gun in hand! There was no intruder. He did it!'

Garrett Mercer's eyes narrowed. 'Quentin, take your friend out of here and calm her down. Mrs Henley is in a state of shock, and by the looks of your date she's helped herself to more than a few drinks tonight. The last thing we want is a bunch of kids in here messing up a crime scene.'

'But Dad,' Quentin began, taking a step towards me. I wished I could stand a little taller, but I had to keep my hand against the wall to stay upright. 'Did you just hear what Maggie said? She wouldn't say it if it weren't –'

'Do as I say!' Garrett ordered, cutting him off. 'Now, Quentin!'

Quentin bristled at his father's verbal attack. Then he dropped his head, shaking it. He took my hand and settled his arm around me as if he just wanted me close. In reality, he was the only thing keeping me standing. Sweat rolled down the side of my face, onto my neck. If anyone cared to take a close look at me at that moment it would have been obvious I was not in a good way. Luckily no one cared.

He walked me back out the door, stopping near his father to say in a low voice, 'You know he did it.'

'Take your friend home, Quentin. And get her under control,' his father said, equally as low, but sterner. Garrett Mercer's piercing eyes fixed on me and I knew that I had become an enemy of his tonight. Guess it was only fair since he'd been my greatest enemy for the past two years. I might've actually tried to say something more, cause a bigger scene … If only I could've caught my breath.

Quentin half laughed. 'It's because they're a true match, isn't it?' he asked, but he didn't wait for an answer before leaving the room with me. He didn't need to. Negs were sent underground and true matches were given a free pass to everything.

Even murder.

Slumping into the passenger seat of Quentin's car, I heard him curse.

'We should get you to a hospital,' he said.

'No,' I responded. 'It's fine. Just take me home.' My eyes drifted open and closed as he jumped in beside me and took off down the driveway.

'Whatever you say, Maggie,' he said, anger pouring from him.

The whole night. The pressure of being at the Mercers' home and seeing Garrett Mercer's corrupt activities in play. In a wedding dress no less! It was all too much. 'That's right, Quentin. *Whatever* I say and don't forget it!' I snapped, needing to distance myself from him and refocus on my objective.

His jaw clicked to the side. 'As long as you get what you're after, right? You don't care about anything – or anyone else – do you? Just your father. Forget about the rest of us.'

By 'us' I knew he was grouping himself not with his family, but with other negs.

His words hit hard. As intended. Anger boiled now and I welcomed it, directing it at Quentin. 'Absolutely. I don't care who I have to mow down on my way.' I half laughed, though nothing about this was funny. 'But don't point the finger at me like I'm the bad person here. I wouldn't have to be doing any of this if the system *your* family so proudly developed and stand behind was in any way fair or honest. You all make me sick.' The last words tumbled out before I could catch them, before I allowed myself that split second to acknowledge that they weren't true. Not where he was concerned. But it was too late.

Quentin's hands gripped the steering wheel. 'Understood,' he said with a tight nod. He did not look at me again.

My stomach turned. I hadn't wanted to say those things to him. I'd just been so angry. So tired of feeling reduced to cruel tactics. So tired of the nightmares I knew would always remain.

Now I was stuck in uncomfortable silence, reliving the events of the night, which only caused my regret to multiply. I should have been more thoughtful. I knew

Quentin was in a bad place himself, struggling to come to terms with his father's actions. I was well aware that he had to be thinking about what would happen to him if his father discovered that he was a neg. And, of course, during my recap of the evening, I couldn't avoid the constant replay of that kiss, and how it had seemed so … right.

Unable to muster the right words, I rested my head against the window and watched the trees and houses whip past. Eventually I gave in to the heaviness and let my eyes close.

I opened them when I heard the click of my car door, and Quentin crouched down beside me. 'Can you walk?'

I nodded.

He helped me out of the car and then put an arm under my armpits to help me into my room above the garage.

When we made it, I moved towards the bed, about to tell him that he didn't have to stay. After the things I'd said, I figured he'd want to get far away from me.

'Wait,' he ordered.

I paused, but before I could turn back to him he was behind me, undoing the bodice at the back of the dress. I started to protest, but he just shushed me and proceeded. After a while, he disappeared briefly.

When I heard the sound of scissors opening and then the cold metal at my neck, I stopped breathing.

'Relax,' he said, his voice flat and not reassuring at all.

Then I heard the sound of material being cut and saw the edges of the halter drop from around my neck.

'Hands up,' he said. His voice was low. Sad. And yet, it was as if he was pleading with me not to rehash the earlier conversation. Not now.

Feeling strangely compelled, I did as I was told, and felt a T-shirt being pulled down my arms and then over my head. Quentin, still behind me, took the weight of my arms and gently brought them back down to my sides.

I looked down, noticing he had chosen a huge T-shirt – one of Samuel's that had somehow ended up in my drawer. It came down to my knees.

I heard him kneel and then my dress was coming down as he gently removed it, cutting again into the back of the bodice to make sure it came off easily. I hadn't seen the price tag on the dress so I didn't know the exact figure, but I knew it was worth more than my entire wardrobe put together. I felt like I should say something, commiserate somehow, but neither of us dared any more words.

When I stepped out of the dress, Quentin stood, kicking it to the side of the room.

'Lie down,' he ordered.

Still at a loss for words and knowing he must be mad at me, I did as he instructed.

He disappeared into the bathroom, leaving me to wonder what exactly was going on. Before long he returned, sat on the edge of the bed, and without another word cleaned and redressed my wound. The reopening of the wound wasn't as bad as I had feared and, now that I was off my feet, I was already feeling better. It had just been too soon to be moving around so much.

It felt like a small eternity passed as I waited for him to say something. I wanted to apologise, but every time I tried, the words got stuck in my throat. What good would an apology do anyway? It wouldn't change what I'd done. What I was *doing*. As more time passed his silence became louder. After he sat me up to take some more painkillers, he refocused on finishing with the dressing. I watched his face as he concentrated on the bandages. He did not look like the Quentin Mercer I had followed and studied for the past two years. The air around me thickened, each breath increasingly impossible as the realisation settled.

I had broken him.

Looking into his lost eyes, I knew I had to make this right. And even more importantly, I knew there was nothing I could do to keep him. Once I told him the truth, I'd lose him forever. My heart ached painfully at the thought.

He stood and moved slowly, returning the medical supplies to the bathroom and cleaning up. He took a long time and somewhere along the way, my eyes began to give into weariness again. He must've thought I was asleep. He came and kneeled by my head, but for some reason, I didn't open my eyes to tell him I was awake. He brushed the wisps of hair back from my face. His hand shook.

I felt the pillow depress by my face as his forehead briefly touched mine. 'I wish I didn't make you sick. I wish a lot of things. But mostly, I wish we'd never met,' he whispered. 'You make it …' He breathed out deeply. 'You make it that much harder to bear.'

He stood and left before he saw the tear slip down my cheek. Because, for his sake, I wished we'd never met too.

Twenty-one

Master Rua shook his head. 'You're not right in the head, Maggie.'

'Well, it's the only head I have,' I sassed.

He moved back into position, expecting another round. Expecting more. I took a deep breath, desperate to centre my thoughts, get them on anything but him.

It was Thursday afternoon. The two weeks since the night of the ball had felt like the longest in my life. Like the bastard controlling time had made the days tortuously slow and the nights lonely and silent.

Master Rua sent a series of jabs my way. I avoided or blocked most, but his knee struck my hip. Twice. He shook his head again. 'You'll be dead in a week if you're this distracted. What's happened to you?'

I wiped the sweat off my brow and walked to the edge of the mat, using the time to sift through my thoughts. 'I'm not distracted, I'm exhausted,' I argued. And I was.

Study, work and training, all while still recovering from my bullet wound, was kicking my ass.

He stared at me in that way he had that left me certain I'd probably get an elbow to my chin soon if I didn't start talking. I put my hands on my hips and looked around the busy gym. 'Things have become more complicated than I planned.'

'When you first came to me, were things uncomplicated?' he asked.

I thought back to two years ago when I'd first decided I was going to try to find Dad. 'This is different.'

I heard him approach me from behind and I tensed for an attack. He prided himself on being unpredictable.

'Maybe it is not the circumstances, but rather *you* who have changed. Are you sure you still want the same things?'

'Yes,' I answered immediately.

'But do you still want it above all else?'

I opened my mouth to answer, but paused, taking another moment. 'The last couple of weeks have just been distracting. Nothing has changed,' I said, but he knew as well as I did that I wasn't being honest.

Confusion about both the kiss and the unresolved argument with Quentin had left me feeling conflicted about my goals. Which was unacceptable. So I'd decided to avoid him, going out of my way to ensure we didn't cross paths at school. Until, of course, I realised there was no need. He didn't try to approach me. He didn't call me. He didn't contact Gus.

Quentin had completely wiped me from his life.

He'd gone back to hanging out with all of his friends, sitting with them at lunch, laughing and flirting with girls who were anxiously waiting for him to turn on his Phera-tech again. On the odd occasion we passed each other in the hall or accidentally caught one another's eye in class, he looked right through me.

Suddenly, I was on my back, the air smacked out of my lungs. Master Rua was looking down at me, shaking his head. 'Sloppy, Maggie. Very sloppy.'

I rolled onto my side, trying to get my breath back. I hated disappointing Master Rua. It had taken months of beatings before he'd agreed to train me, and deep down I'd suspected – and hoped – it hadn't been the bribe that made him give in and take me on. But as much as I wanted to be better, right now the fight was sucked out of me. I turned my face into the mat.

Quentin's behaviour hurt more than I dared to admit. Every day I'd been fighting the urge to run from the school grounds and hide in my garage. I'd tried to convince myself that it was for the best, and attempted to refocus on the tasks ahead to get through the days. But in the end, punching and kicking until I was too exhausted to stand, too exhausted to feel the pain in my chest, seemed to provide the only relief.

I had hoped a sparring session with Master Rua would help clear my mind.

'You should talk to Alex,' he said, giving me a knowing look. 'They might be able to help you.'

I hauled myself back onto my feet, stretching from side to side to ease the pain. 'You and I both know Preference Evolution will be no help to me.'

'That's not true. I've been watching them, and you, for some time now. You could help each other.'

A guy was walking out the door. I could see a pretty brunette waiting for him on the sidewalk and it made me think of ... What was wrong with me? I couldn't get Quentin out of my mind, even mid conversation.

It was just so hard knowing that he hated me.

I mean, I got it. I even understood it. I wasn't sure what had finally tipped him off to me, if it had been the kiss, getting sprung by his father, or if after our fight on the drive back to my place he had finally decided I simply wasn't a good person. He wasn't turning on his Phera-tech so he obviously still believed there was a chance that he'd rate as a neg. I was tempted just to tell him the truth, let him go, but I wasn't a fool. Now more than ever he was unpredictable.

No.

I had to show restraint if I wanted to have any hope of helping Dad. I would give Quentin what he thought was a permanent disruption at the end of this. Then he'd be free of me.

Maybe down the track I could even tell him everything. Maybe he'd even understand.

Or not.

Master Rua cleared his throat, clearly unhappy with my lack of attention.

'How could we help each other?' I asked, trying to stop my runaway mind. I was still unconvinced that Alex, the Pre-Evo front man, could do anything to aid my cause.

Master Rua shrugged lightly. 'You need to do something that brings you balance. Your obsession has led you to do things you would not normally consider. Preference Evolution has access to resources that you don't. They may be able to help you. And, if you worked with Alex, perhaps you could find a way to bring yourself some peace.'

It wasn't as if I hadn't looked into it before. But the resources Master Rua was referring to were seriously lacking. I was willing to bet I had a load more intel than Preference Evolution could ever dream of. Someday I planned to get it to them. But not yet. I shook my head. 'I'm beginning to realise there will never be peace for someone like me.'

'You should give Alex a chance to talk with you.'

'No.'

He took my hands in his. It was a rare display of affection from the Muay Thai master. 'He can be trusted.'

I shook my hands from his, taking up position again in the centre of the mat. 'I said no.'

He sighed, realising I'd closed the conversation and expected another round. Instead of engaging me, he turned away and walked towards his office. 'Get some sleep. You need that a whole lot more than training right now.'

'Fine,' I said, snatching up my bag. 'I don't need your help to train anyway!' I cringed at my behaviour, hating that I'd let him – and Quentin – get to me like this.

He waved a hand in the air dismissively, but didn't slow down. 'No. You don't need anyone's help, Maggie.'

I tied my hair into a tight ponytail at the bus stop and rearranged the contents of my backpack. I hated disappointing Master Rua and his words had cut deep. Blinking a few times, I leaned my head against the wall and looked at the afternoon sky. I was dreading the night that lay ahead.

God, I was in way over my head. Gus had been right.

But there was no turning back now. Gus had downloaded enough content from the Mercer mainframe to give us a good lead on Dad's whereabouts. He was alive. He had to be.

When Gus first told me, I'd felt so many mixed emotions, not least of which was the huge relief at knowing it hadn't all been for nothing. I was going to find him.

Dad's name had shown up in association with the main quadrant, which suggested he was, or had been, in a testing facility. My thoughts drifted to Sarah briefly and I wondered if she had been experimented on.

As much as I tried to ignore it, I knew there was a chance that my father had been tortured and changed. And I had seen that document – the one about 'Population Control'. We weren't able to find many details on it, but what we had found suggested it was some kind of way to use Phera-tech to control breeding in 'undesirable' zones. We needed more information, but I was sure whatever was to come, it was all bad. And considering what my father had been working on in those final months before he'd been taken, I couldn't help but suspect it had something to do with why my father had suddenly turned neg three years ago.

I feared more than ever what they'd done to him.

Was there a chance they'd used Dad to develop more disruptions? It was too awful to consider, and I hadn't dared voice my concerns to anyone else.

Dad had wanted to make a good contribution to the world. But I was beginning to believe they had taken my father for their own greed. For his disruption formula.

I *had* to get him out of there.

'You planning to punch that thing all day, or we gonna go?' Gus said, walking into my garage an hour after I'd arrived home. Sleep might've been what Master Rua thought was best, but I couldn't afford the time.

I rolled my eyes and kicked the bag. 'I still don't see why I have to go,' I said, concentrating on working my right leg, kicking high to strengthen the side that had been shot.

Gus leaned against the garage entrance. 'What can I say? Kneeing a dude in the balls can do strange things to him. Travis has our goods and says he won't deal with anyone but my ass-kicking bodyguard. Though he also made a point of saying if he got whiff of a Mercer he'd be extremely unhappy. And Mags, trust me when I say we might've one-upped him last time, but we do *not* want trouble with the likes of Travis. He has extremely nasty friends.'

No doubt. I knew we'd been lucky last time. I moved over to the small fridge that didn't actually work but was still where I kept a few bottles of water and grabbed one. 'Don't worry. Quentin is done playing with the likes of us.'

'You sure about that, Mags?'

I shot a look at him. 'Yes.'

He shrugged. 'Then why am I certain that when I pulled up, his car was pulling away from the kerb?'

My brow furrowed.

'I take it he didn't actually stop in?' Gus continued.

I shook my head. 'Why would he just be out there sitting in his car?'

Gus held out my towel. 'If he's anything like I was when you first started using me, he's probably out there plotting your gruesome murder and where to hide the body. Mags, even for you, you've really done a number on him. The guy has to be messed up.'

I snatched the towel from him and headed upstairs. The worst part was, I agreed. And not just about Quentin, but about Gus too.

Gus followed me upstairs to wait while I showered and changed.

Tonight was mostly about a trade – we'd scored some extra intel from the mainframe download, like the whereabouts of a number of lust-enhancing labs. M-Corp might not support lust-enhancers outwardly, but that didn't mean they were above producing and making a profit from them. It was sickening.

We were taking money zips to the trade just in case, but I hoped we wouldn't need them. I wanted to leave as much money as I could with Mom. Just in case.

When I emerged from my bathroom in black jeans and a black tee, I sat at my desk and began restocking my backpack. I didn't look over at Gus, who was sitting on my bed typing something into his phone, when I spoke.

'Do you love Kelsey?'

I heard his sharp intake of breath. 'How long have you known about her?'

'Since your first date at Fitzpatrick's,' I answered. That date had been three months ago.

'Guess I'm not really surprised.' He gave another resigned sigh. 'Yes. I think I might love her. Don't bring her into this shit, Maggie. Please.'

I nodded, still focused on my pack, rewinding my rope so that it wouldn't get tangled. 'We're done after this one, Gus.'

Gus half laughed. 'You might not find him, Maggie.'

'I know.'

Digesting what I was saying, Gus responded cautiously. 'I won't look back.'

'I know.'

He waited for me to finally look at him, and when I did his eyes searched mine as only someone who knows you well can.

I drew my hair back into a tight ponytail. 'Get me though this one and we're done. I give you my word.'

Slowly, Gus nodded and cleared his throat. 'Well, it's about fucking time.'

At that, I smiled. We weren't friends, but I would miss him.

'You know you could do with some help when you go down there,' he said.

I snorted. 'Are you offering?'

'Never,' he said with a smile. 'But I know someone else who might be stupid enough to follow you into the depths of hell.'

My smile disappeared. 'No,' I said, ending the conversation.

'One question then, Mags,' Gus said.

'Shoot,' I replied. May as well.

'If someone had a gun to your father's head and another one pointed at Quentin's and you could only save one of them, who would it be?'

Just the thought sent wracking shivers through my gut. 'I … don't … That's a stupid question, Gus!'

He raised his eyebrows. 'One that until lately, I was certain, no matter what or who was in the scenario, your father would be the answer.' He took a deep breath and let it out. 'It's okay to care about him, Mags. It's okay to want to be happy. And you can't avoid him forever – you still need Mercer blood if you want to get in. Every member of that family was on the initial approved entry list.'

I clenched my jaw. Yes, I needed Quentin's blood somehow. But the rest … I couldn't deal with that right now. 'I *am* going to be happy, Gus. My family will be back together and things will be the way they were supposed to be. Quentin is … He didn't deserve to be caught up in this – but neither did we. I feel bad about what I've done, but … that's all.' I shut my mouth and bit my lips together from the inside.

'Okay, Mags. Sure. You're the boss.'

Twenty-two

Travis sent us on a wild goose chase. No surprise there, but even I hadn't expected to find myself trekking through scrublands and dodging the marshes on Theodore Roosevelt Island at midnight.

'This goes beyond reasonable,' Gus grumbled as another tree branch smacked him in the face. 'I really think I tore a muscle climbing over the fence.'

'I'm sure you'll survive,' I mumbled, trying not to think about the last time I'd climbed a fence. Or more accurately, *who* I'd been climbing it with.

'Are there snakes out here?' Gus went on.

I didn't respond. Mostly because I didn't know the answer. All I knew was that we had approximately five minutes left to make it to the southern point of the eighty-eight-acre island between Arlington and Washington DC. Given that the island was officially closed from dusk and easily visible from the mainland, we couldn't even risk the aid of a flashlight to help us find our way.

It felt dangerously exposed, and yet, even as we heard the sounds of the multi-lane highway that travelled over the top of us, the island itself was deserted.

'It should be just through these trees,' I said, pulling out my tranq gun and checking it was loaded. No secret Travis and I weren't besties. I'd shoved my taser in my back pocket too.

Gus and I followed the directions we'd been given and arrived at the small clearing at the highest point of the southern plateau.

'Ever get the feeling you've found yourself smack bang in the middle of a low-budget horror movie, and you're only an extra?' Gus whispered beside me.

I nodded. This was so wrong.

My hands twitched at my side and I was about to give Gus the green light to run screaming when a guy emerged from the nearby trees.

'You Maggie?' he said, keeping his distance and staying in the darkness.

'Yep,' I said, impressed it hadn't come out like a whimper. Yeah, not scared at all.

'Travis is waiting for you. Follow me.' He turned and started walking.

'Maggie, Maggie, Maggie,' Gus groaned as I began to follow. 'We're about to die.'

I shrugged. 'If you'd prefer to stay out here on your own, go ahead.'

Gus ran to catch up.

The guy – staying a few paces ahead – led us into a group of nearby trees and an area that seemed to have more rocks, judging by the amount of times Gus tripped. When I spied a collection of large bricks with tangled vines embedded within, I asked the guy if there had once been something there.

He turned to me briefly, but it was still too dark to get a close look at him. All I knew for sure was that he had a stocky build, wasn't tall and could use a lot less aftershave. Eventually he replied, 'The old Mason Mansion. It was demolished back in the early 1900s.'

The guy looked up at me, pushing back a mass of vines on the ground to reveal a large vault-style door. Through the darkness his teeth shone as he flashed a smile. 'But they missed some.'

'Oh goody. A place that no one else in the world knows exists,' Gus said sarcastically. 'By all means, after you, Maggie.'

The guy chuckled. It wasn't comforting.

'Was this the basement?' I asked, following him down the stone stairs.

'Nah. The house was up over there,' he said, pointing north. 'This was a separate ice house and cellar.'

At the base of the stone staircase was a small room. It fit little more than a set of sofas, a work desk and a small table with four wooden chairs. My attention zeroed in on the fold-up work desk, or more importantly the person seated behind the desk.

I gestured to the sofa, where I'd already clocked another guy, but kept my attention on Travis. 'Blow-up sofas?'

Travis grinned. 'You wanna try carrying a set of lounges all the way here?'

'Not really,' I agreed. There was no vehicle access to the island. It must've been hard enough getting what they had there.

Travis addressed the guy who'd walked us in. 'Ned, go back up and walk the perimeter.'

I kept my eyes on Travis, but heard Ned returning up the stairs.

My eyes couldn't help but flicker to the closed door that sat ambiguously behind Travis's chair. 'Storage,' he said, following my line of sight. I didn't bother asking him to expand on the contents. It had to be black-market goods – it was better not to know specifics.

'Why all the way out here?' I asked.

He placed his hands down flat on his desk, stretching back in his chair. 'It's just one of my locations, but I do like it. It's isolated, close to the city, defensible.'

I wasn't quite sure how it was defensible.

'So, what do you want this time, *Maggie*?' He said my name like he was trying out the sound of it, which made me want to shudder.

'We brought you intel. Or at least, a sample of it and a list of what else will follow.'

'Of course. To sell or trade?'

'Both.'

He laughed. 'Must be good if you think you'll get both.'

'It is.'

'Then by all means, let's see.'

I didn't move. 'What guarantee do we have you won't try to steal it or kill us for it?'

Travis's eyes were twinkling. He was enjoying the conversation and it left me with an uneasy vibe. 'Why would I do that?'

'You won't need to ask that question once you know what the intel is.'

'I like repeat business. And that requires a code of conduct,' he responded, sounding slightly offended.

I glanced at Gus. He rolled his eyes. He already knew I was going to hand the intel over.

'It's delivery schedules,' I said, handing him the information zip.

'For?' he asked, feigning disinterest.

'Lust-enhancers. International arrivals and departures, along with the lab locations.'

He raised his eyebrows. He knew what I meant.

'And access codes,' I added, just in case he wasn't fully salivating.

Travis leaned back in his chair and I imagined it took considerable restraint for him not to fist-pump the air. We both knew I was putting a goldmine in his lap.

He ran his hand over his mouth. 'I'll have to have it verified.'

'Expected,' I responded. 'But you have less than twelve hours before I shop it around.'

He nodded once. 'And in return for this information?'

'You mean in return for making you richer than your wildest dreams?' I smirked. 'Not much really. A finder's fee – I'll consider a fair offer, though if you lowball me, don't think I'll wait around for a second offer.'

'And?'

I placed my hands opposite his on the desk and leaned in. 'Access codes and a clear line through to the core.'

His eyes narrowed. 'Suicide. Even with the line in and the codes, which will cost me more than I care to consider, you'll never make it out alive.'

I shrugged. 'I'll make sure you get all of your intel as soon as your codes check out, or I'm dead. Either way, you'll get what you want. So let's agree to disagree and move forwards.'

Travis seemed to be considering, but was distracted by his phone beeping. Like Gus and me, he had an old-style handheld model.

He stood abruptly. 'Ned says we have company. We need to get out of here now.' He was already moving towards the stairs when he turned to the guy on the couch. 'Activate the mines.'

'Activate the *what*?' I said.

He spun towards me, his teeth bared. 'If this is your doing, you're dead!'

'If *what* is my doing?' I said, holding my ground.

'We've got a raid on the way.'

I shook my head. 'You think I'm that stupid?'

He tilted his head. 'From what I know about you, yes. But you need me more than I need you, so I don't think you did this.' He smiled, his demeanour suddenly carefree. I wasn't buying it. 'Just bad timing, sweetheart.' He gestured to the guy on the sofa, then handed him a package from his desk and instructed the guy to meet him at the safe house later. The guy shoved the package down his pants and disappeared up the stairs.

Travis slung a black duffle bag over his shoulder and turned back to me. 'They'll be here in three minutes. In two minutes their way in will start exploding. If you want to get out, I suggest you start running. Carefully.'

'I told you we were going to die,' Gus said, leaping up the stairs three at a time.

Once we reached the clearing, Travis pulled up suddenly.

'Shit!' he yelled.

'What?' I said, already hearing the steady whop-whop-whop of incoming helicopters and dogs barking in the distance. This was not good. Not good at all.

'I can't remember where all the mines are.'

'Did you hear that, Maggie?' Gus said, sounding like he'd lost all reason. 'He can't remember where the *mines* are!'

'Perfect,' I said. About five hundred metres to the north the first mine exploded.

'Run!' Travis yelled, taking off.

I sprinted after Travis, trying to follow his path. Gus trailed behind as more explosions detonated, each one closer than the last.

When I caught sight of Travis reaching the edge of the island, I felt the first spark of hope and picked up speed only to be thrown off my feet with a much closer eruption.

Flaming debris flew at me as I tucked myself into a foetal position. It only took a few moments to register two things:

One, the blast had come from right behind me. And two, my hair was on fire.

I rolled on the ground frantically to extinguish my flaming hair and jumped to my feet. I could see Travis by the river's edge, signalling for me to hurry. But when I looked behind I saw the explosion site. And the limp body on the ground.

I struggled to regain equilibrium as I staggered to Gus's unmoving body. I dropped beside him. My hands trembled with fear as I felt around his neck.

His clothes were torn and he was black all over with soot and dirt, but surprisingly Gus had a pulse. It looked as if he'd somehow cleared the main blast or been thrown forwards by his momentum. Either way, I still had a big problem. Gus was out cold.

'Damn it,' I said, trying to manoeuvre his body into a manageable position. He was dead weight and, as much as I liked to think of myself as strong, there was no way I'd be able to carry him.

'Sorry, Gus,' I mumbled as I hooked my arms under his armpits and pulled him, legs dragging on the ground, towards where Travis was.

About twenty metres from the river, another set of hands joined me. I spun around in shock. Travis yanked Gus upright and together we dragged him to the river.

Mines continued to detonate to the north and while we could still hear the helicopters, they had moved back, away from the smoke and ash.

'You're lucky I'm always prepared,' Travis said, pulling small tanks with facemasks out of his bag and shoving them in my direction. 'One of them is a full mask, put that on him,' he said, motioning to Gus. 'Have you got a handheld or anything else that can't get wet?'

I nodded, handing over my handheld cell and digging out Gus's – which had miraculously survived – and handing them over. Then, after a moment's hesitation, I passed Travis my tranq gun as well. And my taser. He threw it all into an airtight bag along with his own weapons, and shoved them into his bag.

I studied the facemask and ignored the sinking feeling in my stomach. I wasn't keen on swimming the Potomac River and even less excited about discovering what might be waiting for us on the other side. But it wasn't really the time to deliberate. So I fitted the mask, which had a miniature oxygen tube attached to it, to Gus's face, making sure it was airtight, and then used the remaining mouthpiece for myself.

Before Travis put his mouthpiece in, he threw me a tight smile and said, 'Watch out for water snakes.'

Perfect.

At least Gus wasn't awake to hear him.

Another mine detonated nearby. Together Travis and I dragged Gus into the depths of the water and, holding one arm each, submerged him beneath the surface and swam towards the Arlington shore.

When we were clear of the water and had hauled Gus to the trees lining the riverbank, Travis pulled the airtight bag out and removed his cell, throwing the rest of the bag at my chest.

He moved away to make a quick call and then returned, quickly assessing Gus's condition. 'He's starting to come around. It's a good sign. Come on, I have a car just beyond the footbridge. We need to move fast.'

I didn't need to be told twice. The increasing symphony of sirens, combined with the helicopter lightshow nearby, was excellent motivation.

It was slightly easier moving Gus this time and we reached Travis's Jeep in less than ten minutes. We were on the road moments after, watching as yet another mine detonated on the island.

Shaking with adrenalin, I sank into the seat and concentrated on simply breathing. I was out of breath and shivering from the cold. But even clear of the raid, I couldn't stop the panic.

'What the hell was that?' I gasped, holding on as Travis took a sharp turn.

'That was the nature of the game,' he said, like it was so simple.

'You just blew up the Theodore Roosevelt Island!'

He scoffed. 'Barely. Just put a few holes in it.'

A few holes. Less than two miles from the White House.

'People would've been hurt. Killed!'

He gave me a blank look and a shiver ran down my spine. He was fully aware – and unbothered – by that fact.

My throat was hurting from the smoke and whatever else I'd swallowed in the river. 'Who's after you, Travis?'

He checked his rear-view mirror. 'Could've been anyone. There were definitely government people there, though that doesn't mean it wasn't initiated by M-Corp. If I had to guess,' he smiled slyly, 'it probably has to do with me pissing off the FBI recently. An unfortunate crossing of paths.'

Unfortunate my ass. I could see by his cavalier attitude that whatever it was had been well worth the price we were all now paying. At least the FBI was a lot less of a problem than a full-scale M-Corp attack and we both knew it.

I reached into the back to check Gus's pulse. It was steady and strong; he would be fine.

'Why'd you help us?' I asked Travis. He could've left without us.

Travis looked over at me, his gaze curious. 'Why did you go back and help him? I've heard you're not the type to pick up baggage.'

'Where'd you hear that?'

'Everyone has sources. Answer the question.'

I bit down on the inside of my cheek and looked out the window. 'He's mine. And I still need him.'

Travis chuckled. 'Whatever you need to tell yourself, sweetheart. But you and I both know you ran back there to save him. You might not like it, but you have that never-leave-a-man-in-the-field mentality about you.'

I clenched my jaw, hating to show any weakness.

'That's why I helped you.'

I turned to him, eyebrows raised.

'You never know when I might be the man in the field. Might pay off,' he said, giving me a wink.

If I didn't know any better, I'd say that at some point this evening I'd not only solidified my source, but I'd possibly made a new ally. Stranger things, I suppose …

Gus groaned loudly from the back. 'Maggie?'

'Yeah, I'm here,' I said, feeling more tired by the second.

He groaned again and rolled onto his side. 'I hate you with the depth, breadth and heat of Hell's most torturous pit.'

A smile overtook my face as Travis looked between the road and the two of us. 'What?' he asked, looking disgruntled. 'No thank you? She did save your life, you know.'

Gus snorted, which only made me smile more. 'Which part should I thank her for? Destroying my life, or leading me into yet another death trap?'

Travis shook his head and refocused on the road. 'And I thought *my* crew were dysfunctional.'

Gus pulled up his wet T-shirt to start wiping the dirt off his face. 'You want dysfunctional? Spend a day with Maggie.'

'I just might need to,' Travis said with a small chuckle.

Trying to mask my relief that Gus was okay, I settled into my seat and looked out the front windscreen only to spin back again when I heard Gus start choking on his own laughter. I recognised the high pitch as his happy-at-someone-else's-expense laugh.

'Oh, Maggie,' he gasped, holding his stomach, wincing and grabbing at his ribs before breaking into another hysterical bout.

'What?' I snapped.

Gus let rip a number of successive snorts. 'It's a shame you've already been to the ball. That massive bald spot on the back of your head would have gone perfectly with the hole in your gut!'

My hand whipped to the back of my head. In all the drama, I'd forgotten that at one point my hair was on fire. 'Great,' I mumbled, feeling my way around what was a large area of well-singed hair. It was stupid to care. We'd made it out alive and with no permanent damage. I wasn't vain. I shouldn't care. But my hair was ... It was mine and in that moment I failed to fight the feelings of resentment that I'd lost it too.

'You all right there, sweetheart?' Travis said between fits of Gus's laughter.

'I'm fine,' I said, shutting down the conversation.

'Whatever you say.' Travis pulled into a side street and waited for an automatic garage door to roll open. We were somewhere in Ballston. 'I have to leave this car here, but I have another inside. You want me to drop you two somewhere?'

Gus was still carrying on in the back. 'Warned you just the other day you were going to get burned!'

I think he was delirious.

I considered Travis's offer. I was getting the feeling I might be able to trust him. One day. 'No, we're okay from here,' I said.

He nodded, knowingly. 'Suit yourself. But Maggie,' he looked down, as if contemplating what he was about to say, 'you sure you want to go in there, all the way? I meant what I said before. It's a suicide mission. I get that you must have your reasons, but maybe take a moment to consider all the reasons why you *shouldn't*. And walk away from this.'

The way Travis looked up and held my eyes made me hesitate. I wondered if he'd lost someone important to the tunnels. By the way he was looking at me, I could tell something was haunting him.

'It's too late to walk away, Travis. Nothing and no one will stop me now.'

He took a deep breath and whatever was showing on his face disappeared when he let it out. 'Your decision.' He pointed towards a small café on the corner of the street. 'We can meet there tomorrow night. Bring all of your intel and, if it checks out, I'll have what you need.'

The next day, Travis was so giddy with the intel we brought him, he held true to his word, handing over a collection of money zips that were more than reasonable and a file including all of the entry codes we needed.

His eyes were alight with excitement. I could already see him planning a hit on the couriers and labs that carried the highly desirable lust-enhancers. I knew it was particularly appealing to him because M-Corp would never report it to the police given that, one, lust-enhancers were black market, and two, M-Corp were the last people in the world thought to be producing them.

Both in possession of what we wanted, we parted ways with a handshake. I wished him good luck, he did the same, and I went in search of my brother.

I found Samuel in the back VIP area of Burn and hovered near the entryway until he spotted me. At first he looked happy to see me, then, probably remembering where I was and that in general he chose to hate the world, he scowled.

He stormed up to me and grabbed my arm, studying my M-Band and quickly deciding that it was a fake.

'What the hell, Maggie?' he spat. 'Do you know how much trouble you can get in for wearing one of these?'

Before I could answer, he was dragging me by my arm towards the back alley exit. He opened the door, literally tossing me out, before following me and slamming the door behind him.

'Give me one good reason why I shouldn't tell Mom!'

I laughed. Not meanly, but truly laughed out loud. 'Gee, Sam, when did you start to care!' I yelled between my laughter.

He startled and began pacing back and forth. 'What are you doing here anyway?' His tone had lost its bite.

'I came to see you. I have a bit of a … situation.'

'Is this about that guy you were here to see the other week?'

'Kind of,' I said, and he must have sensed this wasn't an ordinary high-school drama.

'Have you gotten yourself into something, Maggie?' he asked, still pacing and looking unhappy about having to deal with me.

Normally, I'd never turn to Samuel. He was a mess, even more so than Mom and me. He'd worshipped Dad when he was a little boy, but something had changed between them and they'd grown apart before Dad was taken. I don't think Sam had ever forgiven himself for the deterioration of their relationship. Not that he'd actually ever admit that out loud. I wanted to tell him he'd have another chance, but I knew he wasn't ready to believe that.

Every time I'd been into the tunnels, I'd been careful and had solid plans, and even when I'd been reckless I'd felt confident. But this time ... with all that had happened recently, plus the fact I was going into the core, this time I wasn't so sure.

I pulled the money zips out of my back pocket. 'Give these to Mom if I'm not back in a couple of days.'

When he took the zips from my outstretched hand, his eyes widened as he realised what they were. Silver zips symbolised a minimum five-figure value. And I'd just handed him three. I didn't mention exactly how much was on them, but it was everything, even the extra secret stash I'd pulled together by bribing the polished-brogues businessman I'd taken shots of last month. He'd turned out to be the most predictable kind of wanker: the type who believed you could buy your way out of anything. In my case, he was right. But I'd made him pay big.

'Jesus, Maggie, what have you done?' Sam said, looking confused and frightened.

I shrugged. 'It'll all be okay, Sam. I just … I'm going somewhere tomorrow. If for some reason things go wrong, I wanted you to have these.'

'You gotta give me more than that, or I swear to God I am going to put you over my shoulder, take you home and lock you in your room!' He started pacing again. 'Where did you get this kind of money? Did you *steal* it?'

I sighed. 'I know you hate Dad, Sam,' I said, noticing how he stiffened at the name. 'I get it, really. I know you feel abandoned and it's hard to remember all of the good times. But you don't know everything that happened before he turned neg.'

'Maggie –' he started, but I cut him off.

'There's a way to put our family right and I'm going after it.'

He was shaking his head, looking down. 'Don't be a fool, Maggie. You were just a kid when he left. You don't know what you're talking about.'

Now I shook my head, taking a step towards him. 'That's where you're wrong. I was the *only* one who knew, Sam. I get that you don't want to believe me because it will make everything that much worse. Just ... please, look after Mom.'

There was nothing else to say. I could see Sam shutting down, shaking his head. I started walking away from him. When I reached the end of the alley, he must've finally looked up and realised I'd left.

'Maggie, wait!' he called. But I didn't.

'Maggie!' he screamed.

Going to him had been a mistake, but it was either that or go to Mom, and I knew I couldn't have faced her. If Sam caught up to me, he was going to try to stop me, so without another thought I took off into the street, weaving around people and getting lost in side streets until I couldn't hear his voice calling out my name. Until I was alone, again.

Tomorrow.

Tomorrow I would find Dad, along with evidence of his innocence. Then everything would be worth it. My family would be back together and Mom and Sam would heal. It would take time, but we'd be okay. I'd be okay.

I'd be a better person. Maybe we'd move back to the countryside, or maybe somewhere new.

So why the *hell* was I hiding in the corner of the deserted Clarendon Metro, bent over, gripping at my chest, while I struggled to breathe?

Twenty-three

Dinner was in the oven and there was a note from Mom on the countertop amid the dirty pots and pans. She was working the late shift and wouldn't be home till early morning. Her note instructed me to eat properly and that we should go to see a movie on the weekend.

I wanted to clean up the kitchen for Mom. But I was too worried that Samuel would come home looking for me and knew I had to leave immediately. I threw the dinner in the bin and rinsed the plate, scribbling below her message: *Thanks, Mom. Love you loads. Mags.*

I headed up to my room, knowing the hardest task was still ahead of me. But there was no way around it. I needed to find Quentin before tomorrow night and get him to give me a blood sample.

As if the universe had read my mind, when I walked through my door, Quentin was sitting at my desk. I made a mental note to start locking that door.

He was facing towards me, his elbows on his knees and his head hung low. He looked as exhausted as I felt. Although he'd still managed to wrap his exhaustion in a nice pair of jeans and a black shirt, sleeves rolled halfway up his forearms.

By his feet I noticed a bottle of bourbon and pressed my lips together. 'I don't have time for this. You came to the wrong place to get drunk,' I said, dropping my bag and heading towards the bathroom to wash my hands and give myself a moment. It was too difficult to be around him. I couldn't control the way I felt so drawn to him; it made me weak.

'I've been walking around for the last three hours with it in my hand,' he said when I turned off the taps.

'Lucky you. Guess there's some big glamorous party you're supposed to be at,' I snapped, re-entering the room. 'Don't let me stop you.' I kicked my front door open, ignoring the tightening in my chest.

He looked down at the bottle and this time I noticed it was full. The lid hadn't even been cracked.

'There is. And, yes, I'm supposed to be there,' he said.

I strode to my bedside table as it all fell into place. 'And let me guess.' I pulled out the last of the vials and tossed it at him. He caught it easily, further proof he wasn't drunk. 'You can't go without this? Well, there you go, and by tomorrow night I'll have the permanent disruption.'

'What do you mean by tomorrow night?' he said, his eyes narrowing.

I'd considered giving him the disruption – not that it actually existed – before I went back into the tunnels, but I couldn't take the chance. I'd been manipulating people for so long that now I just expected people to do it to me. The way I saw it, once he was home free he could turn on me. I couldn't take that chance with Dad's life.

I turned away from him and started to grab things that I needed from my wardrobe, throwing them into my backpack. 'Gus will get it to you and then you can get on with the rest of your life, just like you want.'

He stood. 'How would you know what I want?'

'I don't! I don't know anything about you!' I didn't even know why my hands were shaking or why I was yelling.

'Where are you going?' he asked, watching me stuff things into my pack.

'Gus's place,' I said, dismissively.

'You're going back underground, aren't you?' It was an accusation.

I glanced up and did my best to keep the emotion out of my face. 'It's none of your business. Our mutual partnership is over.'

He lunged off the chair, grabbing my wrist. 'It damn well is my business. You're not going back down there and that's final!'

I ripped my arm away from him and pushed him back a step. 'Don't even think about trying to stop me, Quentin. Your permanent disruption is where I'm going. You'll never see it if you try to stop me going down there.' I looked him up and down threateningly. 'So if you want to run to your father and tell him everything, it will have to wait until then at least!'

I went back to my bag. Damn it, where did I leave my taser?

'You're so blind, it'd be funny if it weren't so damn tragic. Last time you went down there you almost died. You think I give a damn about getting the disruption when you might never come back to me?' His brow did that furrowy thing while his lips remained parted.

Silence followed his words. They dropped like a bomb and then we both just stood there, dumbfounded, as we watched the smoke and debris clear. But that kind of smoke lingers.

I looked at him in his dark jeans and shirt, his hands balled into tight fists at his sides, his brow lowered in a way that gave off so much raw emotion. I wanted to reach out to him, soothe the furrowed lines.

I covered my face with my hands for a moment, breathing out. It was safer if I didn't look at him. 'I'm going down there, Quin. I have to.'

'Why?' he rasped.

'You know why.'

'Your dad.'

I nodded.

'Fine. I'm going with you.'

My eyes shot up. 'No! No way.'

A smirk was playing on his lips. 'You don't get to be in charge of this. I need something that's down there just as much as you do. I have just as much right to go. And I am.'

I glared at him. 'But I can get what you need without you coming down there. I'm better at this alone and I'm not going to be responsible for you too!'

'Like that girl the night you got shot? Sarah?'

I flinched. I hadn't ever fully explained what happened. 'How do you ...?'

'You said her name in your sleep that night. And I've figured out enough to know you tried to help someone escape.'

'Oh,' I said, averting his gaze as a fresh wave of shame washed over me.

'You told me you never did that, that the risk was too high.'

'And it was!' I snapped. The image of Sarah, shot and falling to the ground, replayed in my mind just like it did in my dreams every night. I wouldn't let that happen to Quin.

'Not too high for *them*, Maggie. Too high for *you*. But you risked it all for her anyway and you didn't even know her.' He dropped his head. 'I was wrong the other night when I said you don't care. I know you do.'

I swallowed uncomfortably. I didn't want to talk about this. All I knew was that he wasn't coming.

Sensing my hesitation, Quentin moved in for the kill. 'Gus told me the other day that if you needed to get into the main quadrants down there, the only hope was my DNA.'

I made a mental note to hit Gus in the face and sighed. 'Would you wipe the shit-eating grin off your face. You're not coming with me.'

'Yes. I am.'

'Do you have a death wish or something?'

'Do you?' He stepped towards me.

'No. Which is why I don't want you down there, slowing me down.'

'I'm faster than you give me credit for.'

Actually, he was.

'We're not even certain your DNA will fly.'

'But my guess is, Gus isn't often wrong and he thinks it will.'

Also true.

'If you get caught …'

'I won't.'

But we knew there was a good chance we'd both be caught. I dropped my bag and crumpled onto the bed. He sat beside me.

'Please don't force this. Once I get Dad I need to be able to focus on him. I can't be … looking after you too.' Because Quentin had turned out to be the one distraction I may not have been able to ignore.

'What if he's injured? He's been down there for two years, Maggie. Even if you find him alive, you'll likely need help.'

I bit down on my lower lip. I'd thought of this myself from time to time.

'Plus,' Quentin continued, 'I'm going down there to get the synthetic chems. I won't let you take that risk for me. I have to do it. We'll go down there, get the disruption and your dad, then we'll get the hell out of there.' He said it so matter-of-fact. As if it would actually happen like that.

I shook my head. 'The risk is too high.'

'I'll make you a deal. If one of us gets caught, we swear, no matter what, we won't turn the other one in. I can keep my word, Maggie. Can you?'

Usually my word meant shit, but on this occasion I could make a promise I intended to keep. Finally I sighed and nodded, even while glaring at him. 'Study the maps,' I said, slapping the file that had been resting on my pillow at his chest. 'So you'll at least have a chance of getting yourself out of there if we're separated. The purple circles are possible exit points. The green circles are the preferred exit routes. The big X's are security stations. Red lines are dead-ends or unknown. We *don't* go near red areas,' I pressed.

'Got it,' he said, taking the file. 'No red.'

I stood up. 'Come on. We have to get out of here in case my brother comes searching for me. We can do this over at Gus's.'

Quentin stood, but instead of heading for the door, he moved into my space, catching me off guard and causing me to back up until I hit the wall.

'If things were different,' he said, his voice low, 'if I wasn't me, from my family or a neg … would things have been different? Is it even possible?' He reached up and played with a strand of my hair before letting it go and dropping his head.

'What are you talking about?' I said, my voice shaking. He was so close I could feel his breath, smell his slightly spicy scent. I could even feel the heat coming off him.

He nudged nearer, his mouth now at my ear. 'How can I know what I am and yet feel every single fibre of my being falling for you?'

I gasped. Speechless. Wondering if I had heard what I thought I did.

'You … you hate me. You've been avoiding me. You wish you'd never met me,' I whispered back.

He hung his head, leaning it against the side of mine. 'Because if we'd never met, I'd just be a neg. But now I'm a neg who knows what I'll never have, even though I want it more than anything. You've asked me to question everything, and I know stuff has been happening that isn't right and that my family is at the centre of that. Things shouldn't be this way, but … nothing has made me question the system more than this thing between you and me. I can't get you out of my mind.'

He was still at my ear, his words flowing like a whispered confession, but when he finished he pulled back to look in my eyes. I wondered if he could see the endless number of thoughts that were running through my mind, keeping me frozen in place.

His gaze was so powerful. 'I've tried to stay away, Maggie. Get you out of my head.' He inched closer still. Our chests were touching. 'If you tell me no, I won't kiss you. But you should tell me quickly.'

When his words were met with silence, his lips brushed mine. 'Please don't hit me.' I felt his lips curve upwards as they pressed to mine, and the world slowed so that all I could feel and hear and touch was Quentin. All I wanted was Quentin. And when he began to pull away, all I could think to do was grab his shirt and pull him back to me. I never, ever wanted to let him go.

But somewhere in the recesses of my mind, I knew I couldn't really have him. I loosened my grip and slowly stepped away from him.

'We need to go,' I said.

He smiled boyishly, looking young. And happy. And I felt a similar feeling inside, even though I worked damn hard not to show it. 'I'm going to be seriously pissed if you get caught or hurt down there,' I said, grabbing my bag and heading for the door.

He grabbed me around the waist and kissed the side of my neck before letting me go again. 'We'll go in together and we will leave together.'

Stunned by his brashness, I closed the door and we headed down the stairs. At the halfway point I paused to look at him and blurted, 'And after that?'

He would still be Quentin Mercer and I would still be me. Responsible for all the unforgivable lies.

Quentin simply reached down and took my hand, starting on the stairs again as he said, 'Together, Mags. Full stop.'

As we got into his car I bit the inside of my lips hard to stop the smile threatening to split my mouth and, instead, turned a scowl on him. 'Just make sure you study the maps properly.'

He started the car and looked at me with a crooked smile. 'Love you too, babe,' he said flippantly. But my entire body tensed and I noticed mine wasn't the only one. I hadn't expected those words from him. Not now. Definitely not yet. I knew he'd said them in jest, but still. Those words.

And what they did to me.

I swallowed and looked out the window, wondering what I was going to do. How could I possibly help get Dad out of there *and* be sure to protect Quentin?

All I knew was that I had to.

If Dad was in there, I had to get him out. I wasn't going to give up on him. But I knew now that there was no way I'd give Quentin up either.

Gus slammed the door in my face not long after he'd opened it. He waited long enough for me to say I needed a place to stay for the night, looked over to see Quentin standing beside me, rolled his eyes and said, 'Ask big bucks here to get you a hotel room. Hell, tell him to buy you the hotel. I've got one bed and since it might be my last night of freedom, I'm most definitely not kicking out my guest, who is currently waiting in said bed, to make room for the two of you.'

Cue door.

'Too much information, Gus!' I pounded my fist against the wooden panelling. 'I'll stand out here and wake up the entire neighbourhood if I have to. Ask Kelsey if that puts her in the mood!'

Quentin chuckled. 'Maggie, come on, we should leave him be.'

My fist banged on the door again. Damn it, he wasn't going to throw me out on the street tonight. God knows I didn't want to go anywhere near his bed after whatever he'd been doing on it with Kelsey, but I had too much work to do and I needed somewhere to stay.

'Gus!' I yelled. I could hear him throwing stuff around in his apartment, bitching and cursing.

I really didn't see it coming.

Gus opened the door, smiled, pointed a tranq gun at me, and shot.

I had enough time to hear him yell, 'Go. Away!' and close the door, before I reached for the dart in my shoulder, slouched into Quentin's arms, and slurred, 'You basssssstard!'

Twenty-four

D*ad had explained enough for me to understand what he was doing. Just like the pesticides he developed, these dosages of 'disruption' didn't attempt to fool the pheromone production from the glands. They worked directly on the way a person received and interpreted a pheromone signature, sending a message that the outgoing signal was strong and positive, causing a mirrored result to the person they were rating with. For months now Dad and I had visited Mitchell's Diner. Each time Beth the waitress had registered higher than normal ratings.*

Sitting in our booth, Dad started to move off his seat. I watched from my disjointed dream position as my sixteen-year-old reflection grabbed his arm.

'Please. I've watched you so many times. I can do this,' I said, impatient to have my turn at the spy game.

Dad shook his head. 'Not this time, Maggie.'

My nostrils flared in frustration. I wanted to participate, and not just for a piece of the action. I wanted a chance to wreak some havoc between two of the more unkind teachers at my school. A disruption of my own could come in very handy if I could create the right scenario. At the very least my BFF, Kaye, and I would have a lot of fun.

I looked pleadingly into Dad's eyes. 'I've been here every single week. I've helped. You know I have. Come on, Dad.'

I watched as he inhaled deeply through his nose. I didn't miss the clenching of his jaw before his expression relaxed and he let his breath go. Dad slid his hand across the table, passing a small vial into my palm. Then he proceeded to quietly give me instructions.

I nodded, feeling a thrill of excitement. When Dad called Beth over to our table, I shimmied out of our booth and strode towards the bathroom, via the register where her drink always sat.

The me that was dreaming watched on separately from my bird's-eye view and felt increasingly restless, knowing where this all led.

I moved clumsily, but remembered how at the time I thought I handled the situation like a pro. I'd seen Dad do it so many times and attempted to emulate the direct yet casual approach he so easily adopted.

Reaching the register, I thumbed off the lid and quickly reached my trembling hand over the counter to pour in Dad's latest disruption. Once done, I basically tripped over my own feet on my way to the bathroom.

It hadn't been the exact plan and I didn't look back in Dad's direction again. I was supposed to go to the bathroom first and drop the disruption on my way back to the table, but I needed the extra time to re-cap and stash the vial – along with its remaining few millilitres of disruption – into the back of my sock.

I watched as I hurriedly checked myself over in the mirror, slowed my breathing and prepared to head back to our booth. The hardest part was over. I bit back a smile, happy with myself. I was already fantasising about what I could do with my secret supply. School tomorrow would be epic.

Barely a few minutes had passed when I exited the bathroom, but instantly it felt like the world had somehow shifted axis. The scene in front of me was one I never would've predicted.

Beth was surrounded by a group of people, all looking wary, their M-Bands raised as they were registering pheromone ratings. The problem really hit home when I saw Beth's wide, frightened eyes as she glanced between the customers and her own M-Band.

I took a step closer and watched as she broke into sobs. 'I don't understand. A minute ago ... and now everyone is rating as ... as negative.'

A local customer barked out a laugh. I reeled back from the venomous sound. 'It's not us who are the negs, honey-bunch. It's you!'

Beth stumbled back, overwhelmed by the customer's looming figure. I saw beyond her, to her almost empty drink by the register. My mouth fell open and I took another step towards her – knowing that something had gone very wrong – just as Dad's hand gripped my upper arm and he pulled me out of the diner and into the car.

We travelled home in silence. Neither one of us missed the two police cars that came tearing down the road from the opposite direction. We knew where they were going.

Once home, Dad cut the engine and kept a tight grip on the steering wheel. 'Did you get rid of the vial?'

I nodded, trembling, too frightened to tell the truth.

'What was that?' I asked.

Dad took a deep breath, letting it out slowly. 'I don't know, Maggie. But I do know we can never, ever tell anyone about this. Do you understand me?'

When I could only stare out the windscreen, Dad grabbed my shoulder, turning me to look at him. 'Maggie, do you understand? You can't speak of this to anyone. You have no idea how dangerous this could be for all of us. Swear to me!'

I licked my lips nervously and Dad sighed, letting go of my arm. 'It's okay, don't be scared.' His expression softened. 'It's just, this is big and there are people out there, people who would do terrible things if they knew that negative disruption was actually possible. I ... I had no idea that it was so powerful.' His back stiffened and I could see his torment when he looked at me again. 'We can't say anything. Maggie, I'm asking you to do this for our family.'

I nodded, tears falling down my cheeks. What had happened to Beth? Was she okay?

'Promise me.'

'I promise, Dad.'

It was the moment everything changed.

The last time I would ever feel like that sixteen-year-old girl.

The last time Dad and I went to Mitchell's Diner.

The last time we ever saw Beth.

I didn't want to wake up. I most definitely didn't want to open my eyes. Didn't want to have to be in the real world. Because wherever I was it was sooo good. My earlier dreams had faded away and I was surrounded by indulgence. Not normal bed soft, but unbelievable cushioning and perfect temperature. You'd expect it to be too hot, because of the sinkability factor, but it wasn't. It was perfect. I wriggled my body, keeping my eyes closed, willing myself back to sleep.

'Maggie?'

It was Quin's voice. I was still dreaming. That was the only possible explanation for the surreal contentedness of this moment.

This dream was so much nicer than the others.

Before I knew it, I was saying things that the real me would never admit aloud. 'So tired, Quin. All the time,' I mumbled. 'I could sleep for years. Want the quiet, so much.'

His fingers brushed lightly across my forehead. It was a good dream.

'Feel guilty, wanting it. Dad's had no peace for so long. But I still want it, quiet from the guilt,' I confessed, burying my face into the silkiness of the softest ever pillow.

Quin continued to stroke my hair. 'I've never known anyone like you,' he said, his voice adequately dream-husky. 'The passion and fierceness you have for the people you love ... He's so lucky.' His voice caught on the words. 'I'd give everything just to have a person put me first like you do your father. You're ... It's everything, Maggie. Everything.'

I scoffed. 'I'm alone anyway. Always alone.'

His hand stilled and he shifted, his voice dropping to a whisper, making me acutely aware of his nearness. 'Not anymore. I promise.'

Okay, even a sinfully sinkable bed couldn't distract me completely from the fact that the voice beside me was starting to say things not even my dreams could conjure.

I cracked one eye open to see Quentin sitting on the outside of the blankets, fully clothed, my files open on his lap. He had a small smile playing on his lips. Then I remembered.

My other eye opened and I rolled onto my back, noting that the magical mattress seemed to adjust of its own accord to accommodate me. 'Gus shot me with a tranq gun.'

Quentin's smile widened. 'Yes, yes he did. It was only an hour shot; he promised you would be fine.'

'Son of a bitch,' I said, but it was half hearted. It was the bed's fault. I was actually wondering if he'd done me a favour.

'Where are we?' I asked. And who do I have to kill to get this bed?

'Sebastian's place in Old Alexandria. He's out of town for a few nights and told me I could crash here if I needed.'

'I think I want to marry him,' I mumbled.

'What?' Quentin said.

Nope. No mumbling for him.

'His bed is so good. Really. Have you slept in this before?' I asked, still fascinated and – I noted later to my embarrassment – still wriggling around. I blame the residual tranquilliser.

'Oh,' Quentin said, now smiling again. 'I have. It's extremely comfortable. I agree.'

I started to get up.

'Where do you think you're going?' he asked.

'Bathroom and then I have to get to work. You're not the only one who needs to look over the maps.'

He watched as I got up and then pointed me towards the bathroom door.

'There are fresh towels under the sink and your bag is by the door. If you don't have anything to sleep in … I could grab you a T-shirt.'

I waved a hand at him as I grabbed my bag. 'I'm all good.' Before I closed the door, I glanced up at him. 'Quin?'

'Yeah?'

'Thanks for catching me when Gus shot me.'

'I'll never let you fall, Maggie. Not if I can stop it.'

'Hmm,' I mumbled, unsure what to do with his response. In fact, I had no idea what to do with our entire earlier conversation. If I'd known I wasn't dreaming, I never would've confessed so much. It was way too exposing.

I ended up staying in the shower for a long time. Long enough to wrinkle and for the water to run cold. Then I stayed in the bathroom after I'd dressed in a singlet top and shorts, sitting by the edge of the sink with absolutely no idea what to do.

I pulled up my top and assessed the healing wound. I had removed the staples last week and only a raw pink scar remained, though it was still tender to touch. For the first time I became acutely aware of how unattractive it was.

My hand gripped the door handle, but I just didn't seem to be able to twist it open. I needed to get my work done. But thanks to Gus shooting me, now all I wanted to do was get back into the world's most squishy bed and sleep. I wasn't the only one inhabiting the bed though. And what the hell did that mean?

I put my ear to the door, but I couldn't hear anything. Eventually I started mumbling to myself in the mirror. 'Stop being a baby. You need to sleep. He needs to sleep.' In the end I just rolled my eyes at myself, threw my shoulders back and opened the door.

Quentin had changed into sweat pants and a T-shirt. He was still on top of the blankets, but the files were gone and his eyes were closed.

I rubbed my hands up and down my bare arms. It was cold in the room and I looked around to see if there was any heating. I couldn't see anything. In the end I gave myself another dramatic eye roll and started heaving the blankets back on my side of the bed.

Quentin turned his head in my direction and opened his eyes. 'You okay?' He sounded groggy.

I nodded, getting under the sheets.

'You sure?'

I bit my lip. 'It's cold. You should get under the blankets.'

He tilted his head, but then seemed to agree because he stood up and drew the blankets down, sliding into the bed.

He rolled over to face me, which caused me to turn away from him and settle on my side.

Such. A. Comfy. Bed.

'Go to sleep, Quin.'

I heard him chuckle behind me. 'Kind of hard with you right there.'

I didn't respond. Not even when I felt him starting to inch his way closer. Not even when his arm moved around my waist. Or when he pulled me in close to him. No. Through it all I was impressively silent.

Of course, he could feel my M-Band vibrating with a heart-rate warning, but I stubbornly ignored it.

'I know it's wrong,' he whispered. 'I know I'm not the kind of guy who is allowed to say this … Even before I knew I was a neg, I never thought I would say it.' He breathed in and when he exhaled I felt his breath warm my neck. 'I honestly believed I'd find my true match, that I would never settle for less. But it's *me* who's less. And Maggie … you're so much … more.'

My M-Band vibrated again. The rest of me was frozen in place.

Quentin's fingers brushed the exposed band of skin on my stomach. 'But I have to say it.'

Oh God. I knew what it was. I didn't even have to think about it. I just knew.

I finally managed to muster one word. 'Don't.' He was changing the game. Changing the rules. And I was crap at this game. Absolute crap. I had to stop him. But I couldn't ...

'I have to,' he went on. 'At least once. At least so if you turn your back on me tomorrow and walk away, I know I said it. No matter what, *I'll* know that *you* know.'

The way he said it, *I'll know that you know*, snapped something in me. I shook my head. 'You're confused. Don't say things just because you're scared. It doesn't make them true and words are dangerous. You can't make them go away.'

His hand travelled up my arm, all the way to my neck before returning back down my arm until his fingers entwined with mine. I still didn't move. Our breathing was in time. Rapid.

'I know you feel it too. I know you missed me like I missed you these past two weeks.'

So true.

'I tried to stay away,' I confessed. 'I heard you tell me you wished we'd never met.' I shook my head at myself, inching myself further to my edge of the mattress. 'You were right.'

'I figured you heard me. I tried to stay away too. Tried to let you go, because I knew I was no good. But … I can't.'

'Quin –' I started, but he cut me off and it was a good thing because I was about to tell him everything.

'I'm not scared of this, Mags. You and me? I'm petrified of losing us.'

In a swift move he used the space I'd put between us to pull me onto my back, and lean half his body on top of mine, trapping me and cradling my face with both of his hands.

'I love you. Madly, crazy beyond compare. I feel like I can't breathe without you, never want to lose you, would run with you, kill for you, die for you, *love* you.' He grinned sheepishly. 'There. Now I've said it.'

His gorgeous eyes, so sure, bored into mine and I knew what he'd said was true. I felt it too. I'd do anything for him. Whatever it took. 'This isn't healthy,' I mumbled finally.

His smile grew and my heart clenched. 'The best things never are. The best things always hover right on the edge of life and death.'

He was right, but why did it seem he was my life and I would only be his death? I wanted to kiss him. His lips were right there and I could just reach up and do it. Kiss him and forget. But how could I when I knew what I'd done to him?

I swallowed, guilt eating me up. 'I wish things could've been different, Quin. I wish we could've been normal, had a normal chance. I wish I hadn't … I've done … so many things in the name of my father. I can't take them back and if you knew,' a tear slipped down my cheek, 'you wouldn't give me those words.'

He pulled me closer, almost rough. 'You just don't get it. I didn't give you those words. You *ripped* them from my heart and soul and now they're yours. Forever.'

Oh. My. God. He meant it. And I wanted to say something back. Something equally amazing. Equally as heartfelt, but I couldn't speak over the thudding of my heart.

Quentin had been such a believer in the system, but his feelings for me had made him question those beliefs. All the while, I'd rejected the system. Yet here I was, completely and utterly in love with him.

I didn't know what to say and part of me was worried that I might burst into tears, so instead I did what I really wanted to. I kissed him.

Twenty-five

'I still don't understand why we can't take my car,' Quentin complained for the hundredth time. He'd just gotten off the phone with his mother, explaining that he had stayed at Sebastian's last night and would be there again this evening. Her responsibilities lecture had been loud enough for me to hear, and yet, surprisingly, she had also accepted his explanation without obvious suspicion. I couldn't help feeling the familiar twinge of guilt. Eliza was Garrett Mercer's wife. I couldn't underestimate her, but there was something about her that seemed genuine.

Hoping to avoid my own responsibility lecture, I had ignored the four missed calls from Samuel. At least it seemed he'd been covering for me with Mom.

I looked to the heavens. 'For the last time, your car has a tracking device on it and we can't risk anyone trying to find you. It's obvious. Plus we need to stay off the main roads.' We needed to stay off roads altogether, but I didn't want to tell him that just yet. It would only lead to more questions. 'We can park it at our first stop.'

'First stop?'

'Trust me.'

He took a deep breath and let it out through tight lips. 'I trust you, Maggie. I'm just …'

'I know,' I said. Because I did.

Quentin followed my instructions, taking main streets all the way to the private parking garage. It was one of those ones where you enter a code for your car and a series of lift mechanisms bring it down to you.

We parked Quentin's car and entered it into the garage for an overnight stay. It had worked out well that his brother was out of town. Sebastian's apartment – and comfiest of comfy beds – wasn't far away, so it wouldn't seem out of place for Quentin's car to end up there. It was important that nothing we did raised any suspicion.

Silently, we watched as his car was lifted into one of the bays and then I entered the code Travis had given me. The mechanisms kicked into gear and we waited as a number of lifts were raised and rotated until finally our untraceable vehicle was delivered.

'I'm driving,' Quentin said. He didn't smile. He didn't leave room for discussion. He just stared at the bike.

'I'm driving,' I replied.

He shook his head. 'I don't think you understand. *I'm* driving.'

'No. You're not.'

His jaw clenched and I knew I was seeing the Quentin Mercer of pre-neg days. The one who was used to getting whatever he wanted.

'I'm the best person to ride that bike. I've ridden one of these before. They're all power. You need to know how to handle it.'

'Exactly my point,' I said, stepping towards the bike and up-linking my M-Band to the starter ignition.

Quentin chuckled behind me. 'I don't think you know what you're getting yourself into here. Maggie, *that's* the new Ducati Hypermotard. It's a lot of bike to handle.' He could barely contain his awe.

'You're not stealing my ride, Quin.' I grinned and hooked my leg over the bike, grabbing one helmet and handing the other to him. 'Get on. I'm sure you'll look hot on the back of my bike,' I said with a wink, starting the engine.

He blinked at first, but when he made the connection he just shook his head with a wry smile and jumped on. He moved in close and wrapped his arms around my waist before leaning into me and murmuring, 'I suppose there are advantages.'

I put on my helmet before he saw my blush. I'd be lying if I didn't admit I saw the advantages too.

We cruised out of the parking garage and travelled through side streets towards the outskirts of the city. I took my time, getting a feel for the bike. Truth was, I hadn't ridden this particular model before – my experience had been with the less valuable variety – but I'd ridden a lot of bikes so it didn't take me long to get a handle on it. I'd been riding off-roaders since I was twelve. Samuel used to be really into it and there wasn't a whole heap else to do out in the country. Sam's friends used to head out every afternoon and take the trails. He had let me tag along every now and then. When he didn't, I made a point of sneaking out on his spare bike and practising, hoping if I became good enough to keep up he'd let me go out more often.

By the time I was fourteen, I had most of the boys beat. I thought it would make them want me around more.

Samuel stopped inviting me altogether.

But I kept riding. I even started working at the local mechanic's, running errands and cleaning the workshop just so I could borrow the crappy dirt bike they kept out the back.

Riding out of town, the wind in my face and Quentin holding tight … the temptation to turn in a new direction, somewhere far away, was strong. But there was no turning back now. Not when I was so close to Dad.

I pulled up at the last set of traffic lights before we hit open road, linked my phone to the helmet speakers, and called Gus.

'Sleep well?' he answered.

'You know I'm going to hurt you next time I see you.'

'Exactly why I plan on never seeing you again. I'm packing my bags as we speak,' he said merrily.

'I'm prepared to patiently hunt you down. It will make my payback that much more satisfying.'

He laughed on the other end. I'm not entirely sure when my threats became empty, or when they started to bring a smile to Gus's face. But it seemed I'd lost my edge.

'I'm hitting open road,' I said, cutting off his laughter.

'All right, all right. Give me one second and I'll check the satellite.'

While Gus did his thing, I reached into the front compartment and grabbed my bottle of water, offering it to Quentin.

'Thanks,' he said, after taking a few gulps. 'You ride pretty well.'

I took the bottle back. Gus was in my ear, giving me the all clear. I lifted my visor and had a drink, knowing we wouldn't get another chance for a while. Before I put down my visor, because I couldn't help myself, I turned to Quentin and gave him a sly smile. 'I'd hold on.'

The Ducati had a lot of power. I'd chosen it partly for that reason and mostly because it was a hybrid off-roader that didn't draw too much attention on city streets. It was a sexy bike, sure. But it was a serious bike too. And as we skidded off the smooth road onto a barely visible dirt track, I couldn't hold back the smile as the adrenalin kicked in. It may also have had something to do with Quentin, who was doing just as instructed.

My smile kicked up a notch when he yelled: 'Next time we take two bikes and make it a race!'

I laughed, hearing him through the helmet speakers. 'Only if you're willing to bet big!' I yelled back.

His arm tightened around my waist. 'For you, there is nothing I wouldn't bet.' He didn't yell it quite so loudly, but I heard. Lost for a reply, I revved the accelerator and moved us beneath the cover of trees, weaving in and out, avoiding ditches and the large rocks, hoping nothing too surprising crossed our path. About half an hour later I pulled to a stop.

Before I'd even kicked down the stand, Quentin jumped off the bike.

'Jesus, Maggie! That tree came damn close.'

I scoffed. 'Barely.'

He raised his eyebrows and leaned forwards, removing part of a stick from where it was wedged in my jacket. 'Pretty close to me.'

I shrugged. 'Satellites move over this area a lot. We didn't have time to dodge everything.'

'Well, for future reference, it's good to prioritise giant trees.'

'Thanks for the tip,' I replied dryly. I pulled our baseball caps out of my bag and handed him his. 'Put this on under your helmet.'

'Why now?'

'Because,' I pointed to the building ahead of us, 'we're going in there and when we take off our helmets, we are going to be seen on cameras. We need to keep our heads down and covered.'

'You do realise *that* is the Dulles International Airport. One of the most highly patrolled airports in the world?'

'It is, and yes I do.' It was no surprise given that Air Force One often landed there, but there was no better way to get where we needed to go.

He put on his cap and slid his helmet back in place before hopping back on the bike behind me. 'You're kind of scary, you know that right?'

I nodded solemnly. 'I do.'

We made our way to the arrival level in the main terminal, heads down and shielded from the cameras. I spotted the baggage carousels and paused at a kiosk, asking for a coffee, preferably not scalding. When they delivered it, I paid via my M-Band, discarded the coffee lid, and kept walking.

'Are you planning on explaining this part to me?' Quentin whispered.

'It's better if I don't. Just be ready to do as I say.'

'We are really going to have to work on your sharing policy, Maggie.'

'Understood. I'm not used to having someone with me,' I admitted. Then, before he could respond, I glanced pointedly ahead. 'See that security guard at twelve o'clock?'

'The one with the ginormous machine gun? Yeah, I see him.'

I smirked. 'Great. Well, we are about to walk past him. Whatever you do, don't let him see your face. Got it?'

I heard him groan before he answered. 'Got it.'

Forcing myself to keep a steady pace, I headed towards the last carousel, which would take us directly past the heavily armed guard. Just as we walked by, I faked a trip and fell into him. He caught me with one arm, not letting go of his weapon, even as my coffee spilled onto the front of his uniform.

'Oh, I'm *so* sorry,' I gushed, keeping my head down as I grabbed his arm. 'Thank you so much,' I added as I slipped my hand into his in thanks, slipping him the money zip.

The guard paused, recognising the transaction. He'd been expecting me, but I was a relatively young girl and that was always a surprise.

His hand calmly closed around the money zip. Yeah, he'd done this before. It wasn't a shock – airport security only made a percentage of their income from their actual salaries.

'You're welcome,' he said. He helped me regain my balance, giving the cameras a good show as he assessed his coffee-damaged uniform.

Quentin, I noticed, had wisely distanced himself from us. The last thing the security guard needed was for the cameras to record a Mercer in the vicinity.

The guard pulled out his radio and looked towards the cameras as he spoke. 'You see that?'

I could hear the person on the other end laugh. 'Highlight of my day! Is it bad?'

'Yeah, I'm drenched. I have another uniform in my locker. You'd better send someone to cover for me.'

'Sure. You go and Russ will head over there.'

'All right, out,' the guard said, putting the radio away.

'Again, I'm so sorry,' I said sweetly.

'Forget about it. I've got another uniform out back and I'm only two minutes from the back rooms.'

That was the first piece of intel I needed.

'Well, at least someone can come to relieve you.'

'Yeah. I'll head off now and he'll be here in a minute,' he said, glancing down as he crossed his arms, leaving four fingers out straight.

And that was the second piece of intel.

I started counting. 'Great news. Sorry again.' I gave him a wave and walked towards the last carousel. I looked around. The area was deserted, none of the nearby carousels were currently in use. It was precisely why we'd chosen this time of day.

Quentin fell into step beside me. 'Making friends?'

'Indeed,' I responded, still keeping count.

We made it to the carousel and I gave the guard an extra thirty seconds, just in case. He'd given us a full two-minute window anyway, so I had the time. When I was certain that our corrupt guard had made it to the back control room to shut down the cameras – a job that even Gus couldn't get done from outside the airport – I elbowed Quentin. 'Move fast and stay with me.'

I heard him gasp when I leaped onto the carousel's conveyor belt and straight into the luggage holds, but then he leaped after me.

Ducking low, we ran along the stationary conveyor belt and into the back area. I spied the doorway immediately and slipped the decoder card into the wall.

'I wouldn't have even seen it,' Quentin said, watching on in fascination.

'They hide the doors well. I've missed a few here and there,' I responded, waiting for the decoder to give me the green light. When I heard the click, I blew out a breath and pushed the door inwards. I leaped in.

Quentin closed the door behind him and looked around, shocked to see the room we'd just entered.

'What is this?' he asked, looking around the large concrete box with low halogen lighting and not much else, apart from the stacked crates along one of the side walls.

I kept moving across the room towards another door, anxious at being so exposed. As far as we knew, M-Corp made a point of not having these areas digitally monitored, but that didn't mean I wanted to risk being out in the open for long. The sooner we were within the cover of the transit tunnels, the better.

'This is how M-Corp bring in synthetic chems and ship out lust-enhancers,' I explained.

We reached the next door, which surprisingly didn't have a lock. I was relieved to see it led into the narrow network of passageways that would lead us to the transit tunnel.

'You must be confused,' Quentin said, following me with less enthusiasm.

'Door,' I instructed.

Quentin, still not overly accustomed to taking orders, paused to narrow his eyes before turning back and carefully closing the door behind him.

I smiled and walked on.

'M-Corp don't have anything to do with lust-enhancers, Maggie,' he said, catching up to me. 'They're black-market products in complete opposition to what we do.'

I cringed at his use of the word 'we'. Clearly he still saw himself as part of M-Corp. 'Well, *you* should know then that while M-Corp actively criticise the use of lust-enhancers, they are also the main manufacturer of black-market products. It is *your* way of controlling both economies and providing rules for society to break while still profiting and controlling the flow.'

He grimaced at my pointed response. 'Why would they do that?'

'Because if they simply made lust-enhancers another accessory then people wouldn't want them so much and they wouldn't be able to charge so much money for them. They wouldn't be so desirable and people would look for something else, opening up other options for black-market dealings. This way, they know they have the best illicit product, but they control it.'

'It's smart.'

'Yeah it is, you should sign up for an internship,' I snapped, stomping ahead down the narrow dark tunnel towards the transit system.

Quentin grabbed my arm and pulled me to a halt. 'I hate them, Maggie. Is that what you need to hear? That I loathe my own family? That I've been fed and raised on blood money? That I'll never be able to look at them again without feeling physically ill? You think because I can acknowledge that my father is shrewd means I admire what he's doing, that somehow I would consider a life that follows in his footsteps?' His chest was moving rapidly and I knew his outburst was filled with raw anger. Anger towards his family, but also towards me.

I stepped back. 'I'm sorry. I shouldn't have said that. You're nothing like them.'

He shook his head, dropping his eyes to the ground. 'Do you know how much I wish I was you? Even with everything you've been through, you have a father who was there for you. He gave you something to fight for and I know that you've missed him and fear for him. Hell, I know it's ruined your family. But at least you can believe in him. You get to fight *for* your family. From here on out, I will only ever fight *against* mine.'

'You don't have to,' I said softly. 'You can take the permanent disruption and go back to the way things were. You can still have everything you ever wanted, Quin.

Maybe … maybe you should.' I realised in that moment that if that was what he chose, I would understand. I had forced him into this world through no choice of his own. If he wanted his former life, I wouldn't stand in his way. I'd never bring him trouble. I'd do everything to protect him from afar. Even his brothers, if I could. Most of all, I realised that if he chose that path, I'd miss him forever but … I'd let him go.

He braced his hands on my shoulders. 'I can never go back. I can never pretend to not know the things I know. I don't *want* to.'

I nodded, unable to hold his eyes. 'We should keep moving,' I said.

His hands slipped from my shoulders and, instead of reaching out, instead of saying something more, I called Gus.

'So?' Gus answered.

'We're in.'

Twenty-six

The airport had been a risk, but even with security cameras and heavily armed guards, it was still the smart choice. The alternative would have been to try to travel the entire distance to Mt Weather in the tunnels. The trip was over fifty miles. We never would've made the distance on the back of a transit pod without being spotted, not to mention it would've been near impossible to hold onto a pod at those speeds for so long.

It was going to be hard enough as it was.

Quentin was beside me as we neared the end of the narrow passageway that led away from the airport and towards the main transit paths. These tunnels looked newer and I assumed the additions had been made by M-Corp when they'd first taken over the underground facilities from the government. Eager to reach more familiar ground, I put a finger to my lips and gave Quentin a meaningful look. He nodded.

We stopped at the end of the tunnel, keeping close to the wall, and snuck a look around the corner. I could hear Quentin's intake of breath the moment we spotted the two M-Corp guards standing a few metres away.

The security was expected. This wasn't just any entry or exit point to the tunnels; this was the international airport – a gateway to the rest of the world. M-Corp would have cargo coming and going regularly and, though our intel told us nothing was scheduled for this time, we'd expected them to keep it manned.

Frankly, I was relieved there were only two.

The trick was to take them down without killing them.

I was confident that I was in close-enough range to get to them and make it happen. The danger would be if one of them pressed an alarm button or got a shot off before I could silence them.

Quentin broke through my thoughts when he took a step forwards, as if *he* was about to approach them.

I grabbed his arm and speared him with a steely look, my challenge clear. This was *my* territory. My call. He stared back at me and waited, no doubt considering all possible responses. Finally he stepped back, but refused to break eye contact as we continued our wordless argument.

My lungs filled with a deep silent breath, but I held my ground. There was no way he was going to take the lead out there. This was my job and I was not about to watch him get hurt.

Not after Sarah.

Especially not him.

I pulled my tranq gun out of my bag. It was loaded with a max dosage, much stronger than the one Gus had shot me with last night. It would keep the guards down for at least six hours, and hopefully that was all we'd need. Quentin's jaw was clenched as he deciphered my plan – which he understood didn't involve him – and he shook his head.

Feigning concentration, I kept my eyes down and on my weapon, attempting to ignore our ongoing negotiation.

Eventually though, I had to accept that I couldn't do it alone without taking a chance. My hands went to my hips and I took a few silent breaths before leaning in and whispering, 'Follow behind. Take down the first guy. Get his gun. Knock him out. *Don't* kill him, it'll activate his mortality zip.' I grabbed his upper arm and squeezed. '… And *that* will be bad.'

All security personnel at M-Corp were fitted with alarms. A lot of normal people elected to be as well – it was one of the popular accessories. I could never figure out why. What was the point in having an alarm that was only activated once you were dead? Not like it could save you.

Quentin nodded, still looking unhappy. Without further delay, I turned the corner, gun low by my side. I moved steadily but fast. It took the guards a couple of seconds to see me, a couple more to realise I was a threat. By then I'd already raised my arm and shot the first guy in the neck – one of the only unprotected areas – with a tranq.

They both raised their weapons. There wasn't enough time for me to aim and shoot at the second guard, but I was close enough now. Behind me, Quentin barrelled towards the first guard, knocking him to the ground. I threw a right hook at the second guard's face, followed by a right elbow jab, utilising his momentarily stunned state to grab his gun and throw it far away.

That was all I had time for before I copped a heavy fist to my left temple. I stumbled back, but recovered and ducked the second swing, stepping close to the guard and delivering a hard and sharp knee to his groin. He bent over and before his hand could make contact with his radio, I grabbed a fistful of his hair and pulled him down while my knee smacked hard into his nose.

He dropped to his knees. Still in motion, I stepped back and spun around, leg out. My foot collided with the side of his head and he went down.

I reached forwards to check his pulse. Still beating. Then I shot him with a tranq and turned around to see Quentin standing over the first guard – who was well and truly out – his arms crossed over his chest, his eyebrows raised.

'Don't think I didn't note that you gave me the semi-conscious one.'

I shrugged. 'I'm a better fighter.'

'Matter of opinion, really.'

'No. It's a fact.'

He groaned. 'You really are trying to emasculate me here, aren't you?'

I smiled briefly. 'Not at all. Now help me move them around the corner so we can get home in time for you to bake a pie.'

'Yes, ma'am,' he mumbled while my smile widened.

We waited in the shadows for a transit pod. Quentin had listened intently to my instructions on how to jump on a pod in motion.

The first pod to speed by was occupied. I only just managed to pull Quentin back before he started running beside it. He missed the second pod, his hand slipping at the last minute, and he landed roughly on his knees.

He wasn't happy with his failure. 'I suppose you got it first go?' he accused, wiping at the blood on his elbow.

I shrugged a shoulder, heading back to my position by the tracks. He took that for a yes. Truth was, it took me several failed attempts and two broken fingers, but that information wouldn't help him right now. He had to believe he could do it.

We waited for the next pod, Quentin beginning before me, my place about fifty metres further down the tunnel. That way, if he made a successful jump, it was easy for me to follow.

Third go was the charm. I watched him sprint. Even in the dark it was an impressive show. Quentin was fast and his strength shone through in his ability to control the speed. I didn't give him enough credit. He leaped into the air like a cougar and, though he grappled, once he got that first hold, I knew he wouldn't be letting go. I started to run. When I made the leap, Quentin's hand gripped mine and he pulled me into place.

Another display of his strength.

It was crazy, but riding that pod, jammed up next to him, taking chances with our lives with no guarantee of any reward … I felt safe. It hit me as a persistent ache in my chest, why being with him was so important.

He'd said as much to me earlier, but I hadn't really absorbed the words. But for the first time since my father was taken, I wasn't alone.

We settled in for a ride that would take about fifteen minutes and watched the junction signs flash by. This was the furthest I'd ventured into the tunnels, by far. It was also the longest stretch I'd travelled. Watching so many junctions speed by, knowing that within each was a community of imprisoned negs, made me sick to my stomach.

Judging by the disgust on Quentin's face, he felt the same. And the ache in my chest increased.

The junction numbers counted downwards. After passing Junction 5, we were both on high alert.

At Junction 3, we jumped. Me first, then Quentin.

I dusted myself off from the roll. Quentin had landed with a light jog. Show-off.

Following the map we'd memorised, we turned off the wider path and entered a complex route of smaller tunnels. The tunnels were only wide enough for two people to pass by one another at a squeeze.

We moved methodically, keeping track of where we'd been and taking corners cautiously to ensure there were no more guards waiting. The advantage of using this smaller maze of tunnels was that they appeared relatively unused; they seemed to be maintenance tunnels.

Nearing the target area, I checked the time. We'd been on the move for hours and it was approaching midnight. The lab should be deserted. I couldn't help but feel a small glimmer of hope that this might all work out.

But when we spotted the entryway into the

'Development and New Projects Lab', Quentin gently pulled me back.

'Mags,' he said, his voice strained. Desolate.

I looked him over, worried he'd been hurt back with the guards. 'What's wrong?' I asked, trying to stop myself from panicking.

He took a deep breath as if steeling himself. 'I was just thinking, *have been* thinking for a while now, maybe … maybe we should just forget about the disruption.'

My mouth fell open as his words sunk in. Was he turning his back on our deal? On us? Or was he just afraid?

'I still have to break into the lab either way. The cell that Gus and I think Dad's in can only be accessed through the lab,' I said, closing my eyes and gritting my teeth. I didn't know what we were going to find in there, but from everything I'd heard, this lab, above all others, meant pain and suffering for its captives. And my father was in there somewhere. I looked back at Quentin warily. 'This is what you came down here for.' I couldn't make sense of it. This meant everything to him. This meant he could have a normal life.

'No, it's not. I came down here for you.' His eyes locked with mine and the connection between us drew me to him. Damn it, I was on the verge of throwing myself at him. I shook my head.

I couldn't let him do this.

I was too close.

If he walked out of here without the disruption he believed would cure him, he might do something rash and expose himself before I could make him understand. There was a small part of me that still hoped he might never need to know the truth. That maybe he'd be fine. But in my heart I had already realised that wasn't true.

I took a deep breath and struggled to find a way through my tangled web. 'You need this, Quin. Your family and friends, hell, the *world* won't accept you any other way and you know it. You deserve a shot at a normal life and I promise you,' I grabbed his hands, unable to stop myself, 'I *promise* you'll have it. Let's get the disruption so at least you have it and know you have the control.'

He released one of my hands to run his own through his hair. 'But what if … what if I activate the adjustment and we … What if *we* don't rate well, Mags? Eventually the *world* you are talking about will find out if we're not compatible. It's more important to me that *we* are okay than how I rate with anyone else. And right now, everyone believes we're a high match.'

His words could not have shocked me more. My voice shook as I spoke. 'You don't want the disruption because … of me?'

'Not if it means having to give you up.' His expression was resolute.

'I love you.' Eyes wide, I slapped a hand over my mouth. But I was too late. The words were out. God knows they were true, but I'd never intended on saying them, not now, *not* like this.

Quentin smiled softly, his eyes warming as the words sunk in. His hand cupped the side of my face. 'Since the moment I first turned on my Phera-tech, I was sure I would never hear those words from another person,' he whispered.

There was a part of me that wanted to silently back up and away from this conversation, or better yet, run down the tunnel with my arms flailing wildly as I screamed in panic. Another part of me wanted to tell him everything. But I was too aware of the risk. I could be minutes away from finding Dad. I had to hold out until we were clear of the tunnels.

Still, I needed to give him something to believe in.

So instead of running, I leaned into him and kissed him. It was gentle to start. A promise on my lips. But the tension and passion that had been building between us for weeks quickly devoured any attempts to be restrained and instead insisted on something altogether more … hellcat-like.

Tucked in the dark corners of his father's underground empire, Quentin's hands were in my hair as mine hooked under his arms and held tight. His lips were as full as they'd always seemed and he knew exactly how to use them. In fact, I suspected they had some kind of magical quality since everything he did with his lips seemed to ignite every part of my body that he wasn't touching. I was lost to him.

Nothing had ever felt so ... real.

A cry fell from my lips and he understood, pulling me tighter. Closer to the brink of no return.

It had only been seconds, but I mustered my own supernatural strength and pulled myself away, catching my ragged breath and wild thoughts.

'We're going in there to get your disruption and when we get out I'm going to tell you something ...' I swallowed the tight lump in my throat. '... that will change everything.' Although for *us*, it would mean the end. 'I promise you will never doubt yourself again after tomorrow.' His brow furrowed and, feeling bold, I reached out and skimmed my fingers over it. 'And you and I will rate ... better than you could imagine.'

'How can you be so sure?' he asked.

Because I'd seen it.

I'd always known.

Because somehow we were the perfect yin and yang –

his light to my dark. His truth to my lies. His sacrifices to my selfishness.

I glanced at the lab entrance then back to Quentin. We had to keep moving. 'Just trust me tonight. I'll tell you everything tomorrow.'

He nodded, all too accepting. He pulled my hand down from the side of his face to his lips and kissed the inside of my palm. 'I love you too.'

I smiled. I was so screwed. 'If you tell me that tomorrow, I'll believe you.'

He stepped in closer, his hand drawing its way firmly around my neck. 'No, Mags, doesn't work like that,' he growled. 'I've already told you those words belong to you. I put them out there so that I could be sure. So that no matter what, I'd *know* that you know. Period.'

He was so adamant and wanted so badly for it to be true, so I nodded and cast my eyes down as I replied, 'We'll see.'

He kissed me again, and despite all my defences he broke through and stole the last piece of my heart I was so desperately holding onto. Tears prickled as I wondered what would be left of us at the end. When inevitability had its way with me.

Then we broke into one of M-Corp's most secure labs thanks to Travis's codes, Gus's tech and Quentin Mercer's DNA.

Twenty-seven

Wₑ held our breath as we entered a decontamination chamber. The doors slid open and then closed behind us. We waited for sirens to blare, for pounding footsteps, the click of activated weapons. Fear baited me, but I held still and waited for the next set of doors to open, granting us entry to the core lab.

A couple of minutes later they did.

The lab was state of the art, and huge. Dominated by stainless steel, it was narrow but at least one hundred metres in length – easily the largest of any M-Corp lab I'd seen above or below ground. It was equipped with lifts that looked like they went both up and down, confirming that in this core section there was indeed another level below. That evidence alone was enough to ignite my hope that this was really it. Both our research from Garrett Mercer's computer along with the intel from Travis told us that the negs would be below.

There was a glass wall on the far side of the lab. My

body twitched; I wanted to get over there and see what it looked out over. But I had to be smart. Now more than ever. So, instead, I turned my back on the glass wall and made my way towards the large compilation of computer screens at the opposite end of the room.

I called Gus.

'Hold on a sec,' he answered.

I heard some rustling, a few choice swear words, then what sounded like a screeching sound.

'Where are you?' I asked.

'Running this show from the road. You didn't think I was going to hang around for juice and cake at the end, did you?'

I bit back a smile. 'No, I suppose not. We're in the lab.'

'Holy shit, Mags.' He let out a whistle. 'I gotta admit, I wasn't sure you'd make it.'

'Didn't think I had the guts?' I quipped.

I heard a strangled kind of laugh over the tapping sound of him on his laptop. 'Oh, I never doubted your guts. Hell, I even suspect you've got a pair down there.'

'Charming.'

'Just thought you might've changed your mind, you know. You can insert the zip drive.'

I plugged the zip into the back of the main computer and watched as a black screen flashed and then Gus went to work, drilling holes into the system to keep us hidden and find a way for me to access the prisons we believed Dad was in. 'I don't know why you thought I'd change my mind,' I responded, even as my fist clenched.

'I guess it was a pretty out-there idea – that *you'd* decide to have an actual life instead of a death wish. Should've known better. Nothing will stop you. Is lover boy still alive, at least?'

I glanced over at Quentin. He was pacing near the entryway, head down, as if petrified to come further into the lab. I wasn't sure he could take much more. My next thought hit me hard.

'I took his family from him, Gus,' I whispered.

Gus sighed. 'Was wondering when you'd let that one sink in.'

'I took everything from him just to get back what was taken from me.'

'He's not the only one you did that to,' Gus said quietly. After a moment and some more tapping, he added, 'Look, Mags …' He heaved another sigh. 'I'm not going to lie to you, you rate high on the bitch scale. You're mean, calculated, unforgiving – the list goes on, but under all of that … there's a good person. You just need to …' He groaned loudly. 'Oh, screw it. I can't do this. Go get yourself a pep talk later from someone who gives a damn. Get your head in the game, Mags. You're underground, in one of the most dangerous and secret sites the world has ever known. You've been to hell and back, and dragged several of us along the fiery path with you to find your dad. Make it all worth something and save the wallowing for later.' He hit a few more keys and I heard some plastic rustle while I remained speechless on the other end.

When he spoke next, it was over a mouthful. 'You're all clear, Mags. There should be a set of elevators you can access, but I don't know what will be waiting for you below.'

Quentin was slowly making his way over towards the glass wall.

'I see the elevators,' I responded, still processing everything Gus had said, but knowing it was the truth.

'Take them down and then – here, I'm sending the map back to your computer there … Whoa, okay, this place is bigger than I – Mags, this is …' I heard him swallow.

The map popped up on the screen and my mouth went dry. 'Oh.'

There was a beat, then, 'Listen to me,' Gus said in a voice I'd never heard before. 'Listen to me, Mags. You need to get out of there. Now. This place is … it's so much worse than we – Mags, we … we're way out of our depth here. Turn around and run! Please!'

But I was already walking towards the glass where Quentin had stopped. His arms were wrapped around his body, his hands gripping his back tightly, as if holding himself together.

'Maggie, damn it! Are you still there?' Gus yelled.

I approached the glass, drawn by a force I was defenceless against. It was dark on the other side, but lit with intermittent floodlights. My gaze started at the bottom and then moved up, and beyond.

'Oh my God,' I said.

We'd always known about the communities. And about the rumours of a much larger community beneath the ground. But this ... this was ...

'It's the size of a small city,' Quentin said beside me. 'There could be a hundred thousand people living here. More.'

We watched as armed guards patrolled what appeared to be a combination of experimental zones, buildings and prisons. The area was massive and broken into grid-like sections. Some of the buildings looked like they belonged in urban settings, though they appeared deserted. To the right of the buildings was what looked like more laboratories and testing facilities; they were the size of football fields and made of dome-shaped glass. At roof height, long metal rods lined the ceilings, spaced like lanes in a swimming pool. Other zones looked more like barracks and, beyond that, row upon row of prisons. All with glass ceilings.

If the devil had a name, I was sure it was Garrett Mercer.

And this was where he lived.

I looked around the carved-out space, searching now at my eye level. Amid the dark black granite I spotted another glass wall adjacent. The lab we were in and whatever was behind that other glass wall overlooked a world where they played God.

'Shit,' I heard Gus mutter, reminding me I still had the phone against my ear.

'What?' I asked on autopilot.

'Maggie, please get out of there!' he pleaded.

Quentin seemed to rouse from his thoughts at that moment and turned to me. 'Put him on speaker,' he said.

I held Quentin's eyes for a moment and knew he needed to understand, to know everything he could. I bit my lip, but nodded. 'I'm putting you on speaker, Gus, and I'm not going anywhere.' Not until I'd freed Dad from this hell. 'So just tell me.'

He was rifling through pages and tapping on his keyboard. 'Okay, okay. You know how we found those population documents on Garrett Mercer's computer?'

'Yes,' I answered. I knew Gus had tried to follow the trail of information and had come up empty-handed.

'It's the reason they introduced the poverty tax,' he mumbled.

'Gus, what are you talking about?' I snapped.

'They're selling a solution! They're offering third-world countries a population control. Oh, it's just so …' He sounded sick. 'For the right price, M-Corp can make a country stop breeding.'

The enormity of what he was suggesting was beyond comprehension.

Quentin paled. 'How?'

'Disruption,' Gus said softly.

I shook my head. 'But they … they can't. Even if they had a disruption that could make an entire population test as negative, it wouldn't stop them from naturally having relationships, especially when they aren't truly negs.' I glanced quickly at Quentin and then away. 'Even if they think they're negs, it doesn't mean they are. Eventually they would realise.'

'But that's what I'm saying, Mags. They *are* really negative! M-Corp isn't just disrupting the signal; they're changing people's pheromones so that they're sending out a clear offensive signature. Their records show it has a ninety per cent success rate on those treated.'

'They're treating us like a virus,' Quentin murmured.

My eyes found his. 'Not a virus,' I said, too many awful thoughts flooding my mind. 'Like insects.'

He nodded, looking back out over the underground city. He gestured to the domed laboratories. 'Those pipes are some sort of delivery system. If it were a time of war, they might be gas chambers, but they're something else.'

I grabbed my side and bent a little, winded by my worst fears.

'And it's not just population control,' Gus added. 'From what I can see here, they have accounts with every major country's defence departments, and even large corporations. They're selling a highly sought-after service. Stripping people to nothing so all they are capable of is work. All the testing shows that once someone's ambition for relationship and family is fully extinguished, they're pliable in many other ways. Most of all, they have nothing to go back to, nothing to leave for, so they offer long term –'

'Shh,' I hissed, my ears catching a faint noise. Gus stopped mid-sentence.

Quentin stood, alert. He'd heard it too. We looked around, towards the elevator, then the entrance we'd come through. We heard another sound and realised it was the outer door. A red light flickered on above the decontamination room.

Someone was in there.

I grabbed Quentin's arm and started pulling him towards the back of the long lab, putting as much distance between us and whoever was coming through that door as I could. I shoved him under a desk to the side of the main computers. After pulling the zip drive from the back of the mainframe, I joined him, ducking low and whispering to Gus to stay silent.

I didn't realise how badly I was shaking until Quentin's hands came over mine, his warmth settling me. It was amazing how calm he appeared. But then I realised it wasn't so much a calmness as a resignation.

Did he think that city of negs below us was where he belonged? Where he would end up?

My eyebrows drew together. God, I wanted to tell him. I wanted to go back and change things. Everything.

We still had a few minutes until the decontamination cycle was completed.

'You okay?' Quentin whispered. 'You've gone pale.'

My lips pressed together in a straight line as I made my choice. 'You were right. This thing between us … It's like nothing I've ever known and I'm so scared. But it was never fear that you were a neg, or weren't enough – it was that I wasn't. *I'm* not enough, Quin. *I'm* not kind, or thoughtful, or girly, or even all that caring.' I glanced nervously at the decontamination chamber. I was almost out of time. 'Most of all, I'm not honest. I made all these sacrifices, gave up everyone and everything to find Dad … Quin, I did something awful to you. I sacrificed you before I even knew you.'

His hand went to my face, cupping it gently, soothingly. 'Maggie, whatever it is, I forgive you. Trust me when I say there is nothing in this world that could tear me away from you.'

I opened my mouth to say the words. Five little words.

You were never a neg.

But just as I did, the red light above the chamber turned green and we heard the door's pressure valve release and slide open.

I squeezed Quentin's hand. Reminding him to stay still and silent.

A single set of footsteps sounded on the marble floor. They reminded me of the clipped sound of Mr Polished Brogues in the parking garage. I concentrated on my breathing. I had the mute upgrade, so I wasn't about to have a beep-off, but still … It was the principle.

We heard some papers being moved about and then the clinking of something like test tubes. I was too scared to look. So we remained hidden. Listening. With any luck, it was just someone who would leave again soon.

After a few more minutes, we heard the sound of a chair being rolled back and then a creaking sound as the person settled into it.

Then finally a voice. A man.

'Please don't hide all the way down the back with your friend. We don't have much time before the others arrive.'

My M-Band started to vibrate. Before I could think about anything else, I stood, my legs shaking, tears already in my eyes.

He looked like a stranger, sitting in the black wingtip chair, white lab coat over what was a very nice steel-grey suit. Short salt-and-pepper hair. A rigidness to his posture and something missing from his eyes, something that made my blood run cold. But the thing that struck me more than anything else …

He had a nice tan.

'Dad?' I whispered.

But the lump in my throat had already answered one question loud and clear. I knew now I would never find the man I'd been searching for, the man I'd spent two years trying to save. Was this what they had done to him? Had they changed him so much? Was there any hope?

'Dad? Oh my God,' I said, my voice trembling and my hand going to my mouth.

But as he stared at me, it hit me, what was missing from his eyes … It was concern. And worse. It was love. For me.

I thought of how Sam and Mom felt towards Dad now, and suddenly I didn't know if the man I'd been hunting for had ever truly existed. If he had, he could never look at his little girl with such disregard.

He continued to stare dispassionately, waiting for me to start putting the pieces together. Once I started, it wasn't as far from my consciousness as I would've liked. I knew that he was smart, that he'd worked hard as a pesticide specialist on pheromone disruption techniques.

I knew that night at Mitchell's Diner that he'd stumbled across the neg disruption.

I'd just never considered that he ...

A hand wrapped gently around mine. I hadn't even heard Quentin stand. But there he was, beside me, supporting me. He had to be working some of it out in his mind as well.

'We're leaving,' Quentin stated, turning us towards the exit.

My father simply shook his head and raised his right hand steadily, giving us a clear view of his gun, which he pointed at me.

'At a guess,' he grinned cruelly at Quentin, 'I'm willing to bet you'll behave as long as I have this pointed at her.' His smile widened, making my insides turn, and he glanced curiously at me. '*You* on the other hand ...' He shrugged. But I knew what he was saying. My father didn't think I'd try to protect Quentin if he had the gun directed at him instead of me.

He'd always said I took after him.

Twenty-eight

In all the hundreds of times, no, *thousands*, that I'd envisaged, prayed for, planned, dreaded and feared this moment, this particular scene had never occurred to me.

My mouth was so dry I wasn't sure I could speak.

'You're Mr Mitchell. You work here,' Quentin said. It wasn't a question. He turned to me, his brow furrowed with concern, and squeezed my hand. 'I've met your father before. At the M-Corp offices in New York.'

Mr Mitchell? I wanted to be sick. He'd named himself after the diner where all of this began.

Dad saw my reaction and the corners of his mouth twitched in amusement. 'I prefer to be based in New York, but there are times I must oversee things down here. Your father is not going to be happy with you when he finds out what you've been helping Maggie with.'

Quentin stiffened at the mention of his own father. 'You mean, finding you? I'm sure I can explain.'

'Were you ever a neg?' I asked Dad, my voice cracking on each word.

'No more than him,' my father said, jabbing the gun towards Quentin.

Saliva rushed into my mouth and I swallowed down the bile. Tears brimmed in my eyes and something I suspected was my heart felt like it was being drowned from the inside out. Like a coward, I stared at the ground as I could feel, almost hear, Quentin's mind trying to make sense of it all.

'You know I'm a ... a neg?' he asked cautiously.

My father snorted. 'You're as far from a neg as I am from the helpless prisoner Maggie here always wanted me to be.'

I flinched at his words.

'I must admit, I always wondered, Maggie. That night at the café, I knew you were hiding something, but even if you had ... Well, I never imagined you'd put the disruption to such ... use.'

'You planned it all.' My words were a plea for him to tell me I was wrong. That he was not a monster. That the things I'd done hadn't all been for nothing.

'It's a new world and tech is its king. I really wish you'd left things alone.'

Anger started to build and I welcomed it. I needed it to stop the world falling from under my feet. 'You disrupted yourself! You left us to deal with everything. Mom works off all your debts!'

'Yes,' he said. 'It was the perfect way for the government to issue me with a new identity.'

I half laughed, sick to the bone. 'I thought you were dead, or stuck in one of the cells. I did everything, gave up *everything*!' A tear fell down my cheek. 'I hurt so many people, left innocent people behind when I could have saved them. Lied.' I looked at Quentin, who seemed to be lost in thought. And I knew none of his thoughts could be good.

'Yes, you did. All to find me. I've watched, Maggie. At first it was pathetic, but then you recruited that man and things became a little more interesting.' He meant Gus. I couldn't believe Dad had been watching everything the whole time I'd been searching for him. 'Of course, once I figured out you were determined to continue on your path … well, I was intrigued to see if you had it in you. And then your big plan.' He gestured again to Quentin. 'It was smart, I'll give you that. But your mistake was going to his house.' He shook his head. 'Bearing a bullet wound no less. You're lucky you made it out of that place alive.'

I glared at him.

He didn't care. 'Garrett was onto you the moment he laid eyes on you. Not to mention you gave away the fact that you'd hacked his computer.'

'The mouse,' I mumbled.

'The mouse,' my father agreed.

I pressed my lips together.

'Your mother had been smart enough to change your surnames to her maiden name, so you disappeared for a while, but after you caught Garrett's eye it wasn't long before he discovered who you were. He asked me if I'd spoken to you since my extraction.' His eyes narrowed and I saw the chilling depth of his wickedness. 'I didn't appreciate the interrogation, Maggie. So I assured him I would deal with the problem. And here we are.'

'How the hell did you track me all this time?' I asked.

He smirked. 'By having better contacts than you. Or more accurately, the same contacts – they are simply more loyal to me.'

'Travis,' I whispered, hurt by the betrayal. The friendship I'd thought we were forming had been just another lie.

Dad nodded.

'And Norton before him?' I asked, wondering now about the contact we'd used before Travis.

Another nod. 'Though he'd become too demanding.'

Had my father had anything to do with Norton's disappearance? Had he killed him?

All this time I'd been so sure I had a handle on things. That I was in control of my world, moving pieces around as I saw fit. I'd lived with regret and self-loathing, but at least I thought I'd done things well. I thought of my phone still lying on the floor under the table. Was Gus still on the line, listening to all of this? Oh God, had Gus been in Dad's pocket too? That thought spiralled and cut deeper than I could've imagined.

'For a time, it was an entertaining set-up.' My father was still talking. 'I sent you on wild goose chases to keep you occupied. Believe it or not, I thought if I gave you enough dead-ends, you'd lose interest and leave it be. But then you went and upped the stakes,' he said, regarding Quentin thoughtfully.

'Will someone *please* explain to me what the hell you are talking about?' Quentin was almost shaking. It wasn't anger, but a need to be informed. Now. 'What was this *plan*?'

'She never told you about disruption, did she?' my father said.

'Yes,' Quentin said defensively. 'It changes ratings. Like a much improved lust-enhancer.'

'Did she explain what I used to do?'

'Pesticides,' he answered shortly.

My father smiled at me and I closed my eyes briefly. 'Well, Maggie. I can see he didn't make things too difficult for you.' He rolled his eyes. 'I made pesticides that taught insects not to mate. To read negative signals from one another and be repulsed. When I decided to start experimenting with human pheromones, Maggie here was my little assistant. The last night we ran a trial, I discovered the formula to create the same reaction in humans.'

'You *make* people negative,' Quentin said, appalled.

My father shrugged. 'I don't often do it personally, but I provide the ability for others to do it, yes. It's a valuable service. You're a smart kid, think about it – industry is up because matters of the heart and the desire to mate do not distract workers. Armed forces have a higher than ever volunteer record, keeping our country and private sectors secure. And our future is protected. Countries with over-population, low resources and economic weakness come to us and we help – we can slow down population growth and provide the potential for a better tomorrow.'

'You disgust me,' I hissed.

He chuckled condescendingly. 'I'm sure it won't keep me up at night.'

Before I could speak again, Quentin took a daring step forwards, jabbing his finger at my father as my breath caught in my throat. All I knew right now was that my father was not who I thought he was. He was dangerous and capable of untold horrors. I didn't want Quentin any closer and I grabbed his arm, pulling him back.

Quentin shook his head sharply and held his ground. 'You're taking people's choices, their *lives*, from them!'

'We are. For the greater good, sacrifices are often made. For Maggie's greater good, you were one of those sacrifices yourself.'

Quentin looked down at our still joined hands. 'Maggie?' he asked. But he'd already figured it out. When I didn't respond, he added, 'The testing?'

I nodded, unable to speak.

He swallowed. 'I was never a neg.' It wasn't a question. He dropped my hand.

'And you've been doing her bidding ever since,' my father rubbed in.

'What about the synthetics?' Quentin asked.

My father laughed out loud. 'Maggie could've been giving you five millilitres of water for all it mattered. The point was that by dosing out disruption to you, she held all the power. She owned you.'

I heard Quentin's gasp as my father told him the truth in its most unforgiving light.

'Maggie …' Quentin shook his head and started to press the screen on his M-Band. 'Turn it on.' When I didn't move, he yelled, 'Turn it on now!'

My eyes lowered and I watched as a tear fell to the ground, followed by another, and another. How could I have been so wrong? About everything?

The next thing I heard was the click of the gun's safety being released. My eyes snapped towards my father as he kept the firearm directed at me. 'Do as he says, Maggie. Others are on the way and I need to ensure I can deliver a fully operational son back to Garrett when he arrives.'

I turned to Quentin. 'I know I betrayed you, but I … I didn't know you. I thought I was helping someone.' I glanced at my father then back to Quentin.

His jaw was locked and he focused on my M-Band, avoiding my eyes. 'Do it,' he said again.

'You don't want this,' I pleaded.

'Turn. It. On.'

I nodded, resigned, and did as he demanded. When the Phera-tech came online, it instantly registered with his, which was also now fully operational, and a series of beeps sounded. Simple factory-setting beeps, but even so, my father must've sensed something because he stood, suddenly intrigued.

'Well,' he said, standing over me, gun still trained towards my chest even as he grabbed my wrist and stared at it. 'I did *not* see that coming.' Just as quickly he dropped my wrist and moved back, his eyes darting between Quentin and me.

Quentin stared at his M-Band, shaking his head sadly as he finally lifted his gaze to me. 'It was never *my* beliefs. Never *my* theory about the system that was being disproved. *Adjusted*. It was yours.'

I bit down on the inside of my cheek, knowing he was right. I glanced at my father, half expecting him to jump in with some cutting remark, but he seemed to be reeling from the discovery that Quentin and I were a true match.

I shut down my Phera-tech. 'I never meant to do this. I never thought you and I would be like this,' I confessed.

'And that makes it okay? To make me believe I was *nothing*?' Quentin accused.

'No. I'm … I'm so sorry. I was wrong. I was wrong about so many things. I should've trusted in us, in how I felt for you, how *much* I feel for you.' I tried so damn hard to hold his condemning eyes, to show him how sorry I was, how much I loved him.

He stared at me for a moment, my father silently watching on, but before Quentin could respond the elevator doors opened and a barrage of armed security guards piled into the room.

More than a dozen automatic weapons were now pointed at our heads. I took two steps to the side, distancing myself from Quentin, and dropped to my knees. 'Don't hurt him.' My voice came out surprisingly even. 'Quentin Mercer is my prisoner. I've had him working for me for the past three and a half weeks under duress.' I had to try. It was too little too late, but I had to try to protect him. And besides, it was the truth.

Quentin took a step towards me. 'What are you doing?' he snapped.

'I'm telling the truth.'

'Well, it's a pretty stupid time to start! Just …' He shook his head, looking furious. 'Just keep your mouth shut!'

I kept my head raised, watching the guards take up formation around us. There was no way to escape. Now, it was just a matter of how badly things would end. 'I won't let you go down for this,' I told him.

Quentin rubbed his eyes. 'A bit late to start putting me first, Mags.'

A guard stepped up behind me, grabbing my arms and lifting me to my feet. He began to tighten a plastic tie around my wrists. But I kept my eyes on Quentin. 'Just ask yourself this one question, Quin. If I had come to you one day and told you the truth and asked for your help, would you have given me the time of day?'

He was silent and we both knew that was answer enough.

'We both changed,' I said.

But there was no more time for talk. The guards grabbed Quentin as they had me, though I noticed they didn't restrain him in ties. I hoped that meant he would be okay.

Another guard arrived in the elevator and strode towards my father. 'Sir, Mr Mercer is on his way. He will arrive within the hour.'

'Of course he will,' my father said. 'Take them to the holding cells. No community,' he ordered.

My mind raced.

Should I fight? Create a diversion so Quentin can get away?

Should I plead for his safety?

I even considered wrestling my father's gun out of his hands and shooting him. The bastard.

But my thoughts proved futile as the guard behind me pushed me forwards, towards the elevator. As I passed my father he grabbed me by the elbow and stared at me.

'You chose this path, Margaret. You forced it when you should've left well enough alone.'

I shook my arm from his hold. 'Did you ever care about us?'

'Of course I cared. But there was no future for me there and ...' He shrugged.

'And you cared more about yourself,' I finished for him.

His lips pursed, but then he nodded curtly. 'I suppose that's a fair assessment.'

'Now you're just going to let them lock me up,' I said, knowing it was true.

'Yes. But I will give you this one gift – let's call it a parting one.' He leaned in close, so only I could hear. 'If, for some reason, you see daylight again in your lifetime, that … rating of yours will be the death of you.'

I half laughed, giddy with the pain of all that had happened. *This* was my father. 'Why?' I spat.

He moved close again and I was tempted to just smash his face with my forehead. It wouldn't do me any good, but it was still an appealing idea. 'Because the Mercer family would *never* allow it. *Ever*,' he hissed.

'I wish I'd never found you,' I said, feeling another tear fall down my cheek.

Wisely, he stood back, crossing his arms. 'And I wish you'd never looked. But you did, and now I'm afraid, you're on your own.'

As if it had ever been any other way.

At that thought I looked at Quentin and realised just how wrong I was. Two guards were leading him in the opposite direction, but perhaps sensing my eyes he looked back at me, then at the guard whose fingers were digging roughly into my shoulder.

'It would not be wise to forget who I am.' Quentin's voice was level and so measured it was almost terrifying. 'If you harm her in any way, it will mean the end of you.' It wasn't just his voice. He radiated authority and strength beyond anything I'd seen before. The guard's grip on my shoulder loosened instantly. I stared at Quentin and, before he turned away, I caught the flash of pain in his eyes and a determination that made me shiver, reminding me he was indeed a Mercer.

And now … he despised me.

The moment I was shoved into the waiting elevator I felt a sharp sting in the side of my neck. Tranq. My vision blurred even as the reality of my situation became crystal clear. I hadn't always been on my own. For a brief time, with Quentin, I'd had everything.

Then I'd thrown it all away.

Twenty-nine

I woke with a gasp, my heart pumping hard as I shot to my feet and looked around wildly.

'Epinephrine.'

I spun towards the voice.

Garrett Mercer.

I put my hands on my knees, trying to slow my breathing and get myself under control. They'd given me an adrenalin shot. I was in a grey cement cell. No windows, of course. There was a toilet in one corner and a narrow bed in the other. Nothing else.

Desperate to mask the tremors I couldn't control, I fisted my hands by my sides and turned back to Garrett. It wasn't a surprise they'd brought me out of the sedation. I didn't imagine he waited for anyone.

I swallowed a few times, trying to loosen my throat. 'How long have I been out?' I rasped.

'Just over a day,' he said, his cold eyes locked on me.

'Where's Quentin?' I asked.

He tilted his head, considering me like a lion stalking its prey. 'You played my son; told him things he wasn't ready to hear or understand. Poisoned him against his family. There will be a price for that.'

'I didn't need to poison him for him to know the difference between right and wrong,' I said.

'And you … Maggie,' he snarled my name. 'Which one are you?'

'Wrong,' I said without hesitation. I studied Garrett in a similar fashion to the way he studied me. Had my father told him that Quentin was my true match? Had Quentin?

'At least that is one thing we agree on,' he murmured. 'The question is: how much damage have you done?' He was speaking more to himself than to me, so I didn't respond. 'And what am I going to do with you now?'

'I'm sure there is a community pod that is due for clean-up soon,' I sneered, knowing that was what he'd probably do.

He smirked. 'True. But first you need to fix the problems you have created for my family. Eliza is very distressed.'

I swallowed, my throat raw. 'What are you going to do with me then?'

Garrett tapped the door, indicating to the guards he was done with me. As the door opened his eyes met mine one more time, his pleasure evident. 'I like to think of myself as a bit of an artist at times. And, like many artists, I find myself indecisive. It could take some time.' His smile broadened. 'It's a good thing I know where you'll be when I reach a decision.'

With that, he spun on his heel and left the cell, closing the heavy door behind him. A moment later the lights went out.

Sweat trickled down my neck as I felt my way towards the corner and reached the toilet just in time to empty the contents of my stomach. It took a long time for the waves of nausea and wracking shivers to work their way through my system.

Time is impossible to track when there is no light. No routine. No sounds. Nothing that your mind can use to confirm the passing of a day. I had no idea how long I'd been locked in the cell. It felt like years. More likely, I reasoned, it was probably weeks.

It was the worst torture.

I'd expected to be paraded around and thrown to the wolves. I'd expected to be tossed into the worst of the neg communities and left to rot until the next cleaning day. I'd expected to be executed.

Instead, my ongoing existence and isolation gave me nothing but time to contemplate all the mistakes

I'd made. The face of every neg I'd turned my back on when I'd gone into the tunnels in search of Dad haunted me. I relived the blackmail deals I'd made with contacts and wealthy businessmen, all to get what I wanted. I hadn't given nearly as much thought to what I'd done to them as I should have. I'd done little more than ease my conscience.

For days, I thought of Gus. I cried when I finally admitted to myself that he was my best friend. That I loved him like family. And yet, I'd held him to ransom and made him believe I'd be his worst nightmare if he didn't follow my every order.

I couldn't blame him if he'd been working with my father this whole time. I probably would have if I were him.

At least I knew he had gotten away. He was out. That was the one good thing I'd done. And, knowing Gus, no one would ever find him.

I was starving.

Food and water were slid into the cell occasionally. But it was nothing more than stale bread. They were keeping me weak on purpose. It was smart. And cruel.

One day, they threw in a bowl with some kind of stew. I'd almost cried out as I crawled to it on all fours and poured the contents down my mouth, barely pausing to chew.

It took about thirty minutes to understand it had only been another punishment. My stomach rejected the rich flavours and I'd spent the rest of the day throwing up.

It was impossible to steer my thoughts away from Quentin for very long. They always ended with him. The look of betrayal on his face. The fear that he was down here like me. Slowly dying.

The only thing that stopped me giving up completely was the belief that, as awful as Garrett Mercer was, Eliza would never allow Quentin to just be left to rot. But if not this, then what? What horrors had he been made to endure? All because of me.

When I slept, I dreamed of him. They weren't pleasant dreams. More like premonitions, knowing that if I ever saw him again he would be my enemy. He would want to destroy me. And I wanted him to. I wanted his revenge. My dreams were violent and I always woke up before the finale.

No one had spoken to me since Garrett Mercer. No one had come near me.

There was a tiny ventilation fan in the ceiling. It made a constant whirring sound. It kept me company.

I looked down at my M-Band. It had beeped a few times and the screen had even flashed up once, causing me a fleeting moment of hope. But it had been disabled since they'd captured me. There was no way to contact anyone, no way to check my vitals or activate my GPS. And yet, I knew they'd somehow hacked into it. Every now and then, I would hear a health screen test. They were monitoring me.

Slowly, I was losing my mind. The fact I understood this was the only way I knew it wasn't already gone. I'd catch myself talking aloud to no one, seeing things in the darkness. Scenes from my past – family Christmases and birthday celebrations – played back movie-style, but in these versions my father now looked evil. And every now and then I'd scratch my arms or legs until they bled. Just to know I was still alive.

The first few days, I expected my father to show up. To waltz on in and tell me there had been a terrible mistake and he would take me home. Eventually I stopped expecting him. He was done with me. *Had been* done with me since that last night at Mitchell's Diner.

I'd fallen to the ground a while ago. I'd been trying to do laps of the cell to keep my legs working. I tried to move as much as possible. But I'd gone downhill, and after I fell I hadn't gotten back up.

After more time than I dared to consider, the door opened. I scrambled back into the corner. Had they finally come to kill me?

A guard stepped closer to me. I squinted up at him, struggling with the shards of light pouring in from the open door. He dropped a fresh bottle of water, a loaf of bread, two bananas and four energy bars at my feet.

'Eat slowly. A few bites every hour.' He turned and left, shutting out the light behind him.

My M-Band. They knew I wasn't holding up.

I studied the selection. Plain food. Even the energy bars were made from basic ingredients. They wanted me alive.

Briefly, I considered denying them even that.

They wanted me to exist, knowing the failures of my life. I was supposed to be defeated. Lost for any cause and at their mercy.

But they had made two mistakes. Now that it was no longer about finding my father, I was finally able to give way to the thoughts I'd held at bay for so long. Finally able to consider what I could do with everything I knew.

My M-Band beeped. I looked down, almost too scared to consider what that particular tone signified. I hadn't received any communication since I'd been in the cell. Slowly, I turned my wrist.

Tears instantly pricked my eyes.

My lips trembled.

My hands shook.

Was it even possible? I shook my head, staring at the message as it began to disappear one letter at a time, as if someone was trying to cover his tracks. Only one person I knew had those kinds of skills. But there could be plenty of M-Corp employees trying to set me up too.

But still.

Those words.

No one else could've given Gus those words.

No one.

I watched as the last letters disappeared, my M-Band going black again. It didn't matter. The words were etched into my mind.

Never forget. I know that you know.

Tears slipped down my cheeks. 'Quin,' I whispered.

I shook my head and wiped the tears away. I couldn't be sure. It could be some cruel punishment. The worst they'd given yet. A way to make me think he was outside and safe. But why? Did they think it would make me stop wanting to fight? Did they want to remind me of all that I'd lost?

Oh God.

I hoped it was real. I hit my chest with my fist to try to stop the ache. God, I hoped it was true. Those words only meant one thing. They were the words he'd given me when he'd told me that he loved …

I swallowed back the thought. It was too much.

I had to be smart.

Who was I kidding? Even if there was the smallest chance he could one day forgive … I blew out a breath, my mind rolling in a state of confusion. I needed to get strong. *Be* strong.

And not for my own selfish reasons anymore.

I managed to crawl onto the narrow cot, chewing slowly on my food rations. I contemplated what would happen if, in my father's words, I ever saw daylight again. I knew it had to be about more. It always should have been. I thought of all of the intel that I'd secreted away over the past two years. All the evidence I'd collated and then ignored. All the innocent faces in so many neg hubs, and some of them probably weren't even negs at all …

I wasn't proud of myself.

There had been too much death. Given the chance, I would not stand by again, but it wouldn't be about revenge. It wouldn't be about me at all. Strange how that it was only then, locked away in my dark prison cell, that my eyes were finally opened.

And if they thought I was going to just give up before I knew that Quentin was safe, they were headed for disappointment.

I took a few sips from my bottle of water and braced my hands against the cold concrete wall for support. I trembled as I took my own weight, but eventually I was standing.

My purpose had delivered a new hope. That one day, I might do something worthy of his forgiveness. Of his love.

That was the moment I made myself a promise. That I would do whatever it took. I'd see this through to the end. Make it right. This promise, above all others, I will gladly keep.

Acknowledgements

As always, it takes a small army to produce and publish a novel, and I have been so fortunate to work with such an enthusiastic, knowledgeable and passionate team.

Huge thanks to my agent, Selwa Anthony. I am incredibly grateful to have someone to turn to who knows this business inside out and can so seamlessly navigate its waters on my behalf.

Thanks to the entire team at HarperCollins Australia. To my publisher, Tegan Morrison, who once again showed her meticulous attention to detail throughout the production process. Thanks goes to CEO James Kellow, head of children's publishing Cristina Cappelluto, project manager Kate Burnitt, publicist Amanda Diaz, editor Deonie Fiford, designer Stephanie Spartels, and marketing executive Tim Miller. I'd also like to take this opportunity to sincerely thank Amy Fox in sales, Elizabeth O'Donnell in international rights, Janelle Garside in production, and children's assistant Gemma Fahy.

Many thanks to my family, who continue to endure early drafts and dare to be honest. I love you all, and your honesty! To my husband, Matt, and our girls Sienna and Winter – you are my everything.

Finally, to all of the readers and bloggers out there who have supported my books, your enthusiasm and support are continually humbling. I hope you enjoy this first part of Maggie's story as much as I have enjoyed writing it.

An internationally bestselling author, entrepreneur and mother living in Sydney, Australia, Jessica Shirvington is also a 2011 and 2012 finalist for *Cosmopolitan*'s annual Fun, Fearless Female Award. Married with two beautiful daughters, she met her husband, former Olympian Matt Shirvington, at age seventeen. Jessica knows her early-age romance and its longevity has definitely contributed to how she tackles relationships in her YA novels, which include the series The Violet Eden Chapters (also known as The Embrace Series) and the stand-alone novel *Between the Lives* (also known as *One Past Midnight*).

Visit her online at
www.jessicashirvington.com
www.facebook.com/Shirvington
Twitter: @JessShirvington

Read the thrilling conclusion to *Disruption*!

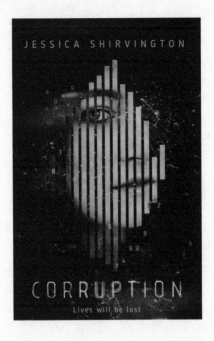

Two years ago, Maggie Stevens began the hunt.

Four weeks ago, Maggie's world fell apart when she finally found what she'd been looking for. And when Quentin, who had blindly trusted her, unravelled her web of lies.

Now, in *Corruption*, Maggie lives in the dark. But she's not about to stay there. Not when she still has to bring M-Corp down. Not when there is still a chance she could win him back.

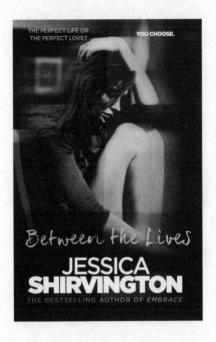

Sabine isn't like anyone else. For as long as she can remember, she's had two lives.

Every twenty-four hours she 'Shifts', living each day twice. She has one life in Wellesley, Massachusetts, and another, completely different life in Roxbury, Boston.

All Sabine has ever wanted is the chance to live one life. When it seems like this might finally be possible, Sabine begins a series of dangerous experiments to achieve her goal. But is she willing to risk everything – including the one man who might actually believe her?